The Story of Drek

By Dan Rempala

Cover Art by Chris Claflin

Author photo by "Hollywood" Ryan Tolman

To Andrew "Rio" Grant and/or his lovely wife, Jenn… whoever ends up picking me up from the airport.

The Story of Drek

Chapter 1:
8:25 p.m.

Sally Forystek didn't know the name of the man standing in the gaping hole where the gym doors used to be. She should have... the bulb of recognition flickered in her head, which meant she was staring at someone famous, but the man's name slipped out of her grasp. It had always been that way with her and famous people. There was this one time, when she went to New York City to visit her cousin, they sat in a restaurant for half an hour before she noticed that the man seated at the next table was none other than Mr. *Saturday Night Live* himself, Joe Piscapo. Couldn't have been more than three feet away. True story. Otherwise, Sally mind wasn't exactly in an optimal state for recognition tasks; after the gym's double doors exploded from their hinges, pinwheeled across the cavernous room, decapitated Marv Cutler and crushed Chet Roberts, she felt a little jittery.

As the echo subsided from the heavy metal door thudding onto Chet's flattened corpse and the hardwood basketball court, Sally just stared at the broad-shouldered, square-jawed man in the dark grey Armani suit with the black, too tight T-shirt underneath. *What's his name?* Somehow, it seemed important. His wore his hair in a buzz cut, which made his head all angles, and she didn't know of any movie stars who wore buzz cuts except the ones who were going bald or were playing a character in the military. The smoke rolling up around him reminded her of the pyrotechnics that rock stars use, but the only rock star that had haircuts and suits like that was Annie Lennox, and that obviously wasn't right. Besides, in this case, the smoke wasn't a special effect, just a byproduct of the exploding doors. Over the man's shoulder, a seven-foot, vaguely humanoid, white mouse stepped into view and held its oversized, red boxing gloves in front of its pink nose in a defensive gesture, and it was at this moment that the man's name sprung into her head.

"It's Dane McVain," Reggie Sleeve muttered from just behind her, echoing her own thoughts, "and it looks like he brought the Knockout Mouse with him." She could barely hear Reggie above the strains of "This is How We Do It" thumping its way through the speaker system and echoing into the recesses of the now still gymnasium. Hopefully, McVain and his minion didn't hear Reggie at all. The audio cover didn't last long, though, because the Knockout Mouse marched over to the DJ table and smashed its boxing gloves down on the CD Player/Turntable combination used to play the music, sending the CDs and the tuxedoed rent-a-DJ flying. The music quite literally screeched to a halt, and silence clung to the cavernous room.

McVain's heavy footsteps filled the audio void as he stepped toward the middle of the gym. He wore polished, black combat boots, which seemed like an odd accessory for a designer suit. "Greetings, Class of '96," McVain said in his thick, Scandinavian accent. His sausage-link fingers curled around the handle of what looked to be a toy raygun, the sort of thing you'd pick up in the discount aisle of Toys 'R Us, but he quickly put to rest any questions regarding its lethality. "My name iz Dane McVain, and dis iz a neural destabilizer," he said, holding the gun aloft. "I'm not a good shot, but even iv I miss you, I'm bound to hit vun uf your complacent, fast-food-eating classmates. Besides, iv I don't keel you, and da Knockout Mouse does not pummel your puny bodies into oblivion," he theatrically paused for a few long seconds, allowing the momentarily dead air to fill with a chorus of guttural quacks resonating from the parking lot, "then da Wolfian Ducks will."

Sally shuffled back a few inches. It was an instinctive movement, distancing herself from the danger, not like she was edging toward an escape attempt. She wore high heels, Prada knockoffs that she bought for the occasion at an outlet mall in Peoria, so making a break for it wasn't an option. The spiky, three-inch heels went well with her little black dress that she was so ecstatic to be able to Atkins herself into. It was important to look good at these things, not only to make Kelly feel like shit for dumping her before her Junior prom, but for more practical, primarily economic, reasons.

Her senior year, she got knocked up by one of the Puerto Rican ringers that attended their school to play baseball. They got married, he got a job operating a forklift over at International Lumber, and two years later, she divorced Jorge and took little Manuel to live with her mother. These days, Manny was in the fourth grade, and Sally had been cutting carbs and hitting the stair climber five days a week for four solid months so she could impress one of these former losers who were now managing department stores. Hopefully, they'd be so excited at the chance to nail the former co-captain of the dance team that they would forget that, once upon a time, she wouldn't have pissed on them if they were on fire.

Whew! The tension of the moment and the tension of her dress made her a little light-headed. Reggie must have noticed her distress, because one of his strong hands closed firmly around her shoulder. The strong hands came from his compulsive weight-lifting. He's sculpted himself into a small tank, but she never got the idea that it was narcissism thing that made him burn away those hours in the gym. After everything he'd been through, she always thought that he was just trying not to feel like a victim. For that reason, she had no qualms about the fact that he was actively trying to compensate for his obvious shortcomings. In this instance, the feeling of those callused fingers closing around the point of her shoulder reassured her. Upon further consideration, though, maybe he was using her to steady himself. That's their relationship in a nutshell: it was difficult to tell who was supporting who.

He was about the only guy she graduated with who she still talked to… meaningfully. She ran into former classmates all the time, and they might exchange a few how-ya-doin's but it was all bullshit. She and Reggie met every couple weeks for lunch because they both felt sorry for the other one. He felt sorry for Sally because she was a single mom working in retail. She felt sorry for him because… he had something wrong with him. Donna Sumner told her that the doctors had diagnosed Reggie as a necrophiliac and he passed out when things got too stressful, but she hadn't seen him have an actual sleep attack in years. She avoided the topic because it made her uncomfortable. When they met for lunch, they both seemed perfectly content to talk about her. Under the pressure of Reggie's fingertips, Sally turned, inadvertently touching her smooth cheek to the rough knuckles of his hand. "What do we do?" she whispered.

"Just sit tight," he responded without moving his lips or looking at her. "Evil geniuses don't normally crash high school reunions. He'll tell us what the deal is soon enough."

Over Reggie's shoulder, at the other end of the gym, a few of the greasy guys who looked like they took auto shop back in the day came spilling out from the hallway that led to the P.E. locker rooms. Even though their hairlines were creeping up, most still looked like they could pose as an overweight Guns 'n Roses cover band, and a few had variations on the Jeff Foxworthy mustache. She would bet anything that they were smoking a doobie in the back hallway, even if they all looked tense as piano wire at the moment. Their wide-eyed visages floated in from the hallway seconds before a pair of females clad in leather cat suits followed in a more measured, almost synchronized, gate. They clicked over the floorboards in their high-heeled boots. One sported long black hair and a red body suit. The other, long red hair with a black body suit. Again, they looked familiar enough that Sally would remember their names if she wasn't so preoccupied with thoughts of neural destabilizers and mutant rodents.

McVain's brain, on the other hand, seemed to be working like a well-oiled machine; this was probably a typical Friday night for him. He did a quick scan of the gymnasium. His left index finger, the one that wasn't touching a trigger, punched the air in front of his eyes, making him look like a muscle-bound secretary with poor typing skills. "Eighty-zix," he ultimately decided. "That's everyone." He turned to the giant rat standing over by the fragments of the DJ table. "Iv you vind anyvun in da hallvays, terminate dem." The rat nodded it bulbous, white head and started to depart before McVain added, "And help Poindexter move his machine in. And take da two bodies and find a closet to shove dem into."

Turning back to the crowd, McVain's pale lips parted and exposed a mouth of big teeth, square and gray as cinderblocks. "Now, Class of '96, you're probably vundering vhat a big, international figure like myself is doing here in Kooterville, Iowa, so I vill spare you da suspense, ja? My assistant, Dr. Poindexter has found a way to trace the residual energy given off by my greatest enemy, and da path has led here." He scanned the trembling cluster of Sally's former classmates, rhythmically moving the business-end of his ray gun like a conductor's baton. "Drck Manifold is somevun in dis gymnasium, and vun vay or da udda, I'm going to vind out vich vun of you he is."

*   *   *

Chapter 2:
8:31 p.m.

He had cool hair. That's what the young man thought the first time he saw Drek Manifold's picture in the paper. He'd read about Manifold's exploits before and heard he looked so much like Richard Marx that tabloid reporters had camped out at the B-list rockers house outside of Chicago, trying to find some evidence of the connection (and making some up when they couldn't find any). Seeing the Tri-Cities' own hero, though, in the grainy, black & white flesh, somehow made it more real, more concrete. There he stood, shaking the police commissioner's hand as the cops pushed the Ice Cream Assassin's head down so they could shove him into the back of the squad car. His naturally curly hair cascaded down to the collar of his jean jacket.

From that point on, Manifold became something of a hero for the young man. He was a hero to a lot of young men in The Cities, so much so that for several weeks, there were lines of teenage boys ten deep at local salons, all waiting to get perms. Barber shops had to start giving them or they would have been run out of business. The world's fashions changed, but Manifold's hair style remained, leading to a lot of jokes from the national media (one headline in the Chicago Tribune *read: "Faster than a Speeding Mullet"). None of it mattered: Manifold remained the biggest thing in town. The Tri-Cities had their share of celebrities, but they all were people who left. Manifold became part of the lives of those who stayed behind. Hell, everyone had their Story of Drek, of how they saw him fly in through the front window and saved the jewelry store on Hayseed Avenue from getting robbed, or how he used their uncle's pickup as a missile to*

knock the Beach Master out of the sky when he tried to cause the atomic silo
over on Old Man Johnson's farm to melt down. Everybody identified with
the Hero of the Tri-Cities because he was theirs. He wasn't Broadshoulder,
zooming in from Chicago for a couple hours at a time. He wasn't the
Cornhusker, Defender of all the Plain States. He was theirs.

For Jack Jordan, though, he was something more. Drek had
appeared right when Jack's brain started to turn to mush, and for Jack, the
appearance of the Mulleted Marvel provided motivation to keep hope alive.
Drek was living proof that miracles could happen.

*   *   *

The giant rat and the two impossibly hot women in leather suits
slowly converged on the middle of the gym, herding everyone onto the
creaky wooden bleachers. "Herded" was the proper term, too, because no
one acted: they just marched to their seats, compliant as sheep. Then, after
everyone had eased into his or her own butt-bruising section of wooden
bleacher, the rat stomped out of the gym doors, reappearing moments later
as it wheeled in a 3 x 5 black box that vaguely resembled the karaoke
machine that now sat inert beneath the still-spinning mirror ball. Everyone
sat silent, tense, and wide-eyed, even though the silence left plenty of space
for the unnerving quacks echoing from the hallway to fill.

The lone exception to this sea of rigidity and shallow breathing was
Jack Jordan. He sat silently in the second row, but it was a serene silence,
not forced, as he breathed steadily through his wonderfully clear nasal
passages and thought about lying on a warm, white sand beach and letting
the cool ocean water trickle over his bare toes. That's what his therapist told
him to do whenever he experienced a psychotic break from reality, which
this obviously was. "Stress makes you hallucinate," Dr. Utley had told him.
"When that happens, you need to de-stress. So, I want you to visualize that
you're in your Happy Place." In the gym, Jack immediately made the self-
diagnosis of psychosis, right after the doors flew off their hinges, but he
wasn't absolutely certain until the rat with the boxing gloves that matched its
beady red eyes showed up. He must have gotten nervous from being
surrounded by all these people, and in his own little world, all Hell had
broken loose.

Most of Jack's hallucinations were of the auditory variety… voices in
the head that told him he was pathetic, that he should hang himself, and so

forth, but visual hallucinations were not exactly a Haley's Comet-rarity. So, while the arrival of the giant white rat unsettled most of his classmates even worse than the exploding door, it convinced Jack that he had better start his breathing exercises. He couldn't be certain what was real and what wasn't anymore, but one thing was clear: things could not possibly be as bad as they seemed.

The fact that everyone seemed to experience the same hallucination failed to deter Jack, because he always could have hallucinated their frightened faces. That's the problem with your brain hating you: it controls your entire freakin' universe. Maybe in the really real world, his classmates all sat on the bleachers and Principle Spaulding read some meaningless tripe out of the ten-year-old yearbook... some of the Senior Superlatives, maybe. That was fine. Jack wasn't going to have to stand up any time soon; Jack probably wasn't anybody's Most Likely to Whatever, unless it was "Most Likely to Spend the Rest of His Life Getting so Doped on Haldol That He Needs Someone to Dress Him." Come to think of it, though, he might have won the award for "Prettiest Smile" and just forgotten about it. He *did* have a pretty smile.

Jack wasn't the sort to attend high school reunions in the first place. In fact, once upon a time, he gave Trevor Okdie permission to shoot him if he ever set foot in Kooterville High again (thankfully, Trevor showed the wisdom to stay home tonight). This was all Dr. Utley's idea, something about drawing comfort from seeing familiar faces and confronting old demons, even if some of the familiar faces *were* the old demons. Jack's episodes started back in high school, after all. Doc Utley used a metaphor to describe Jack's brain: it still needed water to make the gravy, and stress was the water. Thinking back to his Junior year, Jack's parents *had* just joined that swingers group, and he *was* trying to claw his way out of JV Football purgatory... so, yeah, there was something of a river (of stress) to wade through. Plus, over the last few weeks, he seemed to be responding really well to the anti-psychotics, and he hadn't experienced a psychotic break in almost two months, so the reunion seemed like an ideal situation to expand his horizons.

For most people with psychotic disorders, the episodes creep up like a cancer; reality gets thinner and thinner until you're in Hell. With Jack, they were sudden as a heart attack. Most of his delusional themes centered on persecution and grandeur, so one minute, he'd be in the library trying to solve the maze in *Highlights*, the next, he'd be running down the street half a step ahead of fire-breathing dragons or black-clad soldiers firing Mac-10's at him. Then, just as suddenly, they'd been gone. The descents into the unreal used to leave him in a quivering mass, but these days, he had enough experience as a victim to know that he could just sit back and relax, and the Armies of Darkness would pass by him just as suddenly as they came. They were an escapist fantasy, after all, kind of like his super-hero worship.

Jack had moved to Chicago a few years ago to get a job as a toll booth operator, and even though Drek Manifold was the protector of the Tri-Cities, he wasn't above the occasional trip over to the Second City. Having the Holy Roller, Broadshoulders, and Heartthrob protecting the skies was enough to grant anyone a night of rest, but whenever Jack read about one of the hometown hero's exploits, it was still like getting a visit from an old friend (not that he had a lot of experience with old friends… or visitors). Over the years, he had accumulated quite a scrapbook of articles from the *Tribune* and the *Tri-City Courier*. The only way to mark the passage of time was the improvement in the quality of the photographs; Manifold still looked like mid-90's Richard Marx.

The first time Jack ever heard of Drek Manifold, he must have been seventeen or eighteen. A train had derailed at the old depot, spilling radioactive waste into downtown Transverse City. Although there were no camera crews present, the man who would be Drek showed up in flannel shirt and ripped jeans and by all accounts *ate* the glowing green waste. The article in the paper suggested they call him The Human Shop Vac, because everyone assumed he could just consume things, but each time he strolled in to save the day, it seemed to sport a different power, even if his haircut and clothing never changed. Often, like the first time he fought the Knockout Mouse, Manifold showed superhuman strength. Other times, like the first time Dane McVain unleashed the Wolfian Ducks into the Mississippi River, Manifold was able to move so fast that he could run over the surface of the water without sinking… no easy task in cowboy boots.

Sitting in the gym on the uncomfortable wooden bleachers, Jack didn't need a scrapbook to know the major players in this hallucination. Dane McVain was the former-bodybuilder-turned-Swedish-Secret-Agent bent on transforming the world into a Socialist Utopia. His sidekick, Dr.

Poindexter, was an MIT dropout who actually created the Knockout Mouse and the Wolfian Ducks in a genetics lab he assembled in his parents' garage. After taking the "doctor" title for several years, he eventually did end up receiving his doctorate, even if Jack wasn't convinced that the University of Stockholm was a real school. Finally, the two chicks in leather had to be Eva Destruction and Donna Correction, a pair of former fashion models who had been kicked out of the industry for using an illegal, performance-enhancing skin cream that ultimately altered their DNAs. Using the tip of her finger, Eva Destruction could call up an endless supply of ultra-corrosive stomach acid, while Donna Correction could alter the atomic structure of airborne makeup particles to create any object she desired.

It all seemed rather fantastical sometimes, but if the Tri-Cities' meta-humans were part of his delusion, then so were the rest of the world's. And if Jack went that far, he might as well go ahead and assume he had hallucinated his entire life. Reality had to exist somewhere. This moment, though, having a team of earth-bound gods invade the Kooterville High Gym during a reunion social… wasn't that just a little too absurd? Just a little beneath them? Jack thought that even he would know if one of his classmates was Drek Manifold. He wasn't that far gone… right?

Dr. Poindexter plugged the black box into one of the floor outlets, and the purple, cup-shaped antennae atop it began its clockwise twirling.

"Alright," McVain said, holding a yearbook open to its back third. "David Allen. Pleaze ztep forward."

*   *   *

Chapter 3:

8:39 p.m.

"I hate you," Kitty said and threw the Bobby Labonte commemorative plate at Dave.

Dave didn't have third-baseman-like eye-hand coordination, so he reflexively held his bent, quivering hands in front of his face, T-Rex-style, as the plate whistled past his skull and shattered against the wood-paneled wall. "What the fuck are you doin', you crazy bitch?!" Dave yelled. In truth, he wasn't mad about the plate. He had nothing against Bobby Labonte, but it wasn't like he was Dave's favorite driver. Hell, he wasn't even Dave's favorite Labonte. The problem was that Kitty had a case of the screams and Dave's parents were only a couple hundred feet away. Thank god it was a Tuesday and they were watching Diagnosis Murder *with the sound turned up real loud. He didn't want mom and dad to think they were the domestic-violence-type, and he definitely didn't want mom trying to fix his marriage again. Hand-holding and amateur group therapy was a nice thought, but Kitty wasn't real receptive to it, and in the long run, it honestly made things worse.*

Dave took a step forward but froze when Kitty picked up another plate. He was close enough to see that the surface of the plate featured a black car, its roof adorned with a white number three traced in red. "Wait a second, honey," he said, holding up his hands in a steadying, rather than defensive, gesture. "That's my Intimidator plate. Let's think about this shit for just one—"

She cocked he hand back, but Dave sprang forward like a half-drunk jungle cat and grabbed her wrist. "I hate you!" she screeched loud enough

that Dave would know Mom would be coming over tomorrow to tell him
Oprah's latest advice for fixing a broken marriage… something having to do
with throw pillows. Like a man gingerly removing a thorn from a lion's
paw, he wrenched the plate out of her hand. "I hate you!" she wailed.
"You're disgusting! When we have sex, I have to think about Drek Manifold
to even touch you!"

Cradling the plate, Dave paused, even as the butt of her hands
slammed into the back of his head in a series of rapid, weak punches. What
an odd thing to say…

            *   *   *

David Allen used to be a varsity wrestler. He once weighed 162
pounds and came within fifteen seconds of winning the Cloverdale Regional.
He once had a full head of hair that he had kept kind of shaggy (except for
the spring of the Cloverdale Regional, when the whole team shaved its
collective head in an act of solidarity). That's who he used to be, though.
During the last decade, he had magically transformed into his dad.

Three years ago, his dad, Big Dave, had a heart attack while trying to
extricate his arm from the blood pressure cuff at the local Walgreens. The
family had an argument in the hospital waiting room about whether that
qualified as "irony" (they decided that it did). Big Dave survived, but and
ever since then, Little Dave had run the hog farm. He and his wife built a
house on his parent's property, with Mom and Dad still living in the same
two-story, off-white dwelling amid the shimmering methane cloud where his
childhood memories were set. In many ways, not all of them bad, it
constituted a sort of homecoming, but this time around, Dave Allen, Junior
ran the show.

This fate wasn't anything he hadn't anticipated a long time ago. Hell,
by the time he was twelve, he'd given up on his dream of being an astronaut,
and by age fourteen, that ambition shared a section of the fantasy scrap heap
with his dream of forming a band and becoming the next Brett Michaels.
His life's big adventure involved joining the Air Force for a two-year hitch
in Alaska. Sure, it let him visit a third state before he died, but he spent the
entire time feeling so homesick that he would have cut off his pinky finger
to see a cornfield or a Tractor Supply Company Store. Most people never
dreamed of being a hog farmer, he didn't delude himself into thinking

otherwise, but what it lacked in romance, it made up for in security. The
world would always need hotdogs and footballs.

When he heard the big European call his name, he wasn't sure what
he was supposed to do. He glanced around as everyone stared at him, like
some scene straight out of a nude dream, but the audience's faces mirrored
his own confusion. Everybody had showed up in the gym that night hoping
to get a little drunk, a little high, and maybe fuck around a little bit. Nobody
had planned to get taken hostage by super-villains. "David Allen," the big
European said, harsher this time. His narrowed eyes swept the crowd,
finally settling on Dave's general section of the bleachers. Pretty bad that,
even with twenty people staring at Dave, the European still couldn't tell for
sure that an eighteen-year-old version of him stared out of that yearbook.
Dave could probably pick three people in this gym who looked more like he
did when he was eighteen than he did now. The European stepped forward
and leveled his toy pistol at Kathy Reagan-Marshal's shock of curly red hair.
"If I have to zay it a third dime, I'll shoot dis one in da head."

Kathy's freckled face started to shift toward a hue to match her hair,
and her jaw muscles clenched up on themselves like she was about to take a
dump. That said, the experience probably would have been a thousand times
scarier if the guy hadn't been holding something that looked like the kind of
toy people on welfare buy their kids. Before Kathy passed out or crapped
herself in that hideous flower-print frock, Dave forced his legs to make him
stand up. Once standing, it became easier to march down toward the gym
floor. *Act like you're on the "Price is Right,"* he told himself as he adjusted
his belt under the distended belly. He hadn't seen 162 pounds in a while,
and the wooden bleachers eked out an embarrassing sigh with every step of
his steel-toed workboots that contained trace amounts of pig shit pressed into
the tread.

The thud of his boots on the hardwood floor echoed for several
seconds. From the floor, he realized that this McVain character wasn't as
big as he looked from up in the tenth row. He probably went about 6'2,"
225 lbs. Sure, it was probably all muscle, but there were a couple guys in
the bleachers who where taller, and half the men and a few women were at
least that heavy. If they all decided to rush him, even if the guy was holding
a Howitzer, they could easily overpower him. One look at the rat, though,
and its shiny yellow teeth, red eyes, and rapidly heaving chest, and Dave

knew the European could sodomize and dissect him at midcourt and no one would lift a finger. Taking on the European would be scary the same way getting carjacked was scary. That rat was... unholy.

McVain used the barrel of his pistol to gesture toward the orange plastic chair that was probably an orphan from the cafeteria. Dave sat down, grateful that he hadn't taken a tumble in front of all these people. Just thinking about it gave him a half-second flashback to an incident thirteen years ago, during the preview for the junior high band's Christmas Concert. The band members were filing in from the wings, and right when he hit the stage with the rest of the percussion section, he dropped some cymbals, and the noise couldn't have been louder if he'd pulled the fire alarm lever. It was enough to make him give up his music dream and start wrestling. Thinking about the incident, and how he just avoided a sequel, actually made him breathe easier. This lasted for a few seconds, until he was seated, until some dork wearing horn-rimmed glasses on his face and a calculator attached to a cord around his neck started rubbing conductant gel onto Dave's temples and pressing suction-cupped wires into the cool, oozing mess.

Dave's heart thudded against his ribcage so hard that it felt like it was caught in the middle of his throat. *Just like the old man*, he thought. *I'll go just like the old man.* He tried to think pacifying thoughts, things like... how he wasn't Drek Manifold, for instance. He heard of Manifold, of course; everybody had, even the gimp in the wheelchair over by the exit. Dave used to think it was pretty cool that the Tri-Cities had their own protector. Usually it was places like New York or L.A. who had the super folk, but shit, Des Moines and Bransen didn't even have their own super-hero. Something his wife once told him turned him around on the topic, though. That, and an accumulation of inconveniences.

Once, Dave was driving some feed through Woodly when traffic got backed up for two hours because of some fight between Manifold and the Soft Werewolf that caused the timing of the stoplights to go all out of whack. It was a pain in the ass, but you had to expect things like that. Annual super-villain-related fatalities had increased by a factor of three since Manifold moved in. And that wasn't just Dave talking out his ass: that was a big-as-life statistic. Manifold made Tri-Cities *less* safe. Some hero. About the only good things Dave had to say about that faggot was that he

had a nice jean jacket and he once read in the *Daily Harvester* that the Drek
Manifold Museum brought more tourists to the Tri-Cities than the World's
Largest Sanitary Landfill and the Lawn Dart Throwers Hall of Fame
combined. And you didn't need to be an economist to know that more
tourists meant more pork chops and pork rinds.

The nerd in the glasses turned toward the black box that looked kind
of like a mini-fridge and started fiddling with the dials. Dave felt a bit of a
throbbing in his skull, but he wasn't sure if that was a new throbbing or just
the one caused by his heart palpitating. The worst part was that everyone
kept staring at him, like he was full of candy or something. He knew exactly
what they were thinking: *Please God, let ol' Dave be Manifold so the
European will kill him and I can go home to my family.* Sure, he would
have been thinking the exact same thing if his name had been "Yokem"
instead of "Allen," but right now, he hated every single one of them for that
look. The stares made him nervous. What if he did something stupid, like
shit himself? Then, not only would he not be Drek Manifold, he would be
That Guy Who Shit Himself in Public. It may seem strange that this fear of
humiliation superseded a fear of death, but there was no fear of death. The
European wasn't going to pop him with that ray gun because he wasn't Drek
Manifold.

The black box contraption started chirping, and a few seconds later, it
spit out a six-inch length of paper that looked suspiciously like a cash
register receipt. The dork (Dr. Poindexter. That was his name: Dr.
Poindexter) tore it off and looked at the purple ink numbers. Then looked at
them again. "Vhat does it zay?" McVain asked, his forearms folded under
his bulbous pectorals.

Dave's hands began to absently inch up to his temples, where the
wires were attached. *Let me go let me go let me go...*

"Um," Poindexter began, his eyes shifting from the paper, to Dave,
then to McVain, all in the space of a second. *Not a good start*, Dave
thought. *What could possibly be holding him up?* "Um, it detects some
residual radioactivity of the same sort that Manifold produces."

McVain's eyes narrowed, then turned toward Dave, dragging the rest
of his face with them. "Any statement from the devence?"

Dave looked around and huffed. "Wh-Wh-" but nothing compelling
came out. He hoped he misunderstood the European because of the accent,

but he didn't believe that for a second. Neither did his bladder, which, incidentally, seemed to put on about seventy-five pounds in the space of two seconds.

"Dane," Poindexter said, stepping forward, cash register receipt extended, "we don't know the precise nature of this readout." He looked like he was about to set a steadying hand on McVain's shoulder, then merely used it to pat the air around the European's beefy appendage. "If all these people attended the same secondary school as Manifold, they could all suffer the same exposure to the contaminants. We simply have to run more analyses to determine—"

McVain raised his empty fist. "Shut up, you!" he bellowed in his signature monotone before slamming the butt of the fist down on the top of Poindexter's head. With the other hand, he leveled the cute little gun at Dave and pulled the trigger.

Dave had heaved himself halfway out of his chair when the invisible ray struck him. Rather than hit him in any individual point, the beam seemed to engulf his entire body. "Whaaaa!" he bellowed as he collapsed backward into the seat. In terms of actual pain, the blast didn't hurt one bit. At most, it caused an uncomfortable tingle to ripple through his body, from the tips of his remaining head hairs all the way down to his forest of toe hair. His vision stopped working almost immediately, though, and his body processes started to zone out, one-by-one. He had no idea as to the exact nature of the weapon's effect on him, but if someone had explained that every instant, hundreds of thousands of neurons were becoming inert, he would have understood perfectly (as soon as someone explained what "inert" meant), because that's exactly what it felt like.

His motor cortex left the party next, and he flopped out of his chair in a full-body hiccup and slammed onto the floor. Fortunately, the somatosensory cortex blinked offline an instant before his skull bounced off the hardwood. His hearing clung to life for a few seconds, long enough to here McVain explain to Dr. Dorkinstein in a low voice, "I couldn't give him da chance to change. I dell you vhat: if da next person shows da zame readings, I owe you a Coke."

Dave's last coherent thought wasn't of his wife and kids. It wasn't about how he would walk toward the light to meet Jesus or an assessment of all the things he had accomplished or failed to accomplish during his twenty-eight years on the Earth. It wasn't even about the Dale Earnhart plate that almost cost him his marriage. It was simply: *Thank God I didn't shit myself.*

*   *   *

Chapter Four:
8:48 p.m.

His mother didn't even have the decency to knock before she shoved her way into his bedroom, pushing the Eddie Vedder poster on the back of his door against the wall. "Dinner is in five minutes," she announced, wiping her hands clean on her apron. "Wash your hands and put on a decent pair of... What in gods name are you doing, young man?!"

The boy knew he was in trouble. He knew that he would never be allowed to go back to the comic book store ever again. That wasn't easy to take. He lived out in the middle of nowhere, and unlike big city kids, he couldn't just look out the window for his entertainment. His parents had always understood that, which is why, despite being church-going folk, his mother usually bought him a comic book at the grocery store whenever she went to the market, back when comic books were seventy-five cents each. This was like spitting in her face... no, actually, it was a thousand times worse.

There are certain milestones in a child's life that parents want to share so much that they haul the damn camcorder out of the closet and record it for posterity to show absolutely anyone who ventures onto their property. Baby walking. Little Ely riding his bike. Those are fair game. Others though... In fourteen angelic years, this was Ely's first time doing something like that. If only the artists hadn't made She-Hulk look soooo good in that white leotard, the curves of her supple breasts and muscular ass jutting out opposite one another.

He wasn't able to do that again for years. Every time he would work up a lather, the image of his mother's terrified face would invade his brain.

*   *   *

"Eric Atchison," the big guy with the accent said as he loomed over the nerdy little guy fiddling with the dials of the big black box. He spoke in a deep, droning monotone. It was distracting enough for Ely Lisch to forget what he was just thinking about. He felt a little disoriented, like he'd just passed out, but here he sat, in the high school gym, just like he remembered. It must be a pep rally, because a guy dressed in a giant rat suit was walking toward the exit, wearing boxing gloves, no less. Several seconds passed before an aspect of the situation struck Ely as incongruous with the overall perception. *Wait a minute*, he thought. *We played the Harrison River Rats last week.* A second thought followed on the first's heels. *If this is a pep rally, shouldn't the JV team be wearing their jerseys?* He certainly wasn't, even though he was a *starter* on the JV football team; he was wearing a deep blue button-down and a red tie.

At this point, Ely noticed that the Harrison High mascot dragged a limp body behind it, and not fake-limp, either. He could tell. Even if you've never seen a dead body before, there's an intuitive thing about it. It gives you chills. Plus, this body had its eyes rolled back to their whites and its tongue lolling out so far that the tip almost dragged along the basketball floor.

Ely tugged on the knot of his bright red tie as he drew in a breath and held it. His eyes rotated from the rows of faces on his right to the rows of faces on his left. The faces were familiar, but with more lines, bigger jowls, less hair, and attached to far more porcine bodies than he remembered. It all became a bit unnerving, *Twilight Zone* unnerving, but thankfully, a large piece of notebook paper lay in his right hand, and the salutation read "Dear Ely" in his own handwriting. Something in his gut told him that it had the answers he needed. The rest of the note read:

I'll make this quick, because I have to. You have a neurological disorder called "anterograde memory loss." You were in a car accident when you were sixteen and it damaged the part of your brain in charge of making new memories. Now, you can't hold thoughts for longer than a few minutes at a time; as soon as you get distracted, the memory fades (God, I wonder how many times I've written these sentences). Anyway, today, you're at your ten-year high school reunion. Your friend Katy Crenshaw

(now Katy Duncan) picked out your clothes and drove you to the reunion.
She will also take you home at the end of the day. Try to have fun.

Your pal,
Morning Ely

P.S., To be honest, I have no idea why we're going to this thing. We were
never the reunion type. Maybe someone else thought it was a good idea and
told us it was our idea. I don't know. Either way, it's not my problem, and
in a few minutes, it won't be yours either. Cheers.

Ely scanned the back of the piece of paper, looking for something
about giant rats or dead bodies, but it was blank. At least Katy did a nice job
dressing him: the shirt-tie combination was razor sharp. He looked up from
the paper just as Eric Atchison stomped past him down the bleacher aisle.
Eric looked pretty much like Ely remembered: no major changes in weight
or scalp coverage. He looked forty, though. His pale features were drawn
and his gaze was flat. He looked almost... well, terrified.

As Eric's boots thudded to the gym floor and carried him toward an
orange plastic chair, Ely checked his letter again and turned to his left, where
Katy sat looking remarkably pregnant. "Hey, Kate," he whispered, because
that was what he sensed was the right tone of voice to use. "What's going
on? Is this some kind of sketch or something?" Even at a whisper, his voice
carried through the cavernous gym.

"Shut up, you," the big, square-headed guy on the gym floor
bellowed. He pointed a toy pop gun at Ely. For a second, the gun made him
certain that he was watching a comedy sketch, but the snarl consuming the
lower half of the big guy's face, and the fact that everyone seated near Ely
started squinting and leaning as far away as possible, made him rethink the
situation.

The combination of events confused him horribly, like he'd been
dropped into a movie about someone else's life, but with the same actors as
the ones in his movie. Thankfully, Katy saved him from doing anything
stupid by standing up, hands under her belly to accentuate the bulge, and
saying, "Sir, Mr. McVain. Please don't blame Ely. He has a memory
condition."

Memory condition? Ely thought. It sounded familiar, so he checked the letter to himself. *That's right: anterograde memory loss.* The phrase looked familiar, even if he had no clue about its specific meaning. He probably read the word so many times that its image burned its way into his retinas. Was the condition just a passing phase, like a sprained brain, or was it, like, a long-term thing?

"If he can't shud his mout, I'll have to give him a condition... a *permanent* condition," McVain said. Then, just in case his threat proved too subtle, he added, "Death." Despite his idiotic one-liner, McVain's hard stare made Ely feel all squirmy. Speaking of squirmy, Eric Atchison looked the part as he sat down in the orange chair at center court.

"I, er," Katy glanced down at Ely. "I'll try to, but—"

"Allow Eva or Donna take custodial care of him in one of the locker rooms," some nerdy guy in glasses and suspenders off-handedly offered as he proceeded to stick suction cup electrodes to Eric Atchison's sweaty temples.

Mr. McVain inhaled deeply, as if preparing to get loud again, but then he glanced over at a red-headed woman standing over by the drinking fountain and gave a nod toward Ely. At first, Ely could barely see her because Amber Leptin's afro-like head of hair blocking his view like a hedgerow. As she walked, in a gesture straight out of a shampoo commercial, the woman tossed a curtain of wavy hair over her shoulder so she could eye Mr. McVain like a cat eyeing a saucer of warm milk. The woman's high-heeled boots clicked across the gym floor as she approached, echoing all over the gym and competing with the hum of the computer and the heaving breath of the guy in the rat suit as the only audible sounds. *Boy,* Ely thought. *That rat costume looks awfully realistic.*

The woman's boots came to a stop at the bottom of the bleachers, and she stood waiting for Ely with each hand resting on a shapely hip. In that black cat suit, she had more curves than Lakeshore Drive. Sure, she was chewing bubble gum, which struck him as kind of weird and trashy, but a chick this hot would have to be chewing Timberwolf Chewing Tobacco before Ely started caring. She gave him a blindingly white smile that would have sent him down the steps under any circumstances. "C'mon, slugger," she said. "I'm going to babysit you in the locker room."

Katy touched Ely's arm. "It's okay, Ely," she said, forcing a smile. "You can go with her."

Ely sprung to his feet and marched down the bleachers, clutching his note in one hand and his backpack in the other. People watched him with some mixture of envy and distain, similar to the way he used to look at the retards when they got out of school after only a half-day. Once on the floor, he realized that people didn't just envy him for being able to leave the tension of the gym: this chick was model-hot, and he followed her heart-shaped ass to the corner of the gym, then back to the corridor that led to the locker rooms, like a dog crawling after a steak. Along the way, he noticed that someone had torn the gym doors off of their hinges.

This chick, who was far hotter than any of the other chicks who went to this high school, turned to regard him over her shoulder as she strutted. "What does your little note say?" she asked.

He couldn't think of anything clever to say, as usual, so he just handed her the note. Walking toward the locker rooms brought back a flood of memories for Ely. They were especially vivid because they were some of the last solid ones he had. He had walked this path a hundred times on the way to and from football practice. He walked down this hallway to go to P.E., and he walked it whenever he wanted to buy a Dr. Pepper from the soft drink machine. The last time he remembered walking it, he headed to the parking lot to get a ride home after one of the practices for sectionals.

That day, whenever it was, he left the locker room before anyone else because he hadn't bothered to shower. He normally did, being the hygienic sort, but in this case, it struck him as totally unnecessary. He barely broke a sweat during practice because he wasn't on varsity, and all he really did was run around the field a couple times, do some jumping jacks, and stand on the sideline and freeze his ass off for two hours. Yeah, the hallway was almost exactly the same as it had been that day, the fluorescent lighting, the tangy smell… it all seemed so familiar, but not quite right.

After the woman handed him his paper back, though, she continued right on past his old locker room. "Wait a minute," he said as they neared the next wooden door. "That's the girls' locker room. I'm not supposed to go in there."

The woman turned and gave him a sad smile as she ran the tip of her tongue across her upper row of teeth. "It's okay," she assured him, with only a hint of condescension. "We have permission. Besides, it smells about a thousand times better than the boys'."

Ely stopped walking as his face scrunched up. "Wait a minute. Who would give you permission for something like that? Mr. Dowling?" Ely'd never set foot in the girls' locker room before, but without any showering girls in there, his curiosity wasn't exactly piqued. He knew that no cheerleader pillow fights awaited him. It probably looked just like the boys' locker room, except with more tampon dispensers.

The woman closed her eyes for a moment and ran her fingers through her lustrous red hair, visibly frustrated by something. "Just come inside," she said, finally. "I'll make it worth your while. We can make out."

Ely tried to play it cool, but it sure felt like his eyes were going to pop out of his bright red face. *Dear god... that would be worth getting ten detentions!* "Okay," he said, as the woman pushed the heavy wooden door open and held it for him. "When?"

"Oh, in about five minutes," she said, letting the door swing closed behind her.

*   *   *

Chapter Five:
9:15 p.m.

Dane had thought of everything. Uppsala sat crouching like a steel dragonfly on the roof of the Genosha County Bank & Trust with her cloaking device in place. He had hired some low-rent local street toughs to hold some empty guns, and if any of the bank employees or customers got out of hand, they were instructed to pistol whip the idiots back into submission. It was so hard to get good help to run crowd control, but if you got some idiot out of the local crack house and minimized the amount of real damage he could do, fear worked almost as well as competent help.

All the thugs had to do was stand there and look tough, because the cops weren't coming any time soon. Poindexter had created a localized electro-magnetic signal-dampening device to kill the silent alarm before anybody could activate it. It was a handy device for robbing banks or jewelry stores, but with Poindexter on his team, the inventions never resulted in profit for Dane; just "investments" on future devices. This electromagnetic thing cost several tens of thousands of dollars, and if they were lucky, their haul would be five to ten times that amount.

Dane stood in the back of the bank, right in front of the closed vault door, shaking a pill bottle full of metal-eating super termites onto the vault's hinges (yet another investment). It had been a while since he participated in a string of bank robberies like this, and while he got some low-level charge from striking back at the symbol of capitalist decadence, it was slumming and he knew it. He was sick of coming up with small schemes that got snuffed out by one super-powered moron or another, though. The solution was to cover all *the bases, like he was doing now. Even if it took a year, he would accumulated the funding needed to buy every weapon, soup-up every vehicle, and pay every bribe to make his next plan perfect.*

Within seconds, the first vault hinge looked like it had been run over by a tank. The termites were migrating down to the lower hinge when one of the mouth-breathers in the lobby yelled, "It's Manifold!" Dane closed his eyes and waited for the sinking feeling in the pit of his mighty stomach to pass. He felt that sensation more and more these days, and he feared that an ulcer was developing. The second hinge gave way, and the vault door smashed the ground in front of his feet. He felt a rush of air move past his face and opened his eyes in time to see Manifold standing in the mouth of the vault, stupid haircut and all. Dane didn't hesitate a half second to swing his Uzi to his hip and point it at the intruder, but just like that... he was gone.

This version of Manifold moved at the speed of sound, which meant a couple things: 1) the whole scheme was over in less than twenty seconds, and 2) everyone in the bank, perpetrators and hostages alike, all left the scene with bleeding ears. Dane was unaccustomed to getting shoved into the back of a police car like he was nothing more than a domestic abuser in a sleeveless T-shirt, but as Transverse City's finest drove him away, he realized the error of his ways: the key to taking over the world wasn't to accumulate assets, it was eliminating the opposition. He vowed to never make the same mistake again.

*   *   *

Dane McVain grumbled as he pushed the wrinkled American dollar bill into the currency receiver of the Coca Cola machine situated in the hallway circumscribing the gymnasium. Money, paper money especially, was such a dirty thing. Twenty-four hours earlier, some homeless man could have been rubbing it on his genitals before fate sent it through a series of wallets and into Dane's hands. He hated touching the money, and this marked his third attempt at shoving the stupid American dollar bill into the slot. Perhaps the woman in the currency exchange booth at the airport gave him wrinkled money on purpose, perhaps not. The money was not the sole reason for his grumbling, however. Dr. Poindexter had turned out to be correct, as he often was: Eric Atchinson, Suspect Number Two, gave off residual radiation readings similar to Suspect Number One, David Allen. So did Cassie Duncan (formerly) Bane. So did Bulla Boyd.

This finding meant several things, none of them good. First, when he fried David Allen's brain with the neural destabilizer, he may have been ridding the world of some capitalist detritus, but he had not rid the world of Drek Manifold. Second, if everyone in the room exuded trace amounts of the "alpha-2 radiation" (Poindexter's term), Manifold would prove that much more difficult to find and the Knockout Mouse and the girls would prove that much more restless and difficult to deal with. The ragtag group of ne'er-do-wells had formed an uneasy alliance based on a mutual goal, but the longer they remained together, the more tedious the situation, the more the relationship would stretch and fray. At some point, he knew that tempers would flare, and the alliance would snap, and that's when Manifold would strike. The final problem, of course, was that he now owed Poindexter a Coke and did not possess a dollar of sufficient crispness to fulfill his obligation.

Dane grabbed both ends of the dollar bill and rubbed the green paper against the corner of the soda machine, trying to smooth out the legion of wrinkles. He once saw some teenage hoodlums perform the act at a shopping mall and it proved successful in their case. At least this dollar had George Washington on it. Dane had minimal contempt for George Washington and his anti-imperialist leanings. At least it wasn't Alexander Hamilton... that bastard.

The bigger problem, of course, was Manifold. Back in his days as a student, Dane received an 'A' in his class on hostage-taking, and he had retained much of the information (unlike his Fertilizer Bombs 152 class), so there were several legitimate options. One school of thought would say that he should start wasting the people in the gym, just lining them up in the bleachers and firing into the crowd until Manifold appeared, but that struck him as a bit terroristy. Besides, the people in the gymnasium were more than civilians and more than prisoners: they were hostages, and one way or another; they were keeping Manifold from attacking or escaping.

Dane tried the dollar a fourth time, but the machine spit it back out like a finicky prostitute. If he were carrying a real gun, he could have just shot the machine and stole any intact sodas, but he was packing this stupid neural destabilizer, and not even Poindexter knew what it would do to edibles.

Something brushed against his leg and made the hairs of his crew cut stand up like a carpet of needles. He rotated his eyes down toward the floor to find that it was just one of the Wolfian Ducks. It had silently waddled next to him and now stared up at him with pleading yellow eyes and those jagged stalactites of teeth jutting out from its upper bill. Dane reached down and scratched the top of its downy head. It nuzzled into his heavily callused hand and made that adorable, staccato, "quack quack quack" sound. Most people nearly voided their bowls when they encountered the Ducks for the first time, but after the initial shock wore off, the little critters were actually kind of cute. Just a bunch of fluffy, four-legged mutant bastards with webbed feet, wings, and a beak full of razor-sharp teeth. They liked having their head scratched; it was one of their few pleasures since they weren't capable of copulating. "I know how you feel," Dane whispered to the creature, whose eyelids pressed closed in ecstasy.

It was Dane's idea to create them, of course. That was how he and Poindexter usually worked: he came up with the big plans and left the details of making it happen to Poindexter. It seemed like the perfect way to unleash the powers of nature on the Capitalists, and he first turned the Ducks loose on the Mississippi River paddle boats, crippling the dinner/cruise industry in the Tri-Cities and holding the people on the boats hostage. He tried to get ten million dollars from the tri-mayoral council, but an incarnation of Manifold showed up to foil his plan. This version had the ability to mimic duck calls, and he lured several dozen of them into the turbines of a hydroelectric station. From there, Manifold and the Cornhusker tore through the rest of them with brutal efficiency. That was the a few scams ago, but since then, Dane always held out hope that Manifold would once more appear with nothing more than the ability to mimic mutated fowl. On that day, Dane will shoot him in the face and scalp his corpse.

Dane pushed the Coca Cola machine's coin return button, surely the act of a desperate man, but nothing came out. He found it ironic that they only reason he had pulled the riverboat scam in the first place was because Manifold had generated an electromagnetic pulse that damaged Uppsala's computer brain and Dane needed to pay for upgrading it. Then again, he wasn't certain if that qualified as irony; people did misuse the term so often. He would have to check with Poindexter on that one.

Dane wandered away from the soda machine, toward the front
window, so that he could stare out at the American football field where he
had landed Uppsala. Her computer brain still didn't work as well it should.
He'd taken her to several computer experts, even the capitalist Geek Squad,
and they were all so smug and confident that they knew what was wrong
with her, but the repair process always seemed like trading out one problem
for another. First, the voice recognition system wouldn't work. Then it was
the automatic chair massager/warmer that wouldn't respond. The rest of her,
the flight, weapons, and cloaking systems, behaved as perfectly as ever, but
it was tantamount to taking care of a senile loved one. He felt obligated to
play the caretaker, though, because if given the opportunity, she would
surely do the same for him. He put the palm of his free hand flat against the
chilled windowpane and whispered, "Ja, Uppsala. You're da only vun who
loves me."

"Dane?" a smoky female voice said from behind him, near the
gymnasium doors. It belonged to one of the girls, but he had to turn fully
around to see the red leather cat suit before he could identify her as Donna
Correction. Many women wore leather pants during the course of their
lives, but few could do so and actually make it look attractive. Luckily, he
worked with not one, but two women who could accomplish the task with
ease. "Dane, is everything okay?"

"Ja, is fine," he said, turning away from the gymnasium light, in case
the sheen in his eyes became visible.

Too late. "Were you… crying?" she asked, her emerald eyes
widening.

"Of course not," he insisted, his manner hardening. "It vhas da
asbestos from dis under-funded American public school. Vhat are you doing
out here?"

"You were gone so long. I just came out her to check on you," she
said, tilting her head in a sympathetic, very un-super-villain-like angle. Her
shiny, bouncy hair, no doubt treated by extravagant American hair care
products, slipped over her shoulder. He hated those hair care products; a
good Socialist should only need a bar of all-purpose lye soap and time. As if
that weren't grating enough, with Eva babysitting the retard in the locker
room, Donna had left security of eighty people in the hands of a seven-foot

rodent with a brain the size of a walnut. Dane only stared at her, so she broke out in a shy, half-smile. "So, you're okay?"

"Ja. You have a dollar bill?"

Donna held up her hands to expose her skin-tight outfit to visual inspection. "Sorry. Not a lot of pockets on this thing. Besides, I'm a little cash-poor at the moment..."

"Da. I haven't forgotten dat I owe you money," he assured her. He always remained on his guard around her. Out of everyone in the group (for which he still needed to find a catchy name), only she possessed the requisite guile of a rival. Poindexter was smart, Eva was sweet, and the Knockout Mouse was big, but none of them had guile. Donna, though, had guile up the poop-shoot. She could work an angle without you even knowing. "Hopefully, by da end of da month."

Donna waved a hand. "I know you're good for it. I can transmute you a dollar, if you want."

"No need," Dane assured her, tonelessly, as he pressed the handle of the neural destabilizer toward her C-cups. She took the weapon from him, a bit confused until she saw him lift his arm. His right hand contracted into a fist, and he thrust it through the glowing, fiberglass front of the machine. His calloused, muscular hand didn't hurt in the least, but a sliver of plastic almost landed in his eye. That would have been a stupid mistake, even though he *did* always want to wear an eye-patch. Several seconds of grinding, squeaking, and grunting followed, during which the machine inched far enough away from the wall that its power cord popped out of the three-pronged outlet. In the end, though, Dane managed to extricate an almost terminally dented plastic bottle of Sprite.

When he turned, triumphantly holding the green bottle, Donna Correction's full, lustrous lips parted in an expression lingering somewhere between shock and disgust. Usually, women reserved that expression for when he revealed to them that he collected military-grade snuff films for a hobby. "Oh, Dane," she said, shaking her head. "You do have your moments."

"Vhat do you tink about names?" he asked her.

"For...?"

"Da group. Our group," he said, wistfully. "I vas tinking of something like da 'Red Army.' You know, like da hockey team?"

"Yeah, I know," she replied. "The only problem is that I'm the only one who ever wears red. Oh, and you're the only one who's a Socialist."

He shook his head. "No. Eva said dhat she vas."

"Eva says lots," Donna said.

They looked at one another for several seconds before Dane turned away. "Oh vell, da beat goes on," he said, shrugging. He wasn't wild about the name, either, but at least he was trying. They were going to *have* to decide on a name if they managed to kill Manifold; the newspapers weren't going to just list all of them. "It vas just an example."

He strode back toward the gymnasium, and Donna followed in his wake. "Wait a minute," she said when they reached the doorway. "Didn't Poindexter want a Coke?"

Dane McVain paused to hazard a glance back toward the mangled machine. "He changed his mind," he concluded before stalking back into the gym.

*   *   *

Chapter Six:
9:26 p.m.

*"How are we going to fence all this stuff?" Eva asked in a whisper
barely audible above the zipping of garment bags.*

*"I don't know," Donna replied, frantically trying to drape the dresses
securely over the sides of the shopping cart without rumpling them. Some
were too short and kept slipping into the cart. Others had so many sequins
and shit sewn into them that they kept getting snagged on anything with an
edge. "I'm sure there's some way to do it. If worse comes to worse, we can
open an eBay account and ship them from Canada."*

*Eva began chomping down on her bubble gum even harder than
before. Ever since she developed her superhuman abilities, Eva had started
chewing gigantic wads of gum. It used to hurt her jaw so bad she couldn't
sleep, but she got used to it eventually. These days, the more excited she got,
the harder she chewed, until she sounded like an automatic smacking
machine. Nice to know her poker playing career had now gone the way of
her modeling career. Not that she ever played poker, but it's nice for a girl
to have options. "I'm not sure asking for thousands of dollars for a one-of-
a-kind, designer dress is the most inconspicuous way to—"*

*"Okay, then we'll think of something else," Donna snapped, her long
fingers wrapped so tightly around the handle of her shopping cart that it
turned her knuckles white. It was Donna's idea to use their powers to sneak
into the building the night before the fashion show and steal the clothing. It
would probably be her that came up with a decent way to get some money
for them without getting caught. Eva admired that kind of intelligence; it
was the kind that helped you pick up a diploma from an institution that*

existed outside of cyberspace. In the moment, though, Donna proved to be the sort who failed to think on her feet. It appeared that Eva had the stronger stomach, in more ways than one.

"Well, it better get us some kind of money. The model's union stopped paying for my healthcare, and I'm looking to get more than fifty bucks from some consignment shop." Eva put her hands on her hips. They both wore matching black, velour sweat suits that they picked up from Target, so it was fortunate that no one was there to see them. "Where's the jewelry safe in this place?"

"It's in the security office. We'll hit it after I get these loaded in the van," Donna said, pushing the cart with one hand and stabilizing her garment load with the other. "And in case you forgot, I have money problems, too, but my first priority is to not end up in women's prison."

"Then you probabry should have disconnected the sirent ararm," a man's voice said from the shadows. Eva's eyes darted about, and her index finger drifted to her mouth in an almost quizzical pose. When the speaker stepped into the dim light of the red "Exit" sign, Eva saw Drek Manifold for the first time. The jean jacket looked awful, and the hair looked worse, but she didn't have time to laugh. In front of her, Donna clumsily fumbled with her makeup compact, so it was up to Eva to get rid of him with her acid attack. She didn't know he could make his body elastic, though, and the load of stomach acid hit him, bounced off him and splashed onto the pile of garments. It wasn't like they were stealing a shopping cart full of wool and Kevlar, and when the acid hit the flimsy fabrics, it looked like someone had dumped a gallon of boiling water on a pile of toilet paper. A flame-thrower appeared in Donna's hands, all ignited and ready to cook some Manifold, but just like that, he was gone, receding into the shadows. They didn't have long to wait, though, because denim-clad arms shot out from behind them, encircling each of them like rubber lassos and dragging them to the floor.

The cops came and took them away. Eva got her mugshot taken for posterity, wearing a ten-dollar sweatshirt from Target.

<p style="text-align:center">*   *   **

"So, what's your name?" the slightly built, curly-haired yokel sitting across the locker room aisle asked her for the third time. He asked it with the same nervous, feigned nonchalance every time. It was endearing... the first time.

"Topaz," Eva Destruction lied, for the third time, between gum cracks. *It must suck to be him*, she thought. She had pimples and a big ass in high school, and she'd rather slash her wrists than endure that hell for an entire lifetime. This, though, was a whole different ballgame. He probably got a fresh reminder that he was an invalid a dozen times a day. Still, her sympathy for him had worn out around the ten minute mark. After that, it felt like babysitting an especially stupid or annoying child, and she was far from the motherly sort. Her right leg lay crossed over her left leg, and her right her foot bobbed up and down like a metronome. "You want to write it down this time?"

"What?" the hick asked, confused. "Why would I want to write it down?" He absently clutched a backpack, full of god only knew what. What sort of sundries did a brain damage victim need? A pair of jammies and trail mix in case he got lost? A leash with an ID tag so people could call his owner?

"Whatever," Eva sighed as she chomped away on her bubble gum and examined the scuffed cuticle of her right index finger. Must have done that when she was getting out of that damn helicopter. "Just read your letter."

The guy blinked, looked like he was about to ask a question, then realized that his hand contained a piece of paper. What was Eva doing in Nebraska, anyway? She was born in the ass of nowhere, in her case, eastern Virginia, but at least it was close to water. After she got the hell out of there, she never thought life would bring her back to one of these places. It was like falling off the edge of the earth and landing in the Incredibly Boring Land of Oz (or in this case, Land of Ne). "So," she asked before he could finish the letter, "what do people around her do for fun?" She really didn't care; she knew it would be something boring that featured a made-up word like "quilting" or "shucking," but she felt compelled to interrupt him before his face sprouted that look again... the one when he got to the end of the letter... the one that looked like a cross between someone smelling sour milk and dying... again.

"Huh?" he asked, looking up. "Oh, the usual stuff: go to movies, watch TV, go see a basketball or football game... stuff like that."

Eva rolled her eyes skyward but kept rhythmically chomping on her wad of gum and bobbing her foot. "Sounds *awful*."

"Why? What do you do for fun?" the guy asked, genuinely curious, like only a teenager can be. *How old does he think he is?* she wondered. *Did he still collect baseball cards and answer to pet names that his mommy gave him?* She'd already forgotten his name. Something with an "E." *Now who has the memory problem?* she wondered wryly.

"Well, I like to go to clubs a lot," she said, then added, wistfully, "or at least I used to." Being an international super-criminal kind of hamstrings your social life, although there are some weirdoes out there who get turned on by that sort of thing. The Internet's lousy with them. Not surprising, since there are also people out there who get turned on by other people shitting on them (literally or figuratively), but they weren't the sort of people she aspired to associate with. She once dated a "normal" guy for three weeks. He was a soap opera actor. Nice guy. Cute butt. Looked good in a suit. Once, while she was in the shower, he clicked onto *America's Most Wanted* and saw her robbing an armored car by puking on the back door. He was on the other side of town even before she finished toweling off. He was still alive, but they never spoke again. He was undoubtedly terrified, and she was terrified of seeing him terrified. *Damn you, John Walsh.*

Super-villains were more her speed now. She hated admitting it; she didn't want to associate with "those people," and she certainly didn't want to *be* one of "those people." They knew what she was going through. Some of them even had powers that made hers look quaint. Gravitron once crushed an aircraft carrier like it was a Dixie cup, and the Libertine could steal souls. When you rubbed elbows with super-villains, though, you were almost guaranteed to run into someone who was either psychotic, mutated, or stricken with a God complex the size of the Chesapeake Bay.

"I guess you'd better not live here, then," Ely (that was it: Ely) said, then raised an eyebrow. "What are you doing here, anyway?"

Eva smiled sweetly. Poor bastard already forgot he was a hostage. You'd think that if *anything* made it through his thick skull, that little tidbit would. What did he think, that they were on a date in the girls' locker room? Maybe he just got used to being oblivious. She could tell him… anything at all. She could even tell him the truth about herself. Wouldn't that be an unexpected treat? With her "Most Wanted" status, there weren't many therapists she could open up to anymore, but this would be just as good. Better even, like talking to a cat, except you could get some feedback, then five minutes would pass and flush all your demons into oblivion.

Eva leaned back against the row of lockers and changed the cross of her legs. Between the leather pants, the concrete bench, and the metal lockers, it was hard to get too comfortable, but at least they were in a girls' locker room, where people had actually heard of deodorizers. "I'm here because I'm trying to impress a guy I like."

Ely gave a long nod, as though he could totally relate. "Well, I think you're really hot, and if you have to work to impress him, I don't know what his—" His eyes had drifted down to his letter, and he licked his lips and asked, "How do you pronounce this word?"

Eva leaned forward, ignored him staring at her ample cleavage, and examined the word that his index finger hovered over. "I think it's 'anterograde.'"

He nodded. "Sorry I interrupted you," he said, setting the letter down and giving her his full attention, which was worth about as much as the piece of paper the letter was written on.

"Don't worry about it," she assured him, her jaws still working away on her Hubba Bubba cud. Eva wasn't used to working with people as wide-eyed and innocent as Ely. It was a little disarming. Recently, most of the men she encountered and actually spoke to were either cops, mafia assassins, or in a few cases, space warlords. It had probably been years since someone apologized to her and it wasn't an apology like, "I'm sorry! I'm sorry! Please don't disintegrate me!" Besides, it wasn't Ely's fault that fate stuck him with a permanent tenth-grade education.

"I'm going to my high school reunion, apparently," Ely informed her, gesturing with the letter. "Did you go to my high school?"

"No, I went to high school in Virginia. Norfolk."

"Did the guy you're into go to my high school?" Ely asked, leaning back and folding his hands in front of him.

Eva chuckled. She supposed that out here in the sticks, that qualified as a legitimate question. "No," she replied. "He's from Sweden. I don't even know if they have high schools there."

"What does he farm? Corn or soy beans or what?"

That was an even stranger question, but he seemed so sincere. "Oh, he doesn't farm anything. He's a Socialist."

"Socialist, huh?" Ely said, rotating his head back so that he could stare at the dots in the ceiling panels. "We talked about socialism a little bit last week in my econ class, but for the life of me, I can't remember what it means."

"I don't know a whole lot, other than that they're working toward world domination and they…" She smiled shyly and tilted her head back and leaned it on the locker door, the same way he had done. It felt sort of like reclining, except that the headrest was a sheet of steel with holes punched in it. *God help me, talking to this halfwit is like erasing the last ten years off my own life, in a good way.* All the violence and the modeling… there were so many things she would do differently if she had the chance. "Are you sure you want to hear this? I feel like I'm boring you."

"No, not at all," he insisted, shaking his head vigorously. Of course, how do you bore someone who lived life in five-minute chunks? She could tell him the same story five times, and he would find it just as fascinating the last time as the first. Granted, if she was fat and ugly, he probably wouldn't be half as fascinated, but still: what a life.

"So anyway, Dane was trained by his Socialist masters and sent to America to destroy their freedom to choose their own doctor and drive oversized, four-wheel-drive trucks."

"Who's Dane?" Ely asked, innocently.

"The man I'm in love with," she said, clenching her teeth. Just when she started to relax, he had to remind her why this was *worse* than talking to a dog. Maybe this was how bad mothers feel before they shake their babies. One thing Eva knew for sure: this guy wasn't Drek Manifold.

"Does he love you?"

Eva snorted and looked away. "He loves his helicopter," she muttered.

"What?"

"Nothing."

"Why do you love him?" Ely persisted. "He seems like a pretty mean guy, especially the part about four-wheel-drive trucks. Those are awesome to go muddin' in."

Muddin'. It must be one of those Midwestern pastimes, like cow tipping or drinking corn alcohol. She shrugged her shoulders. "He can be mean, I guess, but it's kind of nice when someone you're used to people being afraid of you, and you find someone who isn't. I don't think he's afraid of anything."

"I'm not afraid of you," Ely said, "and I don't know why anyone would be. You seem really sweet."

"Well, bless your heart," she said, her lips stretching into a thin smile, "but that's probably just my Southern charm shining through." Her gum was losing its flavor, and she could really go for a cigarette right now, but her menthols lay stashed in the cargo net on the back of the pilot's seat in the helicopter. She scanned several of the lockers across the aisle. Maybe one of these little sluts had some regular cigarettes. Unlike most smokers, tar and nicotine actually made Eva's breath smell better. Should she tell this one about...Sure. "What would you say if I told you I could projectile vomit onto the door of a bank vault and cause it to dissolve in ten seconds?"

"I would say that that's impossible," Ely said, hesitantly, as if that response was nothing more than his best guess.

Eva stood up, removed a velvet scrunchy from around her wrist, and began to bunch her flowing red hair into a ponytail. He would freak out, they always do. Even high school kids who are fascinated by bodily fluids freak out, and although it made respect and relationships difficult for her, there was something satisfying about the rush of terror that she could cause. The same sort of men who had who ogled her over the years would gasp and clutch their stomachs. Some wet their pants. Some threw up. All of them genuinely feared her, though. Except for Dane. She could still respect Dane.

She took a couple steps to Ely's right, still blocking him from the door in case he showed the running kind of fear instead of the paralyzed fear. After securely tucking her ponytail into the leather collar of her cat suit, she used one hand to scoop out her wad of gum. With the other, she jammed her extended index finger down her throat. If she had to, she could do it by belching, but something about the sensation of a finger pressing against the soft part of the back of her throat felt like home.

There was the familiar tickle, and then the radioactive vomit roared past her lips, maybe a gallon of it, and struck the steel locker in front of her. She could hear the sizzling metal above the momentary wet slap, but she knew what to listen for. The door had melted through even before the last few specks left her mouth. For her part, it always mystified her how her hand could stay dry, but when faced with the impossibility of the big picture, that was like splitting hairs. When she took a step back and pulled the ponytail from her collar, it almost looked like someone had thrown a hand grenade into the locker and slammed the door.

She looked over at Ely, her full, red lips pressed together in her best I-told-you-so expression, but he looked neither shocked nor sick.

"That's… that's amazing," he said, leaning forward, cautiously, to peer through the hole in the locker. The chick whose locker it was used to have some gym clothes neatly folded on top of some gym shoes, but all that stuff was *long* gone. Maybe it was the teenager in Ely that held him in check, the part that still thought that words like "puke" and "cummerbund" were funny.

"Wow," she said, blinking. "I'm impressed. You and Dane are the only people I've ever seen react that way."

Ely turned away from the hole and squinted. "Dane? Who the hell's Dane?"

*   *   *

Chapter Seven:
9:42 p.m.

Heroin detoxification rarely kills you, but it's like spending a few days alternating between thinking you're about to die and hoping that you're about to die. Kelly had to kick in a holding tank more than once, but the events all bled together into a misshapen ball of unpleasantness. There was some vomiting, mixed with a pinch of writhing, and gallons and gallons of sweat. One thing he remembered from one of his detoxing periods, though, was seeing Drek Manifold.

It was back when Kelly was twenty-two or twenty-three, back when it looked like he was well on his way to accumulating an impressive arrest record. The city cops on the Illinois side were releasing Kelly from lock-up because, for once, he'd managed to flush his stash before the cops broke down the door, and this time around, they didn't have enough to hold him. On one hand, he considered himself lucky. On the other hand, he knew he'd be back, regular as a homing pigeon. That's the definition of a loser: someone who repeats his mistakes.

He was snapping his wallet chain back onto his belt loop just as Manifold strode by in his jean jacket and cowboy boots. He was there to interrogate a few small-time thugs who had been working for Methastophales. As his boots clopped past, Manifold glanced at Kelly with something close to familiarity, but kept right on strutting. The look said, "I know what you are; I've seen your kind before." For Kelly, it stayed lodged in his mind as a singular, depressing experience. Objectively, Manifold looked like such a dork, but like those Buckingham Palace guards with the black fuzzy hats, he pulled off the look because he had dignity to spare. A guy like that could wear a clown suit into the Supreme Court and no one would dare laugh. You can't buy dignity, and you can't mainline it, but that's what Kelly would be trying to do the instant he got off the crosstown bus. And it wasn't even lunchtime.

*   *   *

"Jim Bob Duncan," the Swede called out, followed by a fat dude shuffling from the first row toward center court. He wore red suspenders to keep his husky pants up, and he had almost as much hair on his thick neck as he had on his head. In other words, he looked exactly like a Jim Bob should.

Kelly Edwards barely remembered anything about Jim Bob. Nothing, actually, beyond that he had graduated with some doofus whose parents were cruel enough to name their son "Jim Bob." That's what it read in the yearbook, too. For all Kelly knew, that's what it said on the guy's birth certificate. Assuming that wasn't the case, though, it really said something about you when you didn't just go by "Jim" or "James," and what it said was that you were a fucking moron.

They'd dragged David Allen off the floor almost an hour ago, to god knows where, but every time Kelly's eyes passed that spot where Dave flopped onto the floor like a landed marlin, it felt like a phantom corpse still lingered there. From Jim Bob's bloated form, Kelly's gaze continued across the floor until it landed on the guy in the wheelchair. Sitting there, wearing a puffy, Gortex coat and a pair of bright red Iowa State sweatpants, he still looked like a kid. His pale, bald frame probably weighed the same as he did in high school, and unlike Jim Bob, Kelly could actually remember the cripple's last name: Offerdahl, just like the linebacker from the Dolphins who played around that same time.

Kelly popped a wintergreen Ticktack into his mouth and started sucking. He had trouble dwelling on the welfare of others for more than a few seconds at a time. It was too damn depressing. Every class in every high school across this great nation had its share of alcoholics and wife-beaters, but this crew had some serious issues, Offerdahl's probably being the worst. And now these freaks and losers surrounded Kelly like a legion of ghosts. Why did he even come here in the first place?

He shook his head. Beyond maintaining his sunny disposition, a single-minded sense of self-preservation always motivated Kelly. It was even... practical this time. The fact was, he had no idea what that little black machine was. The Swede never elaborated on that point, and he could see for himself that ol' Dave failed the test, whatever it was. Plus, the fact that they were still testing meant that other people could fail it, too. Fact was, something in Kelly's system might set it off. Even though that toy gun didn't look like much, watching it fuck up Dave's insides downright unnerved Kelly. It reminded him of what happened one time when he watched a guy slam a syringe full of Drano into a vein in his armpit. The memory made Kelly shiver so bad that he almost choked on the tiny candy. There were a couple people in the bleachers that he wouldn't mind seeing get toasted, but Kelly still had enough self-esteem to not count himself among them (not much, mind you, but enough).

Kelly cracked the Ticktack with his incisors and popped another. He wasn't much of a drug addict. For this crowd, yeah, he would certainly qualify, but he was a light-weight among people who made an occupation out of it. He liked his highs, there was no question about that, but he had way too much discipline to be a full-fledged junkie (and not enough to be a dealer). He'd been busted on misdemeanors half-a-dozen times since the state decided he was an adult, but his lack of ambition and all-around pathos kept him from doing any hard time.

After a couple times in county lock-up, he realized that not taking drugs for a few days, while unpleasant with a capital "U", cleaned out your system and drove down your tolerance enough so that he could start getting a good high again. He probably first learned about the physiology that undergirded that trick in health class or an "After-School Special" on the TV, but the information didn't stick, because in both of those versions of reality, narcotics might as well have been cyanide. Rotating drugs worked, too, so if things got too dicey when he was going through short-term withdrawal, he could always steady himself enough to go shoplift some Tussin. Most junkies he knew just stuck with their favorite poison and fixated on the moment like a bunch of narco-Buddhists. Kelly, though, he thought about the future.

Fifty feet away, the dude with the glasses attached the suction cup electrodes to Jim Bob's cantaloupe-sized head, but Kelly's thoughts merely noted the fact; he was still busy feeling guilty. Most junkies tell themselves that they can quit any time they want. Kelly, for all his other faults, never harbored that particular delusion. He felt completely satisfied with quitting for a couple days at a time, once every few weeks. He would usually time his kicks with a Bond-a-thon on TBS and sweat it out on the couch for a few days. Like anybody with an obvious bad habit and collapsed veins, he made some half-assed attempt to quit for real, but then a little surge of stress, just a hiccup in his plan, would come along and flatten him so bad that he'd be shooting and smoking himself into oblivion, just like old times. Maybe deep down, he secretly waited for these hiccups, but in any case, he'd usually lose whatever job he'd picked up and have the added weight of failure to smoke away.

Little surges of stress fill our lives. In fact, life isn't much besides surges of stress. It's an endless fire brigade of buckets of stress that hit you in the face when you aren't looking. You can dance around them for a while, but you get tired and sloppy, and after you slow down, the deluge is relentless. Sometimes you see it coming. Sometimes it surprises you. Sometimes, you deserved it because you just didn't think things through.

Case in point: the dick-sucking contest he attended tonight. He fooled himself into thinking he could come back, see the few old friends he had, and forget about the Jupiter-like gravity of his failure of a life for a couple hours. Now, even if Super-Swede and his henchmen hadn't crashed in, Kelly could realize that the plan was stupid. He'd see people like Rob Turner and listen to that grinning jackass tell anybody within earshot about how his John Deere dealership in Woodly was doing so well that he could pay cash for his shiny new extend-cab truck. Even though Kelly couldn't care less, he was surrounded by people to whom that constituted the epitome of "making it." And what could Kelly counter with? "Uh, yeah, and I deliver pizzas and suck down whip-its at long stoplights."

Then there was Sally. He actually dated her for a while, until one of the proms when he got too stoned to remember to pick her up. High school romances don't normally amount to anything except painful lessons, but after she dumped him, she ended up getting knocked up by one of the Puerto Rican baseball players (Julio or Juarez or something). Kelly always felt somewhat responsible for her life getting ruined that way, but rather than trying to fix things, his guilt just made him sink deeper. She looked good tonight, though, in her slutty black dress, and he didn't know if that made him feel better or worse.

Beyond having to talk to people, just sitting in this stupid gym, surrounded by all these stupid people, took him back to a time filled with hope, when he was a three-sport participant with passing grades and friends and healthy veins. If he'd been a little bit better of an athlete, maybe things would have been different, or at least the good times would have lasted longer. As it was, after his sophomore year, he quit sports and found himself playing King Slacker to a bunch of freshmen and sophomores he didn't know. They thought he was a cool for a while, because he could legally drive them out to the cemetery to smoke bud, but it soon became apparent that they were all a bit more on the ball than Kelly, and while meandering through a drug-addled haze proved to be a temporary phase for them, he ultimately would have to switch out of the amateur dope-head crowd and seek out some pros. The rest, as they say, is a long, dull history. On the plus side, at least drugs helped him keep his weight down; he wore the same size jeans as he did in high school.

Speaking of weight, he absently started to lean back and almost ended up in Laney Braughton's fat lap. Either because she didn't like druggies or because she was a Jehovah's Witness and didn't like being touched by males, she didn't cotton to him brushing her knee with his chicken-wing shoulder blade. Kelly recovered fast enough to avoid getting kneed in the back of the head. At least he was still athletic enough to dodge Laney.

He turned and shot her a scowl, wishing he could go somewhere and smoke something. It was pathetic; he couldn't blame his life on his shortcomings at sports. Stupidity and weakness, sure, but not fucking sports. What if he'd been good enough to play another couple years? The minute he left home to go to Northern or State, he would have just lapsed back into his dark little room. The sky is blue, water's wet, and Kelly Edwards needs his insulation from life.

Down on the gym floor, the suction cups came off and Jim Bob ambled back to his seat. *So,* Kelly thought, *Jim Bob passed the Great Swedish Mystery Test.* Kelly felt fairly neutral about that outcome.

"Maxwell Early," the Swede announced, even if the last name came out pronounced *uh-lee.*

Kelly's left knee started bouncing up and down like a paddle ball and his arm veins right in the crook of his elbow began to ache. Great timing. He'd hadn't shot up all day because he wanted to go to the reunion straight.

Look good for all the divorcees. Look like a winner instead of a bug-eyed creep with flop sweat. Same reason he wore the cheap beige sport coat. Brilliant idea, in retrospect, because now with all the sweating and fidgeting, he looked like the guiltiest man in the building. Hell, he might get gunned down before he gets a chance to fail the Great Swedish Mystery Test. *Oh well*, he told himself, as he leaned forward and hugged his elbows. *One way or another, it'll be over soon.*

*   *   *

Chapter Eight:
9:48 p.m.

"Reggie! Reggie, wake up!" Sally called, shaking his shoulder. He was lying on the floor, behind the overturned salad bar at Ruby Tuesday's. Shards of glass lay scattered everywhere. So did shards of cucumbers and cherry tomatoes. "Oh my god, how did you even get here?"

Reggie blinked and lifted the back of his head off the tile a few inches before looking around. The last thing he remembered was the super-villain El Taco crashing through the front window of the Taco Bell across the street. El Taco was a Mexican national who considered his country's food a cultural treasure and had taken it upon himself to steal Glen Bell's fortune, one store at a time. Reggie remembered climbing out of his seat so that he could call the police, but he must not have made it. A year ago, he could have made the call from his seat; he used to carry a cell phone, but people kept stealing it when he would pass out. It wasn't paying for all the 900-number calls that pissed him off, so much as explaining them. "I don't know," he told Sally after a few seconds delay. "I don't remember anything after I left the table."

"It was incredible! Drek Manifold fought Captain Taco right in the middle of Hoyt Street." Reggie glanced past her, through the broken front window. It was as though a small, localized tornado had roared through the middle of the street, leaving half a dozen cars either crushed or overturned in its wake. "Manifold got thrown through the front window, but he dropped a light pole on Captain Taco and cracked his shell, and then just like that, he was gone. It was absolutely incredible!"

"Yeah," Reggie said, dragging himself to his knees. He thought about correcting her, telling her it was "El Taco," but he didn't even have the stones to correct her the previous week when she referred to him as a necrophiliac. He looked around. The sleep attack must have hit him just as Manifold came through the window. Lucky he was passed out and hidden behind the salad bar or else the flying glass might have shredded his face. Lucky Sally saw the fight, too, because now she could think about a real man before she went to bed tonight, not some invalid. "Yeah, I'm sorry I missed it."

*   *   *

"I'm going pass out in the aisle," Reggie Sleeve whispered to Sally without looking at her. "When I get their attention, make a break for it."

The gym was far from silent. No one spoke out loud, and because McVain had everyone turn over their cell phones, there was no subtle, telltale beeping of a text message being written. Every time someone shifted his or her weight or took a deep breath, though, the wooden bleachers let out a series of creaks that was reminiscent of a field of bleating sheep, and the gaggle of former classmates did a lot of shifting. Then there was the coughing from all the smokers who were having their early-stage emphysema flare-ups from not firing up a cigarette in over an hour. The box on wheels that everyone kept getting hooked up to did its part, churning out the beeps constantly and spitting out strand after strand of cash register paper every few minutes. Even the mouse made clicking sounds as it ran slivery tongue over its needle-like teeth. Despite all this interference, Sally responded to Reggie as if someone had strapped a megaphone to her face like a feedbag. "I on't ink at's a ood ieeah," she whispered without moving her lips.

Although he couldn't make out the exact wording of the statement, the wide-eyed, concerned stare that accompanied it provided all the reply he needed. Reggie Sleeve was no coward. Maybe it came from spending a third of his life as an invalid, but he wasn't the least bit afraid of putting himself in harms way. He wasn't especially suicidal; if anything, he constantly sought ways to prove himself to... himself. In this case, though, he couldn't make the break for freedom because of his narcolepsy. He wasn't a neurologist, so he didn't know why what happened to him happened. He only knew that whenever he felt a surge of adrenaline, there was a good chance that it brought an involuntary nap with it. It was completely emasculating and made him feel like the Incredible Reverse-Hulk: when he became angry, he became irrelevant.

Practically speaking, it wasn't that debilitating. It wasn't like being a quadriplegic or having brain cancer. In a good month, he might only get one or two sleep attacks, but that alone kept him from getting a driver's license. He had to move from Kooterville to Transverse City because the public transportation was better. Buses weren't so bad, though. Riding a bus made you an environmentalist without even trying, and there aren't nearly as many chronic masturbators who ride as most people would guess. He still worked out a lot, but he had to lift using the Nautilus machines rather than free weights so as to avoid crushing himself. The worst part of his condition wasn't the inconvenience, it was the waiting and dreading, the expectation that nap time could come at any moment. Since excitement triggered the attacks, he became useless during moments that required the greatest vigilance, moments like... oh, right now.

It was frustrating, to say the least. He would spend half an hour a month enduring a sleep attack and 99.9% of his remaining waking hours worrying about the next one. He held onto the information like a dirty little secret, too, like he'd done something wrong, worked in a Nazi death camp or something, because if the Average Joe or Jane found out about his condition, they'd stare at Reggie, waiting for him to pass out face first in a bowl of soup. When Reggie went to the video store, he stopped renting comedies because every jackass writer in Hollywood seemed to think having a hypocretin deficiency was so freakin' hilarious that they had to put a narcoleptic in every movie. Thank god he didn't have Torrette's Syndrome, because apparently it provided an even better go-to neurological disorder joke than narcolepsy.

Now for the silver lining: this little brain glitch that made his life a walking punchline could finally... *finally*... make itself useful. He could bail into the aisle and act like he had a sleep attack. Enough people knew about his condition that someone would speak up before McVain could use that gun to turn his brain into cornmeal, and by that time, Sally would have slid off the end of the bleachers, crept down the hall to the athletic director's office, and called the police. Easy, peasy, Japanesey... except that, right now, Sally looked too petrified to move an inch in either direction. He'd ask

someone else, but he was right next to the aisle and she was the only person
he could talk to without drawing an obscene amount of attention to himself.

He kept his head still as his eyes moved from villain to villain.
Occasionally, McVain or the brunette chick would make eye contact with
him, but he would quickly look away, the way nervous schlubs do. Maybe
he was kidding himself: the invalid trying to live out the hero fantasy, even
if it was in his own mind. Somebody had to be the hero, though. Marv
Cutler, Chet Roberts, and David Allen were all rotting in a storage closet
somewhere, and god only knew if that bitch hadn't iced poor Ely Lisch back
in the locker room. The only reason McVain hadn't started wholesale
executions was because he didn't want to deal with a human stampede.
Plus, he needed leverage, just in case he was right and Drek Manifold lurked
somewhere in the building. Maybe that's why none of Reggie's classmates
had mustered an escape attempt: they also were waiting for the man himself
to make an appearance. If McVain was wrong, of course, they were all in
for a long wait. And if that was the case, at the end of the night, hostages
would become witnesses, and he didn't seem like the sort to leave witnesses
alive.

Reggie scanned the back of the balding, ball-capped, and Aquanetted
heads in search of something he could tell Sally that would make her willing
to risk her life (although, to be fair, staying in this gym involved risking her
life). McVain was convinced that one of the assembled dudes was Manifold
(assuming it was a dude), but who would Reggie bet on? None of them
looked like the Denim Defender. Reggie had never met the man, but
Manifold was purported to be good-looking, and Father Time and an endless
string of Big Macs had ravaged most of these farm boys. Most of the
assembled guys who were winners sported short hair, they didn't rock the
Richard Marx mullet like Manifold. That meant that, assuming McVain was
right, Manifold could change shape. That meant that it could be a woman,
even if that seemed a little weird. That meant that Reggie had to stop
thinking in terms of external characteristics.

He caught Sally's eye as he scanned, and she gave him a thin, sorry-
I'm-a-coward smile, but Reggie's thoughts had traveled elsewhere, and he
could only manage an automatic nod. Manifold would have to be somebody
who had a lot of time on his hands (or her hands... it was possible).
Eyewitnesses had spotted him in a variety of localities, from Des Moines to

Chicago, often during the middle of the day. Whatever the other faults of the assembled crowd were, they were a hard-working, gainfully employed, primarily blue-collar bunch. Granted, Reggie wasn't the sort to keep tabs on acquaintances after graduation; he didn't see much point since he didn't like most of his classmates (the popularity quotient for narcoleptics hovered somewhere below fat chicks and above retards).

It dawned on Reggie that he had an untapped well of personal information at his disposal. Donna Morgan was the Senior Class Secretary, or whatever the official name was for the jackass who gets stuck with arranging these get-togethers. She printed the little booklets that had everybody's occupation, church affiliation, favorite color, communicable diseases, and whatever else people wanted to brag on. About three rows and twenty people currently separated Reggie from Donna Morgan. She wasn't accessible, but the booklets surely were. Reggie hadn't picked one up, he wasn't the sort to pick up shit like that, but Sally was. He could picture her later tonight, thumbing through it, heaving a sigh of regret as she ran her fingertips over the black and white reprint of her senior photo in the yearbook, pasting it in a scrapbook in its chronologically appropriate place, then never looking at it again.

Without risking another glance at Sally, Reggie's hand snaked out and grabbed her purse. She resisted, probably out of that anti-mugging reflex that women are born with, but after a second of struggle, Reggie's eyes shifted toward her and all but bored laser beams through her face. *Jesus Christ, you crazy bitch! I'm not going to run off with it,* his thoughts screamed. The look injected enough logic into the situation for her to let the purse strap slide off her shoulder.

Reggie made a conscious effort to not look at anything in the purse but the red booklet with gold lettering, and he acquired his target after only a couple seconds of rummaging. Mission accomplished... except that he accidentally saw the conical dish of birth control pills before closing the purse and shoving it in her direction. Despite everything, it jarred him a bit. Who the hell carries birth control pills around with them? The purse was only the size of a sandwich bag and one of the things she decided to carry was birth control pills. In some ways, that's even more embarrassing than carrying half a refill of RU-486 around with you. Does she live at the fucking bus station or something? "Let it go," Reggie muttered to himself as he refocused on the booklet in his lap.

"Welcome Back Chanticleers!" the reunion program's cover announced, the gold letters arching over the head of a muscular, fearsome version of Randy the Rooster, their beloved mascot. In real life, the costume they used for Randy reeked of mothballs and looked a bit less frightening than a rubber chicken. If Cocky, the University of South Carolina Gamecock had been dragged behind a pick-up for a few miles, he would have vaguely resembled Randy. High school wasn't about real life, though. Neither were reunions.

Before he opened the program to Page 1, Reggie made a preliminary prediction. Based on the inherent time constraints of super-heroing, Reggie bet that either Rob Turner or Kelly Edwards were Manifold's alter ego. Rob owned a John Deere dealership and kept his own hours. He always acted like a bit of an ass, though, so unless his abrasive personality was the perfect cover that had developed from childhood on, Reggie had a difficult time imagining Rob doing anything virtuous unless it directly led to him getting laid.

Then there was Kelly. Kelly delivered pizzas (at the moment) for a local pizzeria, which when you thought about it, was a perfect super hero job: erratic hours, minimal supervision, and constant contact with the public. Plus, despite his best efforts, Kelly had yet to smoke himself retarded. The most convincing argument in his favor would be that he looked like he slept about forty-five minutes a night, which was how Reggie always imagined a super-hero's alter ego looking. On the other hand, Kelly had an impressive string of misdemeanors on his record, and in a few celebrated cases, being Drek Manifold would have involved arresting his own drug suppliers. Much like Rob, if Kelly was really Manifold, the acting performance was Oscar-worthy.

Other possibilities existed. Tom Gilmore, for instance, operated his dad's real estate business and made frequent trips to Chicago. He seemed almost too busy, though. Chase Wilder had come to the reunion wearing a suit and a thirty dollar haircut, so he must be important. Eric Atchison was a plumber, so he basically made his own hours, too, but Dr. Poindexter's mysterious machine had already cleared him. No, as far as Reggie was concerned, Rob and Kelly were the favorites. With that as his point of reverence, he turned to Page 1.

*　　　*　　　*

Chapter Nine:
9:55 p.m.

"We almost had him one time," Johnny Cleavage said as he picked up his glass off the lacquered surface of the bar and tossed the rest of the J & B Scotch down his throat. The still intact ice cubes made a clink when he slapped it down on the mahogany plank. It was his third Scotch on the rocks, and he was putting them away so fast that he might as well have started ordering them neat because the ice wasn't diluting a thing. *"The Beachmaster had Manifold encased in cement, buried in the sand, waiting for the tide to come in and drown him,"* he said, using the condensation from the glass to matt down his comb-over. *"I was standing there... waiting for it... waiting for it, and just like that, he was gone."*

"That's a fascinating strategy," Dr. Poindexter pointed out, which was super-villain shorthand for *"why didn't you just shoot him in the face?"* They were all guilty of that, though. When you're analyzing a scenario that didn't work, it's easy to be cold and calculating, as if human nature wasn't involved, but logic and emotion don't mix. In the moment, you want to savor every second. Would receiving a Nobel Prize be half as nice if they mailed it to you? He doubted it.

There's also a matter of one's calling card. A hero winds up dead with a bullet wound, any piker can claim it was his. But if you leave the body with salty sand in his lungs, or a rhinoceros horn jutting from his chest, or whatever, everybody knows who did it. Once, Poindexter had a dream that the cops found Manifold's body turned inside out, like someone had reached down his throat, grabbed something solid, and pulled. *"Faith and begorrah"* one of the dream cops said, lifting his cap to scratch his bald scalp *(in the dream he was Irish)*. *"Well, laddies, only one villain is brilliant enough to pull of that move: Dr. Poindexter." Then, the cop drank whiskey out of a flask and crossed himself. Poindexter woke from the dream with an erection.*

Poindexter knew the temptations of the perfect killing stroke, so he didn't press the issue. Besides, he liked Johnny. Dane never understood how he could be friends with a transsexual, but it was a scientist thing. They were the brains of their respective outfits, and both looked to the other to exchange ideas (despite the version of reality that Dane likes to peddle, the Wolfian Ducks were Johnny's idea: altering genetic codes were his bread and butter). Besides, Johnny always wore a trench coat when he was off the clock, so no one could see his bodacious ta-tas.

"Yeah," Johnny said, staring into the bottom of his glass with foggy eyes. "Because our crew'd been using guns and knives so much, the idea was that he would show up invulnerable, but when he did, he would only be impervious on the outside, like projectiles. Drowning him seemed like a solid plan."

"So how did he escape?" Poindexter asked, taking a sip from the straw stuck in his bright blue frozen Margarita. Pastel drinks were frowned on in the super-villain community, but Margaritas were the special tonight at TGI Friday's. Super-villainy was either boom or bust, and at the moment, Dane's crew had hit a boom. Habits were hard to break, though, and Poindexter always drank the special.

"Shrank," Johnny said, picking up the glass and taking one more, hard slurp in the faint hope of suctioning a few drops of whiskey off the ice cubes. He set the glass back down, looked over at Poindexter, and shrugged. "Not exactly unexpected, but what are you going to do? You roll the dice with that asshole. You never know what ability he's packing, or even if it's a new one or an old one."

Poindexter nodded, knowingly. "Indeed. When you were relating the story, I thought it was going to conclude with him communicating with aquatic life."

"Has he done that with you?"

"No, but once Dane pushed him out of an airplane without knowing that he could liquefy himself in that particular incarnation," Poindexter

informed his drinking partner. "He splashed in the middle of a hayfield and met us in St. Paul when we landed."

It was Johnny's turn to give a knowing nod. The mood had become confessional, and that wasn't good... for either of them. Theirs was a lonely road headed to nowhere, but it was bearable as long as they didn't admit it. Thankfully, Johnny looked up and asked, "You ready to get out of here?"

Poindexter really wasn't ready, he still had half a margarita to go, but if they waited, Johnny would order another drink, and then things where guaranteed to get either bawdy or mind-numbingly depressing. He took one last pull of frozen alcohol through the straw and nodded.

Outside, Poindexter buttoned his sweater to protect himself from the cold Peoria night. His Jane Mansfield tits pressed out so far that they almost closed the distance between the two friends by half. "So," Johnny said, "you never said where you guys are hiding out?"

"Oh, I found a great deal over at this abandoned bakery on 19th. The bread oven is still operational. I haven't deduced how, yet, but I plan to turn it into some sort of deathtrap. What about the Beachmaster? Where is he at the moment?"

"Marion," Johnny replied. He walked hunched over from being too top heavy, and it gave him the posture of a seventy-year-old. "The Federal Penitentiary. The whole crew got boned."

"Really?" Poindexter said, shocked by the unexpected news. He stared across the street, waiting for the white-lettered "walk" signal to illuminate. No point in getting caught jaywalking. "That's horrible. How did that happen?"

"Well," Johnny began, but his voice gradually deepened into an equally familiar rasp, "it turned out that Manifold can change shape." When the inevitable hand dropped on Poindexter's shoulder, it was not a gesture of comfort.

*   *   *

Dr. Arliss Poindexter finished attaching the electrodes onto the sides of Nicki Edmonds' head. There was no telling what her name was now, but ten years ago, according to the yearbook, it was Nicki Edmonds. People change substantially over the course of a decade, and he would guess that one morphological change that took place during the ensuing years was that she had developed an ass the size of a Brinks truck. He couldn't be certain, though; the yearbook photo only showed them from the shoulders and above.

Attaching the electrodes to her temples proved more difficult than normal because conductant had mixed with the layers of clinging sweat and hairspray residue to form a slippery paste. Between the flop sweat and the silent crying, she was probably shedding more water per minute than a marathon runner in Death Valley. "It's alright, Miss," Dr. Poindexter assured her in voice he hoped conveyed mild sympathy. "The alpha-2 reader creates a barely detectable sensation that's not altogether unpleasant. The entire process takes less than one minute."

She turned her mascara streaked raccoon eyes in his direction for the briefest of moments and nodded. Her baby-shit-brown eyes contained a sweet, trusting glow that made Dr. Poindexter curious as to how fast one could develop Stockholm syndrome, but the face they lay imbedded within resembled the Lon Cheany version of *The Phantom of the Opera*. Even her blubbering mug wasn't nearly as frightening as the lantern-jawed visage glowering above her. "Shut up, you," Dane thundered at Poindexter. "Just do da job."

Poindexter nodded silently and retracted his hands from Nicky Edmonds' temples like a seasoned Jenga player anticipating a tower collapse. And... the... wires... stayed in place. With Dane looking on, he returned his attention to the alpha-2 detector. He avoided looking in Dane's direction. Poindexter wasn't a prideful man, but he hated getting yelled at. That's why he preferred to stay in his lab as much as possible: in the lab, it's just you and a bunch of inanimate objects and rodents that don't judge you. At least Dane didn't bash Poindexter's cranium with the butt of his fist, again. How many MIT alums had to put up with that? It didn't hurt, but it usually jarred his glasses off the bridge of his nose, and enduring it in front of all these people, who probably enjoyed physical humor, humiliated him terribly. As he twisted the receptor dials to match Ms. Edmonds' EEG frequency, he reminded himself to focus on life's positives. Only three people had gotten killed so far, and Dane hadn't given Poindexter a concussion. After all, a shout of "Shut up, you," was almost always a harbinger of some physical manifestation of violence, and Dane tended to get nervous on big jobs.

Poindexter sighed. People (the few with whom he interacted) always wanted to know why he worked for Dane. If the question came only from law enforcement officials or crying hostages, he could chalk it up to emotional aversion to Dane, but the few people he knew socially asked it, too. The relationship between him and Dane McVain marked a rarity in criminal partnerships. The Alpha Bitch and Betty were purported to be lovers. The Beachmaster never hit Johnny Cleavage during their entire working experience together, and if he ever accosted Johnny with a harsh word, he usually compensated monetarily by buying Johnny a nice tubetop or something similar. The single question basically amounted to two questions: "why do you align yourself with one so evil?" and "why do you align yourself with one who treats you so deplorably?" These, in turn, spawn another set of latent questions: "why are you so evil?" and "why are you so stupid?"

Poindexter refused to address any question that implied his own stupidity; questioning the intelligence of someone so obviously brilliant merely proved the idiocy of the questioner. As for the other question, one must first ask if evil exists, and if you determine that it does, it's still questionable whether Dane McVain represents said evil. Since the unquestioned goal of socialism is to crush the spirit of corporate freedom and prevent the soul-enriching act of conspicuous consumption, the answer is "probably 'yes,' but maybe 'no.'"

The bigger existential issue involved whether this label of evil could possibly pertain to Dr. Arliss Poindexter. He was neither a philosopher nor an economist, after all. He was a man of science, and his loyalty lay with the search for scientific discovery, but that search contained an unavoidable element of economics. All scientists need funding, and in aligning himself with Dane, he afforded himself not only the opportunity to attain that funding, but to experiment without the cumbersome ethical considerations that most scientists in the public sector must contend with (In fact, he once wrote and submitted a paper to *The Journal of Science,* about how super-villainy had advanced the cause of physics, genetics, and chemistry by several decades, but the editors refused to publish the paper based on their little-known policy about not printing the work of convicted felons).

In any case, the way he lived his life also allowed him to see the fruits of his labor in actual applications. Working for the military, the Wolfian

Ducks probably never would have made it out of the test tube phase, and the Automated Death-Thrower undoubtedly would have collected dust or been shuttled off for use in some Islamic country no one had ever heard of. Yes, his loyalty remained with the spirit of discovery, not to the laws and nations of man, and if he had to play toady to the unstoppable monolith of socialism to see it through, then so be it.

Once the alpha-2 detector was set and the electrodes formed a temporary truce with gravity, Poindexter flipped the switch and waited for the machine to churn out its findings. The process would take almost a minute, so he turned to scan the crowd. Most of the audience had been watching Nicki Edmonds intently, no doubt hoping she was Manifold, but their gaze fell away the instant that Poindexter turned toward them. They feared him, all eighty-plus people in the audience (well, perhaps with the exception of the palsied guy in the wheelchair staring out at nothing). In truth, they probably feared Dane or the Knockout Mouse, but Poindexter was the one that invented the neural disruptor, and without his genius, the Knockout Mouse would have died long ago from rodent rickets or mumps or whatever those cretins at the NIH would have injected him with. So, by proxy, these people were scared of him. Their always bulging, sometimes weepy, eyes flitted from threat to threat as they sat, pale and fidgety, and the scene brought him no small amount of satisfaction. Perhaps that meant that there was more at stake for him in these professional endeavors than merely scientific excellence, but once again, he was no philosopher.

He also was no bully. Quite the opposite, actually, but he came from a town a lot like this by the name of Albany, New York, and he was terribly familiar with the world of public high school. The big ones, like the beefy, slack-jawed moron in the front wearing his sleeveless flannel, used to push a young Arliss Poindexter down in the parking lot and tear holes in the knees of his polyester pants. The handsome ones, like the tie-wearing hair-comber in the second row, used to laugh at him in the Phys. Ed. shower because of his elongated nipples. And the fragrant beauties, lest we forget... why, they were the worst of all. They... like the blonde at the far right side of the bleachers who looked like she used half a bottle of Aqua Net before stepping out the door... they didn't even know he was alive. Even after four first-place finishes in the New York State Science Fair and a private aviary stocked with mutated birds, he remained a shadow at the edge of their spotlight. As the old saying goes: the opposite of love is not hate, the opposite of love is indifference. Well, at least the bullies and the louts had the courtesy to hold him in contempt.

Poindexter sighed and threw the final switch. The woman (whose name he had already forgotten) jumped as though 140 volts of current were running through her (in reality, there were less than eighty). Most of her startle response came from the gurgling sound that the magnificent machine emitted. The paper print-out crept out of the dispenser slot, one centimeter at a time, and... surprise, surprise, her lumpy body did not contain a particularly high level of alpha-2 particles.

Hmmm. A strand of bright pink had begun to show on the paper roll. It was the same sort of paper normally used with cash register receipts (Dane actually had to hold up a Rite Aid in Dubuque just to get a box of them), so the presence of color meant that the roll would need changing soon. Poindexter tore the spent length of paper off the roll, double-checked the results, and gave Dane what was now a customary shake of the head. There was enough room on the roll for at least one more subject.

"Kellen Edwards," Dane bellowed.

*   *   *

Chapter Ten:
10:02 p.m.

The Mustang careened wildly to the side of the road, uprooting a blue mailbox and one of those plastic Daily Harvester *newspaper bins. It was supposed to be a routine beer-run, but some kid on a bike had hogged a quarter of the lane. Chase had been lighting a cigarette as they rounded the corner and didn't see the little puke, but his girlfriend, Shasta, grabbed the steering wheel. That normally would have been a backhanding offense, but Chase was busy right now, trying to keep his year-old car from flying off the Seventeenth Street Bridge.*

The car slammed into the guardrail at almost thirty-five miles per hour and broke through. They were airborne. Shasta screamed her fucking head off, and to be honest, Chase couldn't tell if he had wet his pants. Now, gravity was about to have its way with them, and the only thing between them and hell was fifteen feet of murky water. Thompson and Lindy were in the back, and Lindy wasn't wearing any pants, much less a seatbelt. They'd be killed on impact. They'd have to share a funeral. Chase was too drunk to remember whether he had buckled up or not, but that didn't sound like something he'd do.

Everything seemed to slow down in front of Chase's wide eyes. The Mustang drifted forward as though riding a cloud and tilted toward the ground. Black, choppy water filled his view and the car almost appeared to pause in mid-air. He tried turning the steering wheel, but that only worked if you were piloting Supercar. Then, the car's battered nose dipped toward the ground, and the vehicle... literally paused in mid-air. For real, this time.

Drifting like a leaf on a benevolent wind, the car levitated over the broken guard rail, back onto the street. Its wheels gently hugged the pavement again, right next to the battered boots of Drek Manifold. "Holy Shit!" Chase said, then gulped down a couple mouthfuls of air. In the back seat, Lindy started to shimmy back into her pocketless black stretchpants. "Holy shit. You aren't going to arrest me, are you?"

"No, I won't," Manifold informed him, "but I think you should give me your keys. You're in no condition to drive, and if I'm not mistaken, you aren't even old enough to drink."

Chase obediently removed his key from the ignition, but quickly reconsidered the situation. He'd busted his ass begging his dad to buy him this car, and he'd be damned if this creep was going to deprive him of his right to drive. His fingers closed around the key ring and tucked them against his chest. "Are you fucking nuts, you goddamn piece of shit?" Shasta shrieked, punching him in the shoulder. "Give him the goddamn keys!"

Chase eventually gave the superhero the goddamn keys, and if it had ended there, things would have been cool between the two of them, but Manifold just had to completely ruin Chase's chances of getting laid. After he took the keys, he looked back at the small crowd of gathering teenagers and said, "Remember kids: the path of heroism is paved with disciprine and bravery, not teen pregnancy and Pabst."

*   *   *

Chase Wilder was royally pissed. He'd been talking to Gidget Stoyakovich for over an hour, probably handed out a hundred head nods, seventy-five "Uh huhs," fifty "Oh reallys," and a dozen "Oh! No ways." She just kept yammering away, complaining about how she was tired of being the Channel 5 weather girl and how, since she and her husband were finished, she just wanted to move to a bigger city and start over. Listening and responding to that shit had its own rhythm, like dancing: Blah blah blah. *Oh really.* Blah blah blah. *Uh huh.* Blah blah blah blah! *Oh! No way!* And Chase was a goddamn Denny Tario at it.

The important thing about the conversation, and the reason he invested an hour of his life in it, was that Chase worked as a MegaCorp financial advisor, so he made more money than her fireman husband, and he lived in Omaha, which might as well be Paris compared to the Tri-Cities.

Thus, he fit Gidget's major criteria. Plus, she was still hot (in a heavily made-up sort of way), he took her to the prom their senior year, *and* she touched his arm twice tonight. All this added up to the implication that if he put up with a couple hours of her bitching, he would end the night with a parking lot blowjob from a former homecoming queen. Of course, life doesn't always work as smoothly as the advice of your MegaCorp financial advisor, and since that fucking Nazi in the Armani showed up, Chase got stuck holding Gidget's hand while she forced her knees together so hard she might as well have been cracking walnuts.

Chase stared at the big foreigner, hoping that his eyes smoldered beneath his squint. *I could take him if he didn't have that stupid gun*, Chase thought, but he had always been frighteningly good at deluding himself and dismissing contrary information. As far as he could tell, McVain probably weighted around 225, which Chase could max out on that weight in the clean and jerk back when he was guzzling whey shakes and popping protein pills with every meal. That was back when he had a serious future as a body builder, back before he hurt his knee, got a correspondence financial advisor's license, and the world became his bitch.

Strangely, one of the only things that made Chase think twice about his capacity to kick the guy's ass was the haircut. Crew cuts usually meant a military background, and unless TV and movies had been lying to him for all these years, they taught you some seriously messed up shit in those places. Crew cuts were an indicator of the unknown, like those floppy pajamas that karate guys wear, or slanty eyes. Chase used to have a crew cut, and he would have loved to have gone into the Marine Corp, but his knee was so fucked up. If it wasn't and he had, McVain wouldn't have made it ten feet before Sergeant Wilder had cut him down with an M-16.

There was only one other major warning flag: the guy's foreign accent. It wasn't like Balki's from *Perfect Strangers*, so the guy probably came from Russia, which generally meant trouble. You didn't even need to look outside the action movie genre to know that. Schwarzenegger, Lundgren, and Van Damme... all Russian, and he'd seen somewhere that Lou Ferrigno and Sly Stallone were from the same country... Lithuania, maybe. Besides the haircut and the accent, though, the only other thing that kept Chase from charging McVain and dropping him like a bag of dirt was the giant mouse. What the hell was up with that thing?

Gidget's clammy hand quivered in his, so he gave it a squeeze and gave her a smug smile, like he had everything under control. It was the same look he gave to clients when they came to him because the stocks in their retirement fund were hemorrhaging massive amounts of money. He'd endured situations before where he had to listen to a chick yammer on for a couple of hours and ended up not getting laid, but that was usually because the chick turned out to be a massive cunt-rag. Before the carnival of freaks showed up, Gidget certainly seemed itching for a trip to the nurse's office before the night was out, but even an expedition to scale Mount Wilder can get scrubbed by an act of God.

He almost started laugh-choking when he saw Kelly Edwards shambling up to the testing chair, sweating the way one only can after swallowing a handful of niacin tablets. *Fucking Edwards? Save us the time and the electricity.* Chase had been living in a townhouse in downtown Omaha for a few years now, and he'd lived in the Tri-Cities through high school and long enough to get his associate's degree. So, like most residents, he managed to see Drek Manifold up close a couple times. One thing he knew for a fact was that the only thing that Manifold and Kelly Edwards had in common was long hair, and at least Manifold looked like he washed his.

The dork wore some off-the rack sport coat for the occasion, probably hoping to look like he made something of himself. *We all know you're delivering pizzas, asshole*, Chase wanted to yell. Christ, you could give a guy like that a million dollars, and he'd end up losing it all in his veins. The only reason Chase even remembered Edwards' name was because they played football together for, like, two years, and the only thing memorable about him was how fast he changed. He used to be a runty little schmuck, but a normal runty little schmuck, and then BAM! Like, the next day, he might as well have been staggering around the halls with a syringe hanging out of his arm. If Kelly got hopped up on meth, PCP, and a bag full of glue, he might be able to make like a super-hero as long as the rush lasted, but until then, that machine of McVain's would just be measuring zeros.

It took some doing, but Dr. Dorkenstein found enough dry skin on Kelly to hook him up to the machine. Chase stared, a bemused expression lingering on his lips, hoping that Edwards would look his way so Chase could laugh at him or mimic the International Eat-Out sign. Edwards' eyes never left his lap, though. The machine started its, by now, familiar beeps and churns, then spit out the strip of paper, and that's when a limp body spilled into the bleacher aisle with a dull thud. After that, things got a little dicey.

* * *

Chapter Eleven:
10:05 p.m.

"If you let me go, I'll make it worth your while," Donna Correction said to Manifold. A mass of webbing kept her securely braced against the outside of a brick wall, courtesy of Kid Thorax. She considered herself lucky, though. Manifold could apparently generate ice from his fingertips this time around, and Eva stood encased in a gigantic block of it.

Manifold stood several feet away from her, near in the mouth of the alley, with his arms folded. He didn't seem to hear her as he stared down the street, no doubt listening for the sound of police sirens. A couple overturned cars lay in the middle of the street, but Manifold and his icy touch easily had extinguished the fires. A giant bear trap Donna had conjured lay in the middle of the sidewalk, but like Eva, it was encased in a block of ice and never had a chance to do its job. The silence in the alleyway was awkward enough that Donna considered making her inquiry a second time, just in case he didn't hear her, but Manifold turned and regarded her with those deep, brown eyes. "What do you mean by that?"

Donna licked her lips, wondering how lewd she should be. This was no time to play it modest, but by the same token, she somehow doubted Manifold was big into kink. She had always regarded him as a stiff, the way good heroes are supposed to be, but the way he was looking at her made her wonder if he was a eunuch. "Um, I'll... let you do me if you let me go." She meant it, too. Hell, you could have lined up the Eighth Precinct down the sidewalk, and she would have gone over them like a trained seal to avoid a stint in prison.

"'Do you,'" he repeated, neutrally. "Um, I'm frattered, but no thank you." He turned away and kept staring down the street."

"I'm sure Eva would be down with it, too," she added, trying to stay seductive and avoid sounding desperate. It was hard, though, because she couldn't have been more desperate. She absolutely, positively did not want to go back to women's prison. She didn't have to do solitary time in a special holding chamber to counteract her powers the way Eva did, but general population was no picnic, either. She was real popular with the Jerry Springer *crowd, and without her regular resources (like makeup and Nair) she felt like some sort of cave-woman. "We could go back to the hideout and take our time…"*

"Again, I'm frattered, but I don't see that happening," Manifold said, not batting an eye.

Two super-powered super-models. At the same time. And he didn't even consider it. "Are you a homosexual?" she asked, exasperated.

"No," he assured her, "but if that makes you feer better or protects your reputation, go ahead and use it."

Donna inhaled to make a remark about the variety of sex he probably desired, but the distant sound of sirens muted her. Kid Thorax scurried down the wall from above her and plopped down next to Manifold. If he didn't stand with that pronounced slouch, he was probably 5'10" or so, so he didn't look like much of a kid. He barely looked like much of a human. "What'th the thcore, G?" he asked Manifold. Talking through the mandibles gave him a horrible lisp (which made her wonder why he didn't go with "Kid Arachnid" or "Web-Boy"), but that didn't put any crimp in his social situation that the scaly skin and simian arms hadn't already created.

"I need to be taking off," Manifold said. "Make sure the police melt the ice graduarry: Don't use a sauna of more than 120 degrees and then cut the heat immediately."

"Will do," Kid Thorax said, giving an exuberant salute. "Nice working with you again, Mithter Manifold."

"Rikewise," Manifold said without shaking the boy's hand. Between the two of them, it was like amateur hour at Speech Impediment Theater. As Manifold turned to leave, he gave Donna a thin smile. "Hopefully, someday we can stop meeting like this." She didn't know what he meant by that. Maybe he was trying to appeal to her better nature, like she could make

*better choices and live a better life. She hated condescension, and if she
could have conjured up an ice pick and shoved it through one of those big
brown eyes, she would have.*

*He walked out of the alleyway, into the street, and just like that, he
was gone. He hadn't disappeared, but within seconds, her visual field filled
with goggles, mandibles, and a curly shock of red hair. "Tho thweetneth, I
couldn't help but overhear that the boythcout thot you down. How about
you and the red head get trapped in the Thpider Hole?"*

*For the first time, Donna wished she could switch powers with Eva,
because non-super-powered puke probably wouldn't drive this one away. At
least he'd succeeded in making women's penitentiary looked like a day at
the spa.*

*   *   *

Donna Correction couldn't get the nails on her left hand the same
length as the one's on the right. It struck her as so bizarre; she could conjure
any animate or inanimate object smaller than a Volkswagon out of thin air,
anything she could imagine, but everything about her appearance seemed out
of whack. That was why models needed their stylists. If you stare in the
mirror constantly to make sure everything's in place, that makes you a
narcissist. If you stop caring how you look, that makes you a slob. A stylist
gives you the best of both worlds.

Donna used to have a stylist, because she used to be a model named
Donna Keeler. A *real* model, not somebody that appeared in an aluminum
siding advertisement for the *Hicksville Times.* She still owned her copies of
the issues of *Casino Player, Oxygen,* and *American Spa Seeker* she once
graced the cover of. She kept them in one of the plastic containers in a
storage shed in Tacoma. Maybe she never achieved "super" model status
(which was kind of ironic, now that she thought about it), but she made a
handsome living with her looks. Those were heady times, in retrospect, but
noooo, Donna got too *bored.* Better to use her powers. Better to conjure a
tank to blast a hole in an armored car so that she wouldn't be part of the
meat market anymore.

She kept filing the left index nail and cracking the piece of bubble
gum Eva had given right before they got off the helicopter, well aware that
all the male rednecks on her end of the bleachers were ogling her, waiting to
get home so that they could whack off while they took their weekly shower

tonight. Since the literacy level probably didn't rise above the ability to sign welfare checks, most of the morons in the gym probably didn't know that in about two seconds, she could cause a murder of crows to materialize out of thin fuckin' air to peck out their eyes. That was one of the few advantages of being an internationally infamous criminal: give somebody a dirty look, and it's enough to stop them cold. At least in the civilized parts of the world.

In some rare cases, the reputation could backfire. She'd give someone her patented "I could kill you as easily as look at you look," and in return, she would see a glint in their eye that meant that they were turned on. In those instances, she was the one who wanted to sprint in the opposite direction. Eva had the same thing happen to her a few times, and they would talk about those moments and share a laugh, but deep down, it unnerved them both. She considered wearing outfit that wasn't entirely comprised of leather, maybe a nice poncho or some flower-print maternity pants, but then the pervert bastards would win. Beside, what else was available to super-villains besides leather? Spandex? Thankfully, there weren't any *gigantic* freakshows in this crowd. The only visible evidence of deep-seated masochism involved their willingness to live in this shitty little city in this shitty little state, and the only fetishes probably involved sheep.

She gave a pair of short puffs on the tip of her index finger, and once satisfied, refocused her attention and nail file on her middle finger. She could swear the blonde chick with all the hairspray and the muscle-bound black guy next to her on the bleachers were having a conversation. They sat only about ten feet from Donna, and the guy kept slyly talking out the side of his mouth while the blonde kept staring at him like a fucking Muppet. Couple of super-spies, those two, but were they really trying to be sly, or was it that obvious to them that Donna didn't give a shit?

For the record, they were right: she didn't give a shit. Not for this crime in particular or for crime in general. She had yet to get sent to one of those meta-human women's prisons. Eva did some time in those pits, and it seemed to make her a little extra loopy. It made sense: Donna watched an episode of *Dateline* the other day that took viewers on a tour of the new maximum security holding pen in Shreveport, and it looked like the sixth level of hell with beige paint. Most of the cells were strip cells, and they all had something special to counteract your powers. Stone Phillips, or whoever the commentator was, interviewed the Lorax in her cell. She was in a plastic suit in a plastic room, no natural fibers anywhere. She looked so pale that her skin was almost transparent, chunks of her hair were missing, and the prison doctors fed her vitamin slush through a plastic tube. All that, and the only time the courts convicted her of a crime was when she tried to invade the World Bank summit in Seattle and got beaten down by the Marshall Klan. In the *Dateline* report, they mentioned that the Connoisseur was imprisoned in Shreveport as well... Donna could only imagine the hell she must have endured.

Donna's two stints in the normal, run-of-the-mill women's pen were quite enough for her. Since she used her powers to escape the last time, though, she was surely due for a trip to Shreveport or Wheeling. *What would they do to me in one of those places?* she wondered. They'd take away her makeup, of course, and shave her head. They might even take her clothes, just to be assholes, and assign some masturbating high school dropout to stand guard outside her clear plastic cell. A shudder escaped down the back of her neck and rippled all the way down to her heels. In those conditions, if they were dumb enough to give her any cosmetics, she would create a nice comfy noose and lynch herself with it.

She peeled back her elbow-length glove on her right hand and checked her watch. Seven after ten. As soon as they were done with the needle freak in the chair, they would only be through the E's in the alphabet. She would never knock Poindexter: he could throw together some fascinating junk faster than McGuyver on brain steroids. Unfortunately, whatever he came up with always seemed too big to be practical or took too long to work. Take the Knockout Mouse, for instance. Great for muscle jobs. Loyal. Obeyed orders. But try getting that behemoth from Point A to Point B, and then decide whether you wouldn't rather just give a couple Hell's Angels five hundred dollars and a pair of leather skullcaps to go bust heads for you.

The sooner they got out of here, the sooner they could get on to real money-jobs, and the sooner she could take her cut and retire down to Rio. She'd never even visited Rio, but it seemed so nice in *Wild Orchid.* Dane owed her a shit load of money at this point. She and Eva started working with him almost a year ago, right after she broke Eva out of prison, and he had a strict rule about screwing around with partners, so one night, he called

Donna to his motel room and had her conjure him up some synthetic pussy. She did a nice job, too. Anything Donna could picture in her head, she could turn into reality for a few hours (if it didn't rain). Most of the time, she conjured versions of women she used to model with (especially women she didn't like), and they got better looking as more time went past; gradually, you forget the wrinkles and the lumps and the mastectomy scars.

She certainly had time to practice, because buying artificial sex turned out to be habit-forming for Dane, and he gave her an IOU for a thousand dollars every time she provided this service. They were still the only two who knew about his dirty little habit, but she threw in the secret-keeping part for free. She didn't begrudge him the slightest bit for doing it, either. Hell, she'd had some *nice* little parties in her room with a six pack of Zima and about ninety cents worth of Max Factor. Dane had yet to pay her, though. He'd accumulated about fifty thousand dollars in debt, but every time he came into money, he spent it repairing that damn helicopter.

Donna examined her middle finger, then shook her head. *Still not right.* She scanned for a trash can. Talk about bad timing. Four years ago, before they came out with those counterfeit-detecting markers on the new twenty dollar bills, she could have conjured up all the money she needed. She started strutting down the hallway, searching for a place to spit her gum, and spied a plastic bin wedged between two trophy cases. She could still conjure ones and fives, but paying for an apartment or a sports car with a few thousand five dollar bills that had matching serial numbers and dissolved in water wasn't exactly subtle. She leaned over the trashcan and spit out her wad of now flavorless Hubba Bubba. Besides—

A loud creak and a thud echoed through the gym, and it sounded just like someone had tripped and fallen into the bleachers. A lot more creaks followed as a pack of fat guys around the perimeter stood up and craned their necks toward the middle of the seating area. "Vhat da hell is going on?" Dane called to no one in particular. "Get out of da way."

Jesus Christ, Donna thought, holding her breath*, and here I thought no one else was going to die tonight.* She'd been in the villainy business for some time now, and she'd managed not to kill anyone herself (knock on wood). The cops, the judges, and the prison guards didn't care, but she didn't keep her murder-free record intact to satisfy them. She did it so that she could sleep at night.

Donna cautiously crept back toward the gym and rounded the corner... just as the blonde with all the hairspray crept out from the metal latticework that made up the underside of the bleachers. The shoeless blonde stared at her feet as she stepped gingerly out from under the bleachers and looked ready to shit herself when she glanced up and saw Donna standing in her path, hands on leather-clad hips. "Well well well," Donna said, smugly... right before the wall exploded.

*   *   *

Chapter Twelve:
10:08 p.m.

"He's the spawn of the Satan, you know?" a woman said behind her in the checkout line.

Sally had been reading a copy of US Magazine with Ashton and Demi on the cover, and she was almost inclined to agree, until she realized that the woman was pointing to the box of Alpha-Dreks in Sally's shopping cart. "What?" she said to the vaguely familiar woman. "The cereal? I just got it because it's on sale."

The woman, Myra Offerdahl, wore a shapeless black dress and had her mousy brown hair pulled back so tightly Sally could have counted the comb-marks, had she been so inclined. "Well, I hope you're soul is worth eighty cents."

Sally glanced toward the front of the line. The Pakistani man across from the cash register stood bent over, writing a check. Damn it. Who writes checks anymore? "Look, ma'am," Sally said, sighing, "I just want to buy the cereal and go home. I've had a long day."

Myra Offerdahl arched her disturbingly shaggy, jet black eyebrows. "Normally, I'd be inclined to just go home and pray for you, but in your case, there's a child to think about."

As if on cue, Manny came chugging up to the check-out line, wearing his official Drek Manifold jean jacket. "Mommy can I get a—"

"Not now," Sally told him, gently. "Mommy's talking to a crazy lady."

"Crazy," Myra Offerdahl snorted. "You won't think I'm crazy when you're enduring the ultimate torment for all of eternity."

Sally rested her hand securely on the back of her son's neck and cocked an eyebrow. "I just endured sixty seconds of it and I'm still here."

       *   *   *

Sally Forystek had no idea where the explosion came from, but the instant the woman in the red leather body suit glanced down the hallway to find out what blew up, Sally's fight-or-flight response grabbed a little bit from Column A and a little bit from Column B to get her out of the situation. Not being much of a sports fan, Sally didn't know who Earl Campbell was, so she obviously had never even heard of Isiah Robertson, but sports aficionados the world over would have recognized the similarities when she tucked her pint-sized purse under her arm, lowered her head, charged forward, and slammed her shoulder into the other woman's sternum. And all that while in stockinged feet.

The stupid bitch with her silicon tits didn't bounce when she hit the tile floor, but those high heels were going to make standing up again a real chore. Sally had removed her own heels while still seated in the bleachers, not out of preparation, but out of nervousness. She slid them off over an hour ago and bundled them in her coat because her legs were shaking so badly that her heels clacked against the wooden bleachers like a pair of maracas, and in this crowd, excess noise amounted to an invitation to get shot.

She never agreed to go through with Reggie's stupid plan. Part of her wanted to do *something,* even if it involved shutting her eyes, clamping her hands over her ears, and humming. It hurt her to watch Kelly up there, like a ghost of himself, but not enough to make her leave her seat. As soon as Reggie crashed into the bleacher aisle, though, it was almost like the seas had parted all the way back home to Manny. Not a single soul noticed her as she slithered under the bleacher seat and scrambled to the floor. Before she could even think about maybe she shouldn't be doing what she was doing, she had gingerly stepped through the intersecting metal rods on her way to the side hallway. The dirt and dust collected on the metal rods made her shudder, but the only rat she had to worry about stood in the middle of the gym floor. For about ten seconds, Reggie's plan seemed like the greatest idea since frizz-control shampoo, to the point where she could imagine herself at home, lying in a warm bed with the covers over her head.

Of course, Reggie Sleeve's genius only lasted until the leather-clad vixen popped up out of freaking nowhere, but even that proved to be a minor setback, because now, Sally sprinted down the hall with nary a warm body in sight. She'd successfully bull-rushed a super-villain, and with these freshly waxed floors under her feet, she could stop running right now and slide the rest of the way to the athletic office. A quick phone call to the police station would set the wheels of justice in motion.

The night certainly had turned into an ordeal. God only knew how it would shake out. Maybe Sally would gain a newfound appreciation for life. Maybe it would bring the Class of '96 closer together and they'd start having annual get-togethers. Maybe she can meet Drek Manifold or get on the six o'clock news. The splendid thoughts kept right on coming, right up to when she saw the squat, four-legged, feathered monstrosity lurking at the other end of the hallway. *Is that... a platypus?* she wondered, but then remembered the appropriate name: a Wolfian Duck. It looked almost cute in a mongrel-dog-in-the-rain kind of way, until it started to growl/warble, flashing its row of ivory, razor-sharp teeth.

The... thing started waddling toward her at an unnervingly fast pace, scurrying almost like a centipede, but Sally was only two steps from the office door, and only one thing could stop her from reaching it safely...

She gulped down an air bubble as she twisted the knob. A lone message bounced around in her skull: *It isn't locked.* The athletic secretary left the office unlocked most of the time so that the little jackasses who played sports could call home and have mommy or daddy pick them up if they had a late practice. If any room in the entire school was unlocked, it was usually this office. Sally clutched the slick, metal knob and swung herself inside and slammed the door so fast that she missed shattering her ankle by half a step. Forcing herself to breathe, she slowly and deliberately watched her shaking fingers move upward and flick the silver latch on the door knob from the nine o'clock to the three o'clock position. Her ferocious pursuer had all the motivation in the world, but its webbed feet and ninety pounds body mass meant that Sally now stood safely behind the locked, metal door.

Sally pressed her hands against the wonderfully solid door, and from the frisk position, she glanced over her shoulder. The four-line phone waited on the secretary's desk like the Holy Grail, but Sally took the time to

let her head drop and unleash a throat-clearing cough/sob. The air rushed
back into her lungs in a long, rasping breath, almost like she hadn't used her
lungs since she left her seat. It couldn't have been more than ninety seconds
ago, so maybe she hadn't. Until that moment, she had no idea how keyed up
she was, but her heart hammered against her ribcage, and a cold, slimy sweat
permeated every inch of her skin and made her dress cling to her legs as if
she'd worn it into the shower. When she reached for the arm of the metal
chair nearest to her, her hand shook so badly that she would have had an
easier time snagging a plush bunny with one of those mechanical claw
machines at Denny's. *I would have made a lousy spy*, she told herself as her
trachea expanded, slightly, to the width of a coffee stirrer.

However hysterical, her reaction made perfect sense. While she was
still in elementary school, she once spent a summer with her Aunt Marnie
and Uncle Martie in Racine, Wisconsin, and they took her to Six Flags, once
in May, for her birthday, then again in August, for her cousin's birthday.
Before this time, the only roller coasters Sally had ridden were at the Iowa
State Fair, and let's be honest: they were the kind of roller coasters that were
constructed to prevent lawsuits. When she rode the roller coasters at Six
Flags for the first time, it felt like she'd been strapped to a rocket. She
walked around all day like someone had shot a load of cocaine into her arm.
The air smelled sweeter, the sun shined brighter, and she felt as alive as she
ever had. When she went again in August, it was fun, but not life-expanding
fun: she had gotten used to the buzz. These days, working all day at the
bank and coming home to watch *Hope & Faith* and tuck her son into bed
hadn't prepared her for a night like this, and her body simply rebelled. It
didn't make her a weakling or a bad person; she just wasn't used to... all
this. Hell, in the last three years, her most exciting moment probably
involved asking for a Brazil wax.

Sally twisted around and collapsed backward into the metal chair and
might have pulled a Reggie Sleeve and passed out had not the frantic
scraping on the door squeezed a few more ounces of adrenaline into her
system. She sprang to her feet too fast for her squirmy legs, and she nearly
pitched forward onto the thin carpet. "Qwarl! Quarl!" the creature called
from out in the hallway. It wasn't that loud, but a pack of Doberman's
clawing at the wall would have been more reassuring. Doberman's, at least,
were predictable.

Sally's hand went to her chest as she steadied herself for the final push. Even though the gauntlet she had already run barely stretched a hundred feet, it felt as though she had run the first twenty miles of a marathon and hit the proverbial "wall." She stepped to the edge of the desk, picked up the telephone receiver, and with a wildly swerving index finger, managed to dial a "9", followed by a pair of "1"s. A click resonated on the other end of the line, and a more metallic click ushered forth from the other side of the door.

"9-1-1," the female operator said in her most toneless, bureaucratic voice that she must use to scare off the prank-calling delinquents. "What is the nature of your emergency?"

"Wh-Wh," was the only sound Sally's suddenly dry throat could muster as the door crept open. Thankfully, the mutant duck didn't come charging in, but was the appearance of the model in the red cat suit any more reassuring? "Put that phone down," Donna Correction stated, each word deliberate enough to form its own sentence. She didn't look injured, but Sally found her rigid expression hard to read. At least the tone was familiar. It reminded Sally of how she would speak to bank customers' misbehaving children on borderline-migraine days. They would bat the pens on the chains and screw with the deposit slips. The only reason she could stay so calm was because parents would sue if she slapped the little bastards around.

Donna Correction stepped into the room, holding a silver key in her hand, almost as though it had materialized out of thin air. At least Sally now knew how her panic room had been breeched.

"Ma'am?" the operator's voice spilled from the receiver, threatening to sound animated. "I can't help you if you don't—"

"I have to go," Sally whispered into the receiver before setting it on the metal desk with the plastic, wood-pattern top. She stepped back as Donna Correction took another step forward, almost like they were engaging in a poorly-rehearsed dance.

Donna Correction set the receiver back on the cradle, grabbed the phone cord and ripped it out of the wall. Sally let her. Even if the spirit had still been willing, little fight remained in her body. For some people, the mutant duck lurking in the hallway would have served as the main deterrent to causing any mischief, but for Sally, it had become the woman. Like some sort of Reverse-Jiminy Cricket, she seemed to pop up every time Sally thought she was in the clear, and if she chose to kill Sally, her only dilemma would involve the method of execution.

"Relax," Donna Correction said, searching for a place in her skin tight outfit to put her door key, then shrugging and dropping it on the floor. "I'm not going to kill you, but I'm not taking you back into the gym either, because then you'd definitely be dead." Sally nodded but continued slowly backing away, palms at her sides, until her fingertips touched the wall behind her. She watched as Donna Correction removed a bottle of cheap perfume from one of the few crevices in her outfit. Sally tensed, wondering if the bottle would release noxious gas or battery acid or something similarly awful, but the woman didn't even point it at Sally. She directed the spray toward the left-hand wall, and the misty substance that exited the bottle smelled an awful lot like Georgiou. The drifting liquid particles seemed to hang suspended, glistening in mid-air for half a second under the luminance of the fluorescent bulbs. Then, they soundlessly sucked together to form a pair of metal handcuffs.

The woman casually snagged them out of the air before they dropped to the thin, gray carpet, then worked both cuffs into the open position. Her movements were nonchalant, as though she had produced the steel handcuffs from the recesses of her purse and not some parallel dimension.

"How—How did you do that?" Sally asked, numbly.

"I don't know the physics of it," Donna Correction admitted as she stepped forward, holding the handcuffs in front of her. "We might as well call it 'magic.'"

The damn Duck stood wheezing in the doorway, looking for all the world like it was grinning at Sally through that bill of razor-like teeth. If a dog and a real duck had been fighting, then got run over by an eighteen wheeler, the result might have looked like that thing, or if someone had sent them through a pair of teleporters, like in the movie *The Fly.* Its dark brown eyes flickered with intelligence, though, and it stared at Sally, judging her. The only judgment possible was that she failed. That was her conclusion, as well. What else do you call someone who has a goal and doesn't reach it? A participant? She needed to call the police and she didn't git 'er dun, thereby leaving almost eighty people (and dropping) to the mercy of a Swedish psychopath. Then again, the police may not have faired too well against monsters, people who had weapons with names consisting of words like "neural" and "destabilizer," or with women who could transmute a dose of Primo into a land mine.

Donna Correction put a hand on Sally's shoulder and led her over to the metal chair near the door, and gently pressed her down into the seat. The plastic seat still contained some residual warmth from the mini-breakdown she'd endured earlier. Donna Correction snapped one cuff around Sally's limp, clammy left wrist, and passed the other cuff under the chair arm before snapping it around Sally's equally limp and clammy right wrist. "What are you going to do to us?" Sally asked, trying not to sound too whiny, as the woman checked the security of the bonds and the chair arm.

Satisfied with the situation, the women held Sally's pathetic gaze long enough to spit out an answer. "I don't know," she said with a shrug and looked away. "Hopefully nothing. Believe me when I tell you that slaughtering a few dozen people at a high school reunion isn't a real reputation-builder in the super-villain community." She frowned, thinking. "Then again, what is? The only things I can think of are beating the heroes or conquering the world."

"I wish I could help," Sally offered, and on some level, she meant it. If she was offered an honest-to-god wish, she'd wish for a magical baseball bat so she could bash their collective brains in, but unless the chair produced a genie when she rubbed it, her chance at heroism had come and gone. The most she could hope for, though, would be to get back to little Manny without getting maimed or turned into a turnip. And if she had to roll on Drek Manifold, Broadsholders, or the president of the United States, she would do it.

"Well, you can't. Not unless you know who Drek Manifold really is," Donna Correction said, with a mirthless smirk. Then the smirk fell away and she turned to Sally, squinting suspiciously. "You don't, do you?"

"God no," Sally admitted. "As far as I know, I didn't graduate with anybody who had superpowers. What does he look like?" She knew, of course. Even though she had never seen him close up, everyone knew that he was the spitting image of Richard Marx. An artist's rendering of his face sat stamped on her kid's cereal box for Christ's sake. She wanted to keep her captor talking, though, because it seemed like a good idea: with the woman here, the duck wouldn't eat her.

"Well, obviously, he can change his appearance," Donna Correction began, crossing her arms under her unnaturally perfect tits and getting a distant look in her eye. "In my experience, though, he has dark curly hair down to his neck, like in the 80's. Almost a mullet. Every time I saw him, he was wearing faded blue jeans and a matching jean jacket. The weirdest thing was how he moved. It was kind of jerky, like... almost like someone with a mild case of Parkinson's disease."

Sally nodded, intently, even though she didn't know anyone with Parkinson's disease (*That isn't what Reggie has, is it?*). She tried to keep her eyelids relaxed and tried to keep her focus on Donna Correction, because standing in the hallway, right behind the mutant duck, was the man she was describing. "How old was— is he?" Sally asked.

The duck sniffed the air, curiously, then left out a soft, "Quak?" before the man lifted one of his brown, weather-beaten cowboy boots, and with a dull thud emanating from the creature's midsection, sent the Wolfian Duck skidding down the hall. "Quaaaaaaak...."

"What the—" Donna Correction began, but Manifold took a long stride into the room, balled his hand into a fist, and without the slightest hesitation, sent a bone-jarring haymaker into her solar plexus. Despite everything, Sally found the attack shockingly uncouth. In the movies, Sean Connery might have backhanded a sexy Russian spy who was acting up, or maybe even blown up the car she was driving, but this looked downright savage, like something a drunken trucker would pull on his "old lady" in the parking lot of a Texas Roadhouse (at least Manifold dressed the part). Besides, Donna Correction had been relatively nice to Sally, and... let's face it: she was really pretty. Way too pretty to be lying on the floor of the athletic office, curled into the fetal position, groaning and coughing. Watching it made Sally so uncomfortable that she was almost relieved when Manifold lifted the disconnected, four-line phone over his head and sent it crashing into the back of the former model's skull.

Manifold let the phone tumble out of his hand and turned to Sally. She should have felt grateful, what with the hero showing up to rescue her and all, but he moved in those jerky snippets that Donna Correction just described, and not to be redundant, but it reminded her of Jeff Goldblume's character in *The Fly*. Plus, there was the whole Richard Marx resemblance that was downright uncanny. "You need to go to the porice," he said, pointing behind him, in the general direction of virtually everything.

"What's that?" Sally asked, wrinkling her nose.

"Po-reece," he said, more slowly this time, as though that solved the problem. "Raw enforcement." Sally thought about nodding politely, like she would in a normal situation, but this was no time to humor him. Thankfully, he saved her the trouble of asking again by twirling his finger over his head and mimicking the sound of a siren. "Wreee! Wreeee!"

"Oh, the police!" Sally said, nodding. "Yeah, sure, just get me—"

Before she could finish the request, Manifold reeled backward, clutching at the air over his shoulder, making some bizarre gurgling sound. The mutant duck had leapt onto his back and chomped its bill into his shoulder blade. "Go! Go!" he commanded between gurgles. That, she understood.

Manifold staggered forward, further into the athletic office, with the extra body clinging to him. She waited for them to pass out of the doorway, then gathered herself for the exodus. Still in her stocking feet, Sally slid into the hallway, dragging the metal chair along with her. The chair proved more awkward than heavy, especially since she had to carry it by grabbing one chair arm with both hands. Making matters worse, her feet kept getting tangled in her purse strap. Even though her purse was the size of a dinner napkin, she probably shouldn't have taken it with her; it was such an instinctive thing, though.

The Kooterville police station stood only a few blocks away. She knew the way because during the last weeks of her relationship with Kelly, she once had to sneak out of sixth period study hall to bail him out of jail. She wore tennis shoes and wasn't dragging a chair at the time, nor did she have to worry about super-powered models or Scandinavians blocking her path. A glance toward the gym revealed that none of the above advanced toward her. Not even any giant rats with boxing gloves. She turned around to bump the glass door open with her cushy ass, and welcomed the chill of the night air blasting her sweat-soaked face.

Her feet shuffled in tiny steps as she scurried over the sidewalk, but the chair kept dipping down and its legs scraped against the concrete. On a pair of occasions, she almost pitched forward over the top of it, so in a moment of inspiration, she lifted the chair up and balanced the seat on the flat part of her head, like those African women carrying water jugs back to their village. Her increased stride took her down the sidewalk much faster now, but not fast enough to outrun the Wolfian Duck that burst from the hedgerow behind her. It had only to flap its wings a couple times to glide close enough to her to chomp a hunk out of her left butt cheek. She'd never been bitten by an animal before. The pain was excruciating, like she had sat on a bear trap, but she managed to keep running a few steps before her balance completely left her and she pitched forward.

All four chair legs struck the sidewalk at the same time and sent her and the offending duck flipping over the hedge. She did half of a somersault before the trailing chair slammed against the ground and almost separated her shoulder. She landed on the grass, bleeding, disoriented, and covered in twigs, but at least the fall dislodged the duck's teeth from her ass. It recovered almost immediately, though, and resumed its advance. "Quaark!" her attacker snarled as it waddled toward her. The steel handcuff bit into Sally's right wrist as her hand strained to reach the boxcutter in her purse (her mother had given her some mace as an anti-rape tool, but she always thought that a razor served as a better deterrent when dealing with men). A few, scattered spit flecks from an opening duck bill splashed against her cheek. No time to discriminate, she thought, and swung the metal chair in an arc. The duck sidestepped the attack and dove toward her throat, only to catch a mouthful of purse. It snapped its jaws closed on her handbag, and as Sally was soon to discover, the pepper spray canister attached to her key ring. The canister exploded, and there wasn't a dry eye on the lawn.

*   *   *

Chapter Thirteen:
10:14 p.m.

"Why do you do it?" McVain asked Manifold as the other man lay
bound to the metal table beneath the primed, industrial strength cutting
laser. "With your powahs, you could be a king?"

"I do it," Manifold began with his usual, unnerving calm, "because
someone has to protect the weak against people rike you."

"But dey wouldn't do da same for you," McVain insisted. "None of
dem would. All dey care about is their X-Boxes and their sport utility
vehicles."

"When I call them weak, I don't mean those without powers,"
Manifold explained. "I mean the one's who are too afraid to stand up.
They need to be shown a different way. They need to be inspired. The small
soul can only take, but onry the broad soul knows true sacrifice."

"How's dis for a sacrifice?" Dane said and punched the bright red
the "discharge" button with his fist.

*   *   *

This night seemed destined to become a low point of Dane McVain's
criminal career. He could feel it building like a charge of static electricity
before a lightning strike. A high school reunion... Some balding moron
with a Master's degree in Education from the University of Northern Iowa
could make these troglodytes sit down and shut up, yet they reduced the
great Dane McVain to stalking them through the hallways on a search and
destroy mission. He always wondered what his low point would turn out to
be; context is important when discussing any issue, even the sum of his
existence. The high point of his villainy arrived either when he tricked the

Atom Ant into getting run over by a New Jersey Transit train, or when he
blackmailed the Canadian Prime Minister into accepting state-run health
care. Those were great accomplishments by themselves, but trekking over
the dirt-toned carpet of Kooterville High, they seemed light years away.
With a fiasco like this on his record… he'd have to incinerate the United
States Capitol Building to make up for this.

It only took roughly thirty seconds for everything to unravel.
Poindexter was about to start the alpha-2 scan on someone named
"Edwards," who represented the final person whose last name began with
"E." Before that could happen, though, some idiot passed out and dropped
into the bleacher aisle like a fat capitalist having a heart attack at a fast food
franchise. Dane shoved through the crowd of gawkers, and on the one way,
he heard someone mutter, "He's narcoleptic." That wouldn't have saved the
collapser from receiving his punishment for the distraction, but before Dane
could reach the body, an explosion tore a hole in the wall of the locker room.
He knew that it had to be Manifold, even before the building stopped
shaking.

Eva came staggering out of the hallway and quickly confirmed his
hypothesis, even if that was the only thing she did right. She claimed that
she was filing her nails in the locker room and when she looked up,
Manifold stood in front of her. Before she could react, the wall exploded,
and Eva took cover under the concrete slab running in front of the lockers
that normally acted as a bench. By the time the dust settled, she had
recovered her wits enough to decide to blow her toxic chow at him. She
crept out from behind the rubble, index finger poised by her mouth, only to
find that he had vanished, along with the guy with the memory problem.
Neither of them stood in plane sight, anyway; the ringing in her ears had
reached such a pitch that they could have led a brass band through the aisle
of lockers behind her without her knowing. She ran out into the hallway in
search of Manifold, and that's where Dane found her.

Manifold almost always manifested his powers as flight-plus-one.
Sometimes he didn't fly (which didn't mean he couldn't), but beyond the
flight-plus-one principle, he never manifested two disparate powers. Dane
didn't know whether Manifold had turned invisible and used some explosive
to blow up the wall, or if he had the power to make things explode and just
snuck up on and snuck away from Eva, but consistency wasn't exactly

Manifold's trademark. All told, though, Dane considered this outstanding news. If Manifold turned invisible, as long as they contained him inside the building, invisibility wouldn't do shit against the Knockout Mouse's vasoreceptors. If he had explosive abilities, he would have a hard time using them without hurting civilians.

After Eva's status report, Dane spent a few moments herding the hostages back onto the bleachers. He quickly discovered that, during the commotion, Donna had disappeared, and more than a dozen of the capitalist pigs had fled the gymnasium. He wasn't so terribly worried about them leaving the building (the Wolfian Ducks would tear them apart if that happened), but if they walled themselves off in the recesses of this cavernous, drafty public high school, that could add hours to this already time-consuming ordeal of testing them all. In Al-Salim's *Insider's Guide to Hostage-Taking,* Rule #1 was: more time = more chance something will go wrong.

So, being the hands-on leader that he is, Dane left Eva in charge of the sheep remaining in the gymnasium with audible instructions to "vomit them back to the Stone Age" if anyone so much as left his or her seat. Meanwhile, he and the Knockout Mouse proceeded into the darkened hallways to trawl for stragglers.

Dane stalked in the shadow of the rippled, muscular shoulders of the six-and-a-half-foot rodent. He initially thought about splitting up to cover more ground, but even while clutching a neural destabilizer, Dane didn't like his chances facing an invisible Drek Manifold in a dark, strange environment. Inside Uppsala, he felt so invincible that he sometimes would spend hours fully erect, but down here, he was just a normal human with a powerful gun. Dane crept along, ignoring the rows of four-foot lockers that were too narrow to contain an adult. Manifold was… something that spewed alpha-2 particles like an old man unloaded drool, but he certainly wasn't human. Sure, Dane used to compete in the World's Strongest Man competition, but he was also a Socialist, and being a Socialist, Dane liked things to be stilted and predictable, and strange people with strange abilities made him uncomfortable. Maybe Lord Osis or the Male Splitter were the sort of other-worldly beings who could walk down any darkened hallway they wished, but Dane would stay in the shadow of the Mouse, thank you very much.

Dane could have followed the Mouse with his eyes closed. The
gigantic rodent had a rasp to his breathing like an eight-pack-a-day smoker,
and when he exhaled, the stench of Gouda clung to the air with a death-grip,
along with the assorted other cheeses he scarfed down from the gift basket
Donna bought him for his birthday. They passed under a yellow banner with
red lettering that urged one of the sports teams to "Smash Smithville" in a
classic use of secondary school alliteration. Suddenly, the mouse stopped its
lumbering and sniffed the air.

"Vhat iz it" Dane whispered. He wasn't much of a whisperer, though.
No matter what the environment, his powerful voice tended to carry as if he
were standing in an empty tunnel.

Instead of replying (as if he could), the Knockout Mouse slammed his
gloves together and stepped toward one of the nondescript closed doors.
The small plastic sign to the right of the door read "Art Room." The
Knockout Mouse didn't possess opposable thumbs, so it couldn't turn the
doorknob, and its stumpy legs prevented him from kicking in all but the
flimsiest barriers. It looked over its shoulder Dane, its beady red eyes
imploring its human comrade for his assistance.

Dane sighed as he leaned forward and turned the knob. He didn't
have to let go of it because the Knockout Mouse jarred it from his hand as it
sprang forward into the darkened room. The metal door hit the far wall and
slammed closed. Inside, a pair of muffled screams followed (one being
more of a feminine shriek) followed by a lot of thuds and a big crash. Dane
planned to take his time entering the room so as to avoid any errant attacks
or debris, but he had to resist the temptation to reach inside, turn on the light,
and enjoy the show. Few things brought him as much pleasure as watching
The Mouse work over a couple warm bodies. If it was Manifold in there,
though, he didn't want to give the slippery capitalist any advantage. So,
instead, he checked the setting on his weapon (it was still set on "kill") and
impatiently shifted his weight from one foot to the other.

The crashing abruptly stopped, and a few silent seconds passed before
Dane reached forward, twisted the doorknob, and nudged the door open a
few inches. The only sound inside the darkened room came from the
Knockout Mouse wheezing itself back into a calm state. Dane flicked the
switch on the wall and watched the fluorescent lights struggle to life. A
table full of drying ceramic mugs had tipped over. Amid this mess lay a

young man with a paintbrush mustache and a woman with a wild shock of red hair, both unconscious. The male's Mac USA blue jean pants sat in a puddle around his ankles, so either they had somehow skipped the action in the gym or were among the escapees and, in the moment, were enjoying the aphrodisiac of anxiety. Dane had left his copy of the yearbook in the gymnasium with Eva. He certainly didn't recognize either inert body under their fresh set of bruises, but all Americans looked alike to him, with their Jordache jeans and freshly tweezed eyebrows.

The Knockout Mouse twisted its snout toward him, expectantly, as it braced its gloves against the clay sink. Dane shook his head. Those two troublemakers certainly weren't Drek Manifold (neither had the hair for it), but at the very least, they didn't follow rules and needed to be punished. Dane gripped a dial above the trigger of the neural destabilizer and twisted it down from "kill" to "retard" setting. Without the slightest hesitation, he discharged it, first on the man, then the woman. Since they were unconscious, the neural destabilization produced no immediate, visible effects. He knew that the internal impact was almost instantaneous, though; the two rabble rousers had roused their last rabble. At best, the pair could look forward to washing dishes in a group home for the rest of their lives. Given their fashion sense and the beating the Knockout Mouse inflicted upon them, though, it probably marked a short trip down the intellect ladder.

*   *   *

Chapter Fourteen:
10:16 p.m.

Kelly's black Grand Tereno slowed to a stop just as the traffic light clicked over to red. He pushed in the cigarette lighter and started screwing with the silver radio dial before it could get beyond the first few bars of Cold as Ice *by Foreigner. Just as the cigarette lighter popped out, one of the windows of the retirement castle across the street exploded and a tongue of flame leapt through the open space.*

It was really an awesome sight, objectively. No one liked to see old people burn to death, but the fire just looked really cool. The flame swelled and burst every few seconds like it, and not the old folks, was hooked to a respirator. There had to be a shit-load of flammable stuff in those placed, what with all the compressed oxygen. Kelly didn't have his cellular phone on him, but a Super Test station sat two blocks up the road in the direction he was headed. He could call the fire department from there, but somebody else probably already did. Besides, he was already running late for Sally's birthday dinner. Instead of driving to either locality, though, when the light turned green, he crossed the street and parked the car in the lot for an apartment complex.

The burning building stretched to either end of the panorama of his windshield. Kelly's eyes stayed fixated on it as his hands absently worked like they were on autopilot. They reached into the glove compartment, removed his little black shaving kit, and began to assembled his rig. He noticed what his hands were doing and didn't disapprove. Just the thought of the needle in his arm made him halfway high. The Halcyon Meadows Inferno would be his own, private Pink Floyd Laser Show.

*   *   *

It was the cripple, Kelly Edwards thought as he scrambled down the dimly lit hallway. He stared over his shoulder so often that he might as well have been running sideways. Whenever he saw those horror movies that featured people who couldn't elude supernatural killers who walked like they didn't have any knees, he always noted aloud how stupid their reaction was:

1) Shuffle a few feet, usually in a zigzag
2) Glance behind
3) Repeat

He always told himself that in the unlikely event that fate deposited him into a similar situation, he would pick a direction and haul ass like a steroid-addled Ben Johnson until his tar-soaked lungs gave out on him. Despite this vow, there was Kelly, careening down the hall like someone auditioning for "Decapitation Victim #3" in *Friday the Thirteenth: Part Ten.*

As so often happen, being self-critical made him lose his train of thought. In this case, though, he only needed a couple seconds before the thought found him again: *It's the cripple. The cripple is Drek Manifold.*

Back in the gym, Kelly sat in that orange plastic chair at center court, generating a small lake of sweat. He could hear his own breath like he was wearing a motorcycle helmet, but then everything slowed down, and the events evolved around Kelly with crystalline clarity. First, Reggie Sleeve took a fake spill into the aisle (but at least it sounded real). When the blast came from the locker room, the big Swede, McVain, bolted toward the back hallway that led to the locker rooms. Not two seconds later, the instant Poindexter looked away, Kelly hopped out of the plastic chair, tore the electrodes off his face, and sprinted in the opposite direction. It was just a reflex. If he'd given it some thought, he probably would have frozen up. Now, though, he would have to live with the consequences.

Past the auxiliary gym, right where the science department began, Kelly ran into Jeff Levine (literally). He helped Jeff up, and after a brief palaver, they decided to haul balls down to the north side of the building, where the art room was located, and climb through the room's fold-out windows. The building was air conditioned, and all of the new rooms didn't

have opening windows, but the art room resided in one of the original parts of the building, built in the late sixties. It was a pretty good plan, all things considered.

They took turns kicking in the door to the art room and broke through after a half dozen tries. The pop-out window left them a little more than a foot to work with, and the more slightly built Levine led the way out. He made it close to halfway outside before a mutant duck tore his leg off and dragged the rest of him outside. A lot of screaming and bloody Plexiglas followed. Kelly concluded that it was the sort of sight that only a thousand dollars of smack would drive away, but since that much opiated goodness would not be forthcoming until he could sell his Grand Tureno, the image of Jeff, Jeff's leg, and the duck would linger in every shadow or blink of the eye. So, this is why Kelly fled like an idiot.

He didn't know where to go or what to do when he got there. One thing he felt sure of, though, was that the cripple was Drek Manifold. He didn't mention it to Jeff. Not many people even would have noticed it. Hopefully, none of the members of the traveling freak show holding them hostage noticed it, because only Manifold could get the Class of '96 out of this slaughter house alive, but Kelly noticed it the first time he glanced over his shoulder. The bleacher crowd instinctively divided itself into two distinct groups of the Clichéd Animal Kingdom: rats off a sinking ship and deer in headlights. Needless to say, Kelly proudly counted himself among the rat species, even though the deer outnumbered them by a five to one count.

Not to get technical, but when he sprinted out of the gym, Kelly felt more like a gazelle on crank than he did a rat, but the principle still held. Right when his scuffed brown dress shoe tread over the red out of bounds line, he glanced over his shoulder. Amid the flurry of activity, something in the corner of his vision caught his attention: the wheelchair parked next to the left-hand corner of the bleachers had lost its cripple. It was tipped over, and the cripple wasn't lying on the ground next to it. As far as Kelly new, the cripple hadn't had a voluntary muscle movement from the nose down since high school. So, unless somebody took the time to pick him off the floor and drag him down the hall while psychopathic killers gave chase, he climbed out of the chair by himself, and if he had that trick up his sleeve,

Kelly would bet a crisp ten dollar bill that he pulled it off before the wall exploded.

Kelly slowed to a jog as he neared the cafeteria, more to accommodate his burning lungs than because he considered himself safe. It was important to keep moving, though, and at least in the cafeteria, with its clear sight-lines and sound amplifying high ceiling, he could detect his pursuers coming from a mile away while he took the time to recover. He waded through the shadows and the circular tables and metal chairs until he found a spot roughly equidistant from the four ramps that fed into the cavernous cafeteria room. Here, he climbed onto one of the thigh-high, navy blue tables and with shaking fingers, dipped into the inside pocket of his beige sport coat and removed a soft pack of Camel Wides and a Zippo.

Strange as it seems, firing up a smoke and drinking the noxious air into his lungs actually made him breathe easier. He'd once read an explanation for that phenomenon on WebMD, something about the blood vessels expanding, but most of it was over his head then, which made it completely unfathomable now. After only two drags, his hands stopped shaking. After three, he felt steady enough to feel guilty about thinking of Navin as "The Cripple." He not only knew Navin's full name, he not only knew that Navin Offerdahl wasn't always a cripple, he even remembered the day it happened...

*   *   *

In Kelly's memory, the sky was blue, but since the story takes place in early November in Iowa, around six p.m., it would have been slate grey at best. Jack Jordan was driving them back from JV football practice in his dad's pick-up. All of the kids in that truck either lived on farms or right next to farms, not like the hoity toity suburbanites who could walk to and from school, and only Jack owned a driver's license.

Their relationships with one another ranged from almost warm to indifferent. At worst, none were enemies and few were friends. Kelly supposed he would have classified Reggie Sleeve and Ely Lisch as friends with one another. They had a lot in common, what with their both playing defensive back and both showing goats in the 4-H Fair. The rest of the crew that bummed rides from Jack were more like transportation allies: Jack would drive them home, and they collectively covered his gas bill for the week. The only real moments of solidarity came when Chase Wilder and the

IROC crowd took turns dumping on Jack's truck. They took a strange sort of collective pride in that truck, more pride than they took in wearing those helmets with the stupid rooster on the side. It was a primer gray Dodge with over 100,000 miles on the odometer, but it never broke down in all the time that Kelly rode in it, and more importantly, it represented the type of vehicle all of them expected to be driving within the year.

They took turns reluctantly riding in the back (it was the epitome of a quasi-legal act; it was illegal, but in Iowa at least, the cops punished it less than moonshining). Jack was a good driver, to the point of boring the hell out of his teenage passengers, but late in the football season, it got cold as shit sitting in the flatbed with the forty mile per hour winds snaking through every crevice in your clothing. Anybody stuck in the back automatically started praying for a first-round sectional loss so he could start taking the bus home after school. As fate should have it, on that probably slate gray evening in early November, Kelly was riding shotgun, Ely was riding bitch, and Navin and Reggie Sleeve rode in the back. Navin came from a real religious family... creepy *religious, hardcore Mormons, maybe, which basically made him a dork. He drove Kelly absolutely bat-shit crazy. Reggie was the sort who could get along with a Nazi, though, which was good, because the kid wouldn't shut up, so* somebody *had to talk to him.*

On that day, they were on the way to drop Navin off at that gigantic modular unit he lived in with his five sisters, his dad, and at least one scary ass mom. They were turning down a dirt road. To Kelly's right, he saw a "School Bus Turn Around" sign peppered with shotgun holes. Jack was chewing Skoal Long-Cut Wintergreen and periodically spitting into a used Burger King cup. With all the sensory stimuli that had faded or bled together over the years, that smell (stench?) remained so vivid it might well have been solid.

After the uncomfortable silence that follows when you're riding in the middle seat of the truck and the driver has to shift gears, Ely said something like, "Can you believe they're making us keep practicing?" to no one in particular. "The JV season ended two weeks ago, but we still have to go out and freeze our asses off three hours a night."

Kelly replied with something along the lines of, "No shit. They don't even use us as tackling dummies; we just stand on the sidelines holding our dicks." He wasn't a very good swearer back then; he'd put too much

emphasis on the swear words, like people do when they trying to talk using a
Foreign-Language-X-to-English Dictionary.

Jack took his eyes off the road long enough to spit into his Burger
King cup. "Shit," he snorted, "beats workin' on the farm." That was
Jack's catchphrase, like "Boom!" is for John Madden.

The wheel went into a small, gravel road pothole, which was common
enough on these stretches of road that county trucks seemed to go down but
once a season. This time, though, Kelly could have sworn the truck
exploded. There was a flash of orange, and in that half-second, a thousand
possibilities went through Kelly's head. Did we run over a landmine? Did a
rocket explode into our windshield? Did somebody in the back
spontaneously combust? *None of these possibilities could have left them*
half an hour later with the front of the truck wedged in a ditch, but that was
exactly where they ended up. At the time, they didn't know it was half an
hour later, because the clock in the truck was blinking "12:00." They would
have to wait to find out the time from the EMT, who soon arrived after Jack
staggered down the road to the farm house about two hundred yards away
and made a phone call.

The cop who showed up on the scene acted like his name was Officer
Dickhead. He wanted to breathalyzer Jack twice, even though he passed the
first one, and even though they could have found fifty people who saw him
twenty minutes earlier at football practice. All things considered, they felt
pretty lucky. Jack and Kelly were both wearing their seat belts and came
out of the accident shaken but not stirred. Ely shattered the windshield and
his elbow and sprained his neck. Navin and Reggie got thrown from the
truck bed and landed in a muddy field. Reggie had a sprained wrist and a
broken arm. Navin landed on his head, but showed no visible problems for
days. After that, though, the deterioration came quickly. First, he kept
spontaneously falling asleep in the middle of the day, just like Reggie, but
then it got even worse. He would freeze up for minutes, then hours, at a
time. Finally, before their sophomore year was half finished, his parents
pulled him out of school altogether. For the Navin and the rest of them,
nothing was ever the same.

*   *   *

As he exhaled his last dose of smoke through his nose, Kelly slowly
ground his cigarette out on the top of the cafeteria table, acting out a

childhood impulse. His heavy, clingy thoughts lingered like the tobacco smoke, and he kept grinding away until he had bent the remainder of the Camel Wide into a "V" shape. Somewhere in the building, the guttural quack of a mutant duck resonated for a second or two, but sounded no closer than the last one, so Kelly fired up another Camel Wide. Kelly loved the Wides; they were almost like smoking a cigar.

Twelve years ago, everybody, Kelly included, thought it was getting thrown out of the truck that did Navin in (they thought the same about Reggie, but no one talked about Reggie's problem to his face because he'd threaten to kick their ass... and usually pass out). Ely's memory problems started, and he slowly slipped away and before long, wasn't much good to talk to. Jack felt horrible about the whole thing, as if it could have been prevented if only he'd followed the Iowa State Vehicular Safety Laws a little more closely. He was the responsible sort, anyway, and this Act of God may have led to his series of stints in the loony bin.

Kelly felt guilty, too, not for causing Navin's injury, but for thinking he was a complete dork before it happened. He actually tried visiting Navin at the hospital every once in a while, but since he was the only one doing it, the Offerdahls became creepy-nice to him. Ms. Offerdahl was especially nuts. She always wore these black dresses, even before the incident, and she reminded Kelly of the chick who played the Wicked Witch of the West (the human version.... before Dorothy went to Oz... the one who rode a bike, not the green one). Whenever Kelly stopped by Navin's room, she'd always grab his hand and make him pray over Navin's limp body with her. Sometimes Kelly actually did it. Sometimes he just closed his eyes and thought about Nirvana lyrics until Ms. Offerdahl finished talking. Eventually, when Navin got sent home with his family, Kelly stopped visiting altogether; it would take a hell of a lot more than bone-crushing guilt to send him into the Offerdahl House.

Kelly never had much success solving his problems, but he turned out to be a savant at avoiding them. He happened upon a strategy that worked (i.e., getting stoned out of his gourd) and stuck to it like a leach. Even this strategy had its problems, though. Kelly grew to hate himself for his drug problem, not because he thought that it was inherently evil, but because, of the five people involved in that accident, only he *chose* to turn himself into an invalid. Those other guys were permanently impaired, and Kelly, without any effort or virtue, walked away from that mess spotless. The question always lingered: *Why do I deserve my relative health?* And the only answer he could come up with was, *You don't.*

Now, though, he had to wonder. What if that flash of light turned Navin into Drek Manifold, and what if it had rubbed off on the rest of them in some way, like radioactive fallout after a nuclear explosion? It didn't fuck any of them up as much as it did Navin, but it did a pretty thorough job, one way or the other. It fucked up Reggie's ability to stay awake. It fucked up Jack's ability to think. It fucked up Ely's memory. Maybe, if he continued on with the theory, it triggered something in Kelly, some part of his brain that craved numbness and distance from the world… or needles. Maybe he wasn't the loser his mom said he was, or at least, maybe it wasn't *totally* his fault.

"Quark! Quark!" The sharp sound broke him out of his trance. Either there was a hell of an echo in the cafeteria, or two ducks were waddling toward him. If his sound localization worked properly, they were coming down two different ramps of the gym. Maybe they were smart enough to plan a pincher movement, maybe it was just coincidence, but the only place Kelly could retreat was toward the Industrial Tech wing. Kelly didn't know his way around this end of the building too well, but unless the school underwent a drastic renovation in the last ten years, the halls would still be arranged in a capital "A" formation (actually, more of a capital "H" with another bar across the top). This meant that the paths could double back on themselves, so if the ducks started chasing him, he could buy some time and hope that Drek Manifold would show up to save his former JV football buddy. Plus, if just one of those dozen or so doors were unlocked, he might find a hammer, crowbar, or acetylene torch to kill those creepy fuckers with.

A giant, duck-billed, waddling shadow crossed the wall above the southwest ramp. With those fangs, it looked like the shadow puppet from Hell. Kelly silently snuffed out his half-smoked cigarette and gently eased off the table without causing a chorus of creeks. He didn't know whether ducks had a powerful sense of smell, but wolves certainly did, and Kelly reeked of cheap American tobacco. He crept toward the nearest set of silver Dutch doors that led to the Industrial Wing. *The name of the game is to buy time until Navin saves us*, he repeated to himself. He kept repeating it like a mantra, and his nerves jangled a bit less every time he said it, until he pushed open the Dutch door and it struck an inert form… Navin's inert form… with a thud.

*   *   *

Chapter Fifteen:
10:25 p.m.

"Why don't you stop committing crimes?" Manifold asked as he stood beside the wall of her prison cell, preparing to dematerialize through it.

Donna sat up on her cot, mildly surprised that all their talking had not roused her lesbian pyromaniac cellmate. Manifold had materialized through her floor about twenty minutes ago. He was looking for the Spice Weasel and stopped in to ask if she knew his whereabouts. She and the Spice Weasel briefly dated, and when Manifold asked her the first time, she told him to go to hell. When he told her that Darren (the Spice Weasel's real name) was in danger, though, she informed him that he was studying holistic healing in Northern California. She didn't need an elaborate story to convince her. Whatever his other faults, Manifold was the honest sort, so she believed him when he said he wasn't going to arrest Darren. If he'd just left it at that and went on his way, it would have been a pleasant little visit, but when people tried to play amateur shrink and delve into her motivations, that just annoyed her. "Why do you care?" she asked.

"You're hurting people, so I have to care," Manifold explained as he made this slightly jerky, back and forth motion with his upper body, "and you aren't doing yourself any favors, either. It seems rike such a shame, because you don't seem like a bad person."

She smirked. Do-gooders were all the same. Villains may be despicable people, but at least they had reasons for what they did. Delusional, megalomaniacal reasons, sometimes, but at least they were interesting. The heroes always did the same thing (enforced the law) for the same reason (because someone once told them it was the right thing to do).

"Someone... probably my parents, once told me that you had to use your talents to make a living for yourself. That's what I did before I got these powers. That's what I'm doing now. Besides, I never killed anyone."

"Pro-greed, anti-murder," Manifold observed, evenly. "I guess there are rower standards."

"Thanks for sharing," she said, easing the back of her head back down onto the thin pillow. "Feel free to fuck off now."

Manifold nodded and stepped through the wall.

*   *   *

"Vhat da hell happened?" Dane McVain barked at Donna Correction as she sat the Athletic Secretary's chair with a runny ice bag pressed against her bloody, swollen temple.

"What do you mean, 'What happened?'" she said, removing the ice bag long enough to gingerly touch the puffy lump with her well-manicured fingertips. "He appeared out of nowhere... I mean literally, out of thin air... then punched me in the face and beat me over the head with a phone." She propped her elbow on the desktop and lowered her head into the back of ice, breaking into a fresh wince when the numbed flesh contacted the plastic. He really should be yelling at Eva. She lost track of the guy with no memory, and he still hadn't turned up. For god's sake, keeping tabs on that guy was about as tough as baby-sitting a pet rock. Donna just got beat up by a super-hero; that shit happens. "That's all there is to it and there wasn't a hell of a lot I could do about it."

"Vhat do you mean?" Dane persisted, flinging his arms wide as he brought his big, square face within a foot of hers. He had to leave the Knockout Mouse to patrol by itself, and that made him even less happy than did leaving Eva in charge of the hostages, but it was necessary for him to have a private conversation with Donna. He had worried about her for some time, her enthusiasm in particular. She seemed disinterested with the general mayhem they had been causing of late, almost as though she wanted out of The Life. Did she want out so badly that she would steal a comrade's helicopter and leave him at the mercy of his arch-nemesis? He wasn't sure, but something about her story rang false. "You say dat you tracked da blonde here?"

She exhaled a gust of air and rolled her eyes in a way that Dane did not find the least bit endearing. "Yes. She left. I found her here. I handcuffed her to the chair when Manifold appeared and clocked me with the phone."

"Vhy vere you handcuffing her?" Dane asked, slowly, his eyes narrowing to the point to where he reminded her of one of those giant heads on Easter Island.

Donna tried to give him a hard look, but between the cranial trauma and the fluorescent lighting, that made her head ache. Instead, she took a deep breath and closed her eyes against the offending sights for a moment. "Because I'm tired of people getting killed," she admitted. "It just makes me sick. And you knew that about me when you recruited me for this..." she wanted to say "freak show," but didn't, "... collection of people." She needed a drink... or at least some gum. *I should go ask Eva for some gum,* she thought. "And it wasn't like I was letting her go. She obviously wasn't Manifold; if anything, my getting beaten with a phone proved she wasn't Manifold. She was just a scared woman trying to survive. I would've done the same thing in her position."

Dane folded his arms and squared his legs in effort to magnify his menace. It worked, too: he looked like the Colossus of Rhodes in an Armani suit. "Vhat if he vas in luff vit her?"

"What?" she said, opening her eyes and giving him a weary gaze. "What could his being in love with her possibly have to do with anything? Look, you said yourself that Eva lost the guy with the memory problem. I mean, why aren't you yelling at her?"

"Manifold attacked her. The hostage got avay. Don't change da subject." Dane pounded the back of his hand into his palm. "Haven't I taught you anytink? Vonce you get da luff interest, you get da capitalist, because dey are all about personal gratification."

"Yeah, it looks like that rule has really panned out for you."

Dane paused, upturned palm in midair, and gave her a look that probably could have melted some of the softer metals. This had been a very difficult year for him. He lost a lot of his retirement fund when Volvo's stock dropped, and just last month, Sweden got voted out of the Axis of Evil. His prostate was still swelled to the size of a football, and there was the whole mess with Uppsala's computer... Donna knew about all of these things, and might have been baiting him, but she *really* didn't like being threatened. "I don't fink you haff da stomach vor dis verk."

"I think you're right," she said, careful of the words she chose, because when Dane's accent started to take over, that was the official signal that he had metamorphosized into his "pissed off" stage. This would be a bad time to get confrontational... or to bring up the money he owed her for the synthetic pussy she conjured up for him on a regular basis. As soon as he put that neural destabilizer down, though, she might reconsider. She completed her statement with an optimistic addendum. "But I'm a professional, and I'm going to finish this job." Dane started to speak again, but she cut him off. "And you can relax: I'm not trying to steal your fucking helicopter."

Dane gasped. "I never zed—"

"You were thinking it," Donna said, disgusted, as she held the ice bag with her other hand. "Hell, that's all you ever think about."

Dane stalked over to the doorway of the Athletic Office so that he could check the hall and avoid her for a couple seconds. He would rather deal with the Knockout Mouse than with Donna (as long as he didn't have to clean up its droppings). She had proven every bit as erratic as most American females. As most females, period. In fact, he would have to talk with Poindexter about genetically engineering him a female human for him. If they could remove the Smallness Gene and the Quadruped Gene from a lab rat, couldn't they remove the Sass Gene from a human female? When he stepped back in the room, Dane refolded his arms under his massive pectorals. "Dere's just vun think I don't get: how did Manifold blow a hole in da vall und turn invisible?"

Donna considered the question for a moment, then admitted. "Okay. I don't follow."

Dane sighed. "Each dime he appears, he has a different power, but he only has dat vun power. Now, he does two powers in five minutes."

"Well, did it ever occur to you that maybe the guy with the memory problem turned *into* Manifold and that's how he appeared in front of Eva?" Donna offered.

Dane looked bewildered. "She never said the hostage disappeared before the explosion."

"She never said he didn't," she countered.

"Vell, vhat about when he attacked you?" Dane said, pointing to the doorway of the office. "You zed he appeared out of novhere?"

Donna gave it another moment of thought. It was a difficult question, considering that they had no idea who Manifold was, how he got his powers, or how he changed powers. "That... I don't know," she finally admitted, and the two villains sat in the Athletic Office in silent contemplation.

*   *   *

Chapter Sixteen:
10:27 p.m.

Manifold had a specific scent. It was different from most humans. It was like iodine.

The Knockout Mouse hated iodine. It smelled like needles.

*   *   *

The Knockout Mouse was a simple creature. In most respects, his abnormalities came from basic genomic transplantations and substitutions of equally basic structures. Biologically, he was essentially a large rat. Behaviorally, he boxed using combinations, which most professional fight trainers would tell you requires a lot of eye-hand coordination, but does that really constitute complex thought? Humans who make their living inflicting and receiving minor concussions are not the most intelligent creatures, after all. Maybe, the Mouse fought as well as it did because boxing was a simple stimulus-response, fixed-action pattern just waiting for the right situation to release it, and perhaps having boxing gloves taped onto his forepaws created part of that situation.

He remembered few specific details from his life as a lab rat. Back then, he gained sustenance from a bowl of food pellets and a drinking tube, but his keepers eventually replaced those with tastier, more reinforcing versions of the same thing. What he really missed from those days was the treadmill… wiggling into that thing and running to his heart's content, not trying to get anywhere, just running. In his current incarnation, hitting the speed bag marked the closest he could get to those carefree days, but it wasn't the same. Running provided such a natural release. He could still plod forward on his hind legs, his altered genetic code allowed him to do that, but it didn't satiate his desire to run. He had lots of unfulfilled desires building up inside him. That was the most difficult part of being a genetically engineered wrecking machine: there was no way for him to articulate his wants and needs. Of course, even if he could communicate these to his colleagues, there was no guarantee that anyone would care.

The Mouse could still creep. Most humans don't think of rodents as predatory, but that's because the rodents that most people see are creatures $1/1000^{th}$ the size of an adult human and locked in a cage. It's different story in nature, and in the sewers. They don't live on cheese any more than monkeys live on bananas. When the Knockout Mouse smelled the distinct tang of nicotine in the air and heard the heavy breaths of an errant human making its way toward the darkest recesses of this gigantic burrow, it was not fear that smoldered in his glowing red eyes, but some other, sharper emotion.

As he drew closer, his hind claws digging for purchase into the thin carpet, he could see the back of a skulking, medium-sized human, could see it flinch every time another duck sent another unnerving quack echoing through the empty halls. Normally, even the Knockout Mouse found the ducks unsettling, but with the scent of panic-sweat tingling in its nostrils, he was far too preoccupied to care. He might take his time with this one, maybe just work it over with his left paw for a while… toying with it like he liked to do with stray cats.

Something up ahead bumped into something else, causing an audible thud. A squeaking followed, like when he and Dane robbed that Super Walmart and pushed a shopping cart with a loose wheel. The Mouse froze. The human's heartbeat quickened. The human had pushed the door open, and the door had struck something, something surprising. Scraping sounds now. The human was dragging the blockage beyond the arch of the door. The Mouse crept to the corner of the ramp. Perhaps two body lengths separated him from the human now, plus a flippy silver door. The Knockout Mouse crouched down on all fours, wiggling his tail out of the way. The position felt somehow natural and uncomfortable at the same time. From there, instinct took over, and he shot forward through the doors, gloves first.

The doors flew open, one nearly smashing the human in the head. The human, Mr. Nicotine (not to be confused with Captain Nicotine from Raleigh, NC), let out a gasp, and its face shifted into an expression that normally corresponded with this species producing involuntary droppings, but in this case, nothing competed with the nicotine scent. Mr. Nicotine held another human male, limp and unconscious, by its armpits and was dragging it down the hallway. The dragged human was small and strange with no head hair. When the Mouse took a moment to collect himself, Mr. Nicotine let the inert human drop to the floor and scrambled down the tile hallways in a disorganized flight.

Marching on its hind legs, the Knockout Mouse was not fast over long distances, but the element of surprise remained valuable as ever. Mr. Nicotine blindly staggered into a large red metal box jutting out from the wall, and when its skull crashed into the metal, the human fell to the tile floor in a pose similar to the limp, hairless human's.

The Knockout Mouse loomed over the stunned human, but was enough of a sportsmouse to wait for him to rise. The human, though, lacked any vestige of mouse-like pride, and when it had gathered most of its wits, it chose instead to crab-walk in the opposite direction. With no sparring to be done, the chivalrous part of the Mouse receded, and he stepped forward to snap his jaws around the human's shoulder and drag it to its feet.

"Ahhh! Jesus Christ!" the human wailed. The Knockout Mouse could understand human language fairly well. He had close to a five hundred word vocabulary, and "Ahhh!" constituted one of those words. It meant that he had wounded the human. He also knew that "Jesus Christ" meant that the speaker was angry. Despite these impressive linguistic skills, there were still moments of contradiction and confusion in the life of the Mouse. For instance, one of his colleagues, the human female whose hair smelled like peaches, once presented him with a kitten. He ate it, and someone said "Jesus Christ."

The Knockout Mouse stuck a pair of left jabs at the standing human, who blubbered and tried in vain to protect its face. The shots popped off its shaggy skull in rapid succession. The Mouse dropped his right shoulder and looped a beautiful shot into the human's solar plexus, lifting the human off its feet. If the concrete wall had not been in place, Mr. Nicotine would have gone to the canvas... make that "tile"... again. Still, with those soft abdominal muscles Mr. Nicotine sported, not to mention the lung capacity of a meadow vole, this was not destined to be a good workout. Such a shame, too, because after being stuck in a helicopter with four humans for the last few days, he really needed a good—

The Knockout Mouse's nose started twitching, as if it knew something he did not. That smell. He had smelled it before, and it guaranteed more fun than a treadmill the size of a tractor trailer.

Iodine…

The floppy door shook, as if pushed by a strong wind, but stayed shut. The Knockout Mouse turned and saw… absolutely nothing. The limp, hairless human still lay where he had been dropped, but the sound of boots on tile and the smell of iodine drew closer. The word "confused" resided in his vocabulary, as in, "The Knockout Mouse was *confused* when the fist smashed into his eye socket."

The word "invisible," however, did not.

*   *   *

Chapter Seventeen:
10:28 p.m.

"And so Manny's teacher told me that he was having trouble with spelling, and I just know that it's..."

He wasn't trying to ignore her. Quite the contrary: he thought about her the entire time while she spoke, he just didn't think about the stuff she spoke about. She always talked about the same stuff. Job. Kid. Ex-Husband. Mother. Usually by that time, their lunch would be over. Reggie didn't mind; he liked being her shoulder to cry on and he liked being needed. It just wasn't that interesting. Sometimes when she rambled on, his mind would drift, and he'd imagine what it would be like if they were together. It seemed like a win-win situation: she wouldn't feel like shit from people mistreating her and he would feel needed on a regular basis for once. At most, fantasies like that would give a couple minutes of happiness, and we have to take our bliss where we can get it, but eventually, reality came crashing down on him.

And the reality was this: he was Sally's buddy. Someone to talk to until she found someone to get serious about, and the instant that happened, he would get dropped like a bag of dirt. In some ways, he could accept that, because he wanted to be bigger than any petty selfishness he might be prone to. It was emasculating, though. The main reason she couldn't see him as an option was because she needed a man, and Reggie was a half-man at best. No amount of effort could ever change that.

*   *   *

Reggie Sleeve watched his captors tick through the yearbook again. Sally had been gone close to half an hour. An optimistic part of him could

visualize her sitting in a police station with a thin blanket wrapped around
her while in the background, the members of the SWAT team slammed
rounds into their automatic weapons. His pessimistic side just whispered:
she's dead, because if the Ducks got her, they wouldn't leave enough left
over to imagine. Several other particularly ambitious or frightened
classmates had made a break for it when the locker room wall exploded, but
McVain had taken his toy gun and giant mouse and stalked after them.
Somewhere, a small pile of bodies formed, building skyward like a satanic
pyramid. In any case, events back in the gym had settled into their lockstep
to the point where Dr. Poindexter and the red head in the black cat suit
rattled off names again.

　　　"Um, Charles Gradkowski," Dr. Poindexter said as he looked up from
the yearbook. Unlike McVain, Poindexter didn't have the voice for this kind
of work. Charlie Gradkowski still sauntered down the steps for his reading,
but his gate registered less terror than it would have if McVain had remained
the ringmaster. Poindexter spoke with the sort of indecision one would
expect from someone dialing up some phone sex for the first time. Reggie
knew what that felt like, but that was years ago; these days, he was a bit of
an old hand in the 1-900 game. He constantly worried about having a sleep
attack during orgasm, and although passing out during a four-dollar-per-
minute call can rack up charges on the ol' phone bill, he vastly preferred it to
falling asleep and having a hooker steal your wallet. Can't exactly file that
complaint with the cops or the Better Business Bureau.

　　　He'd had relationships with real women before, and he didn't see the
narcolepsy itself as a huge impediment, not directly, anyway... but he
couldn't drive, and there was always the looming anxiety whenever things
got physical. While the male stereotype is to fall asleep after sex, falling
asleep *during* sex probably created something of a turn-off, and it caused
him a great deal of performance-destroying fear. Since he could never go to
a good college and he couldn't perform any dangerous (i.e., high-paying)
work, he couldn't hold down a job that paid worth shit. So, his condition
left him as the poor guy who might fall asleep during sex and who rode the
bus. Not exactly the stuff personal ads are made of. If he'd been
independently wealthy, a woman might have been able to put up with his
condition (or any condition... just look at Larry Flynt), but Reggie's father

cut hair for a living and his mother waitressed at a Denny's, and his wasn't the kind of condition you could sue other people for.

Maybe if he kept trying the dating scene, he eventually could have found somebody with a terminal illness or someone trying to work out a guilt complex that would have accepted him, but he wasn't a robot. A person can't keep punching the same buttons with the same gusto. Humiliation, disappointment... they wear you down. Each failure is like a kick to the balls, and eventually, you start cringing every time someone pulls their foot back, to the point where a night comprised of a couple hours of TV and a Red Baron Pizza doesn't look that bad.

It now struck him as mind-numbingly optimistic, but when the night started, he actually had a hope that something serious would start between he and Sally. He knew first-hand that her personal life was a wasteland of bad dates, and some of it had to do with her being a single mother (Single-mother? Big deal. Reggie would crawl naked across a field of broken glass for a single-mother.). He noticed how dolled up she got tonight, almost as if tonight constituted one of her last chances to impress people before her looks started to go. So, he had the desperation thing in his favor. Plus, she and Reggie were familiar with one another; when you know someone for fourteen years, you can assume that there aren't any nasty surprises lurking in the bushes. The trip to the reunion itself was almost a couple-thing, a kind of "this is going to suck so let's stick together" event. When she drove him home at the end of the night, he actually thought about asking her to be more than lunch buddies.

Things hadn't been clicking, though, even before the gym doors exploded. Sally'd been droning on in the regular loop. First, it was her ex-husband for five minutes, and then five minutes of talking about the heady days when she was dating the quarterback for the Tri-Cities Arena Football team, the Trinity. A guy can only endure so many war stories, but when you're a half-man, you don't have much clout to dictate conversation. Over the years, she probably developed the mindset that, "This guy's narcoleptic; he has to listen to whatever I say." And she was right. In fact, thank god for those doors blowing up: after she got bored with him, there's no doubt she would have started making the rounds, and he would have had to stand there and take it.

He shook his head in disgust. *That was a stupid, selfish thing to think. What? She can get killed just so you don't have to feel uncomfortable?* He wished Sally was sitting next to him right now. He'd do anything to make that happen. It was his idea for her to make their break for it, after all. Sometimes, when you have a disability, you try to overcompensate, to try to be the hero, when the best thing to do is just sit back, ride it out, and not make things worse. That strategy tore at Reggie, though, because he'd been sitting back and riding out the last decade, and it wasn't working. For once, he wanted to save the day.

McVain strode back into the gym from the direction of the athletic office. He didn't look panicked, like one might if one couldn't account for a dozen people. He didn't look happy, but he probably never looked happy. The brunette in the red cat suit followed in McVain's wake and took up her position in front of the silver drinking fountain. While McVain still had his back to the bleachers, Reggie shifted a few feet to his left until he was positioned right next to the metal guard rail. He threw a couple glances at the brunette, trying to make eye contact. McVain leaned forward and inaudibly discussed something in the yearbook with Poindexter. Reggie took a deep breath and whispered toward the drinking fountain, "Hey. Um, excuse me?"

The woman's eyes swept the area, instinctively searching for the violator of the silence. When she saw Reggie and the direction of his gaze, she touched her chest with her fingertips and mouthed the word, "Me?"

Reggie nodded.

The woman's eyes drifted toward center court. "Are you out of your mind?" she hissed. "Just sit still and shut up and this will all be over soon."

Reggie ignored the warning, both because he didn't believe it and he didn't care. "I was just wondering… my friend, Sally, she ran out of here when everybody freaked out. Did you happen to see her?"

The woman gave Reggie a long look that said, *I knew you were faking.* She licked her glossy lips as she contemplated her answer. For each second that passed, his heart sank deeper into his stomach and his stomach sank deeper into his feet. Then, McVain's voice hit shattered the relative silence like a sledgehammer. "Jack Jordan," he thundered. "Come on down."

Wow. McVain with an attempt at levity. That's rich. Reggie's upper lip lifted into a sneer, and for the moment, he forgot about Sally. *Easy to joke around when you're built like a tank and holding a ray gun, huh, asshole?* In a perfect world, pieces of shit like McVain, and to a lesser extent, smaller pieces of shit like Chase Wilder, would eventually get what was coming to them. The reality they occupied was far from fair, though. Call it "survival of the fittest" or "shit luck" but being a massive dick seemed like a massive advantage. This life was more like a rigged game of Russian Roulette than a pasture of apple blossoms and candy canes.

Jack sat in the first row, and when he heard his name called, he flinched and glanced around on a three-second delay. When he finally remembered where he was, he got up and shuffled forward like a drunk. Sally told Reggie she heard that Jack had spent a few years in the Halcyon Lawns Home for the Emotionally Troubled. Reggie knew all too well how wildly inaccurate random rumors could be, but Jack certainly looked like someone doped him up with enough medication to take down an adult rhinoceros.

While Jack plodded across the out-of-bounds line of the basketball court, Reggie remembered that he had risked his life asking a question and hadn't bothered to wait for the response. When he looked over at the women in the red cat suit (he had no idea whether it was Eva Destruction or the other one), her expression turned grave, and she deliberately mouthed the words, "I don't know."

Reggie gulped down the tennis-ball-sized lump in his throat and resumed staring at his lap. Not the euphemistic response he was hoping for. You have to develop a sliding scale for assessing information in a dangerous situation. In this situation, the scale kept right on sliding. "She's great" means "we implanted a microchip in her skull and can control her thoughts." "She's fine" means "I personally decapitated her." "I don't know" probably means something like "the door to the wood shop closed, and I heard someone start the lathe, but I don't know for a fact that she's dead."

"Hey," he whispered to the now visibly annoyed woman. "Hey," he repeated at a slightly louder volume. "What did—"

Someone slapped him in the back of the head. Hard. The offending hand belonged to Chase Wilder, straight out of a time warp, except that he now wore a cheap suit instead of a letter jacket. "Shut the fuck up, Sleepy," he growled under his breath. "You're going to get us all killed."

Reggie gave Wilder a hard look, but his eyes eventually fell back to the balled fists sitting on his tensed thighs. That's how confrontations always ended for Reggie, with him swallowing his emotions, then tamping them down so he wouldn't pass out. Around strangers, he could act big and dangerous and avoid other people's shit. Wilder knew about his condition, though, so Reggie's could only try to minimize his humiliation. Besides, in this case, ol' Chase may have had a point. Even if the woman had said, "Sally? Oh, yeah, she's bleeding to death in the ladies' room," what was he going to do about it?

Just as Reggie was rationalizing his heart rate back into the normal range, Poindexter yelled out, "Holy Cow, Dane! He's registering 8.7 Geigers of alpha-2 radiation!"

McVain raised a fist over Poindexter's head. "English, dammit!"

"It's him, Dane," Poindexter said, cringing, as his voice echoed through the silent gym. "It's Manifold."

*   *   *

Chapter Eighteen:
10:35 p.m.

"So, you're from the Tri-Cities," the woman Chase met on the Internet but whose name he now couldn't remember said. "Did you ever meet Drek Manifold?"

Chase finished cutting his steak so that he could have time to think of an answer. He knew the theme of the answer, just not the specifics. "Yeah," he replied. "I'd rather not talk about it, though: he's a bit of an ass."

Bonnie (that was her name: Bonnie) furrowed her brow. It wasn't a good look for her; it sent a lot of lines in a lot of different directions. She wasn't an unattractive woman. Her hair looked kind of plastic, though, and those pictures she posted on her page must've been from five years ago. She was the sort he'll probably bang and not call again. "What do you mean?"

"Well, you'd always hear things, but you didn't know what to believe, y'know?" he waited for Bonnie to nod. "Once, I was driving my buddy Thompson home from the bar," he looked up and gave a helpless shrug, "and we saw this ambulance was on fire. So we, like, got out and pulled this guy who had a heart attack and this EMT out of the ambulance."

Bonnie rested her fingertips on her sternum, right above her bulging tits. "Oh. That's so brave."

Chase nodded as he swallowed his steak, then checked out her hand placement. Maybe he'd bang her twice... "Yeah, well, it turns out Manifold got in a fight with one of those super-villains and caused the ambulance to overturn and didn't even do anything about it. The doctors said that if Thompson and I hadn't been there, those guys would've died."

"Oh my god," Bonnie said. "You are so brave. And lucky, too."

Chase wedged another hunk of steak in his mouth and glanced over at her, quizzically. "Hmm?"

"Well, my brother's an EMT," Bonnie said, "and he's never seen an ambulance blow up, but he said that it's a huge concern, because not only do you have the gas tank to worry about, you have all those oxygen tanks. So, it's really kind of weird that there was open flame in the ambulance and it didn't explode in all the time—"

As soon as Chase swallowed, he held up his hand. "Check please."

*   *   *

Chase Wilder remembered Jack Jordan from the days of high school football. They both played linebacker, but in Jordan's case, "played" meant that he dressed up and stood on the sidelines. He was one of those kids who hit his growth spurt early, so he had two years of being a decent athlete before his genetics shot their wad and he became a complete waste of space. Most people have to end their athletic careers at some point during high school, and they always find another group to latch onto, whether it be motorheads, farm kids, druggies, or "theater types." In Jordan's case, though, he just kind of disappeared. Earlier in the evening, Chase heard from his buddy Thompson that ol' Jackie J got checked into the nuthatch and spent the better part of his twenties there. That kind of surprised Chase; he always thought that you had to be sort of interesting to go crazy.

When Poindexter announced that a superhero sat in their midst, though, it dawned on Chase that Jackie's boring craziness might be an act. If someone asked Chase which member of the class of '96 was Drek Manifold (which, McVain essentially did), Jordan would have been his 100th guess, and their class only had 106 people. That put him about one slot in front of the Short Bus Posse, a couple fat chicks, and not much else. Now, though, he saw the whole situation in a new light. After all, isn't that the point of a secret identity, for people to not suspect you?

Still, even though everyone in the gym heard Poindexter label Jack as the source of all their problems, even while the murmur in the bleachers built into a roar, Jordan kept sitting in the chair like an idiot, and Chase had to wonder if Captain Geekboy down there didn't punch in the wrong numbers on his giant calculator. That was right before bright red eyebeams flew out of Jack's freshly mulletted skull and struck the big black computer.

Amid a shower of sparks, there he sat in all his glory: Drek Manifold. His artist's renderings in the newspaper made him look kind of like Richard Marx, so did the more recent camera phone images, but those were always blurred, like pictures of the Loc Ness Monster. Neither did the man justice. He *was* Richard Marx (and since no one had heard from Richard Marx in ten years, maybe this was literally the case), and he hadn't aged a day since the first time Chase saw him, almost a decade ago.

Chase expected the eyebeams to turn the computer consul unto a Roman candle on wheels, but it would have to be gasoline powered for that to happen. As it was, the red lasers hit the plastic side of the machine and sent an arch of sparks spraying out of its metallic front. It only took a couple seconds for the beams to melt their way through the far side, and the computer gave little protest. The eyebeams shut down, and an instant later, Manifold tipped his chair backward to avoid the stream of projectile vomit that tore past his face.

The plastic chair hit the hardwood floor with a crash that echoed for only half a second before the thunderous stampede of humanity drowned it out. Chase left his seat as fast as anyone in the gym and started weaving his way through the mass of doddering sea monkeys on his way to the bottom of the bleachers. He should have tried this the first time, when Reggie Sleeve took a spill into the aisle and the doper in the chair bolted. That time, Chase froze because it caught him totally off guard, the same way this whole string of events caught McVain now. The big jackass just stood there, his wide, rectangular eyes darting around and his ray gun hanging limply at his side as if it were a bottle of Febreze.

The instant Chase's black wingtips hit the floor, he started taking exaggeratedly long strides to keep up with the bulk of people flowing toward the front exit. He hung in the middle of the pack. That way, any random raygun shots from behind him would pick off all the non-him people and the first few people in front would be the one's to get eaten by the mutant ducks. A few classmates in front of him had the same idea, and a few more behind him. They were tentatively jogging at a stunted pace, like escaped prisoners trekking through a mine field, but right after they finished rounding the corner and headed toward the concession area, the wall of people at the front of the pack slid to a halt. "What the fuck?" some dude near the front shouted in exasperation. "When did we get a moat?"

Chase went about 6'1", and from his vantage point, he could smell the cosmetic foundation particles floating in the air and see the dark, fetid moat and the electric eels sluicing through it. The moat went about ten feet wide and ran from the fire extinguisher near the exit to the drinking fountain at the edge of the gym. The exact number of eels was hard to determine because the thick, brackish water looked like someone had emptied a dozen Port-o-Johns into it. Random sections of the snake-like bodies poked out of the water, so there were either a dozen or so small eels or a handful of gigantic eels. Hard to tell which provided a better situation.

Vern Williams stood at the front of the pack and almost fell into the moat from the crush of people charging up from behind him. As is the often the case in life, the woman in the red leather bodysuit acted as the voice of reason. "Turn around and go back to your seats," Donna Correction said from the other side of the moat. Her voice came slowly and deliberately. It sounded almost like she was just your average flight attendant, and they were no more hostages anymore than most airline passengers, and those weren't zap and puke sounds resonating in the gym behind them. The entire pack hesitated, probably making the exact same calculation that Chase was: if they could shove Vern and a few more people into the moat, the rest of them could use the bodies to hop across. Chase leaned forward, pressing against Paul Durkis's fleshy back, and hoped a few other people would give an encouraging shove, but regardless of how many people had the balls to do the right thing, it wasn't enough.

The crowd began to inch around so that about half their noses pointed in the direction of the gym, and Donna Correction continued in a soothing voice. "That's the way. Even if you got over the moat, the Wolfian Ducks are roaming all over the halls and outside. I know this isn't easy, but you'll just have to sit still for a couple more hours. At the most."

There was another long pause, but the life had gone out of the jailbreak. At this point, the people in the back waited for the people in the front to do something, and the people in the front waited for the people in the back to tell them to do something. A chorus of mumbles punctuated the confusion, but the only audible voice came to them in the form of Donna Correction's insistent, authoritative tone. "That's right, the rest of you," she said. "Back it up. *Beep. Beep. Beep.*"

As Chase and the rest of the mavericks completed their transformation back into cows, he creaked his way up the wooden bleachers and back to his seat, not at all sure of how big of a pussy he should feel like. With a running start, he could have easily jumped across the moat (or pushed Vern in and stepped on him to get across), but that chick was right about the Ducks. He saw a show on the Discovery Channel where they dissected one, but he didn't know how fast they could run... or fly... or much of anything about them. Plus, in that situation, he would have had to fight through a couple layers of lazy idiots, and trying to jump without any momentum might have landed him in a pile of eels. Rationalizing made him feel a little better, but he still didn't feel *good*, so he scanned his immediate surroundings for someone to bust on.

"Hey, narco," he said to Reggie Sleeve, slapping him on the back of the head a second time. Sleeve looked like he worked out seven days a week and had a chest you could land a plane on, but his brain condition made him about as dangerous as a ten-year-old girl. "Nice of you to stay awake."

Sleeve did a slow turn until he could glare at Chase with red-rimmed eyes. He looked worn out, but that wasn't why his eyes were red. Only then did Chase realize that the fight sounds from out on the basketball court had stopped some time ago. McVain stood on the crimson and gold rooster at center court, looking at the floor, ray gun in hand. The weapon's spiral-wired barrel faded from glowing gold to dull white. Dr. Poindexter stared at the floor, too, from behind the Karaoke table. So did Eva Destruction, from her post over at the drinking fountain. The spot they stared at, right around the three point line of the west end of the gym, contained Jack Jordan. Jakie J's body looked like it was made of wax and his right arm and half his chest had been held over an open flame. As if that weren't a sufficient indicator of his state, his tongue lolled out of his mouth and his eyes were rolled back to their whites and pointed at the bleachers. He couldn't have been deader.

"Sweet," Chase thought. "They'll send us home soon."

*   *   *

Chapter Nineteen:
10:38 p.m.

The evening news flickered on the TV screen in front of him, the sound-bite-laden stories coming and going faster than he could take notes for them. Even in his most fatalistic moods, he still took copious amounts of notes, so he knew he'd already tried dozens of schemes, desperately attempting to make the memories stick. Familiarity was his latest weapon. Tonight, he would watch the news and take notes. Tomorrow, he would watch the news and rate which stories seemed most familiar. If the stories he rated as familiar were ones he'd watched the previous night, then that meant that something, however slight, was getting through.

The newsman with the gray suit and the colored hair consumed the screen. "Lindsy Walker, the woman who was left in critical condition after the car accident on Sixteenth and Willowby, was released by the hospital today." The camera cut to a scene of a thirty-something woman in a beige overcoat being pushed toward the parking lot in a wheelchair. It was a sunny day and the sidewalk was empty. She smiled like someone who loved life and waved to the camera. "Ms. Walker, if you remember, was pulled to safety by Drek Manifold an instant before her vehicle exploded. There were no casualties from the ensuing fire."

Ely gripped his pen tightly. The woman... she looked familiar. The story seemed familiar. Maybe that meant that something got through. Unless he was fooling himself. Maybe he'd already tried this trick in the last week, and maybe he couldn't even remember that. Maybe it worked so badly that he became frustrated and destroyed the notes of how badly it worked.

Ely sighed and stared down at the frantic scribblings on his notepad until his mind turned to blank. That's odd, *he thought.* Why was I taking notes on the news? And why do I feel so angry?

*   *   *

On some deep level, Ely Lisch had gotten used to "waking up" in strange situations. He might wake up on the toilet and not remember getting up to go there. Or he might wake up in the morning, ready to shave, only to find out that it was two p.m. and he had shaved hours ago. He'd spent almost half his life existing in five minute snippets that seemingly had little to do with what had come before, and he'd grown used to it, even if he usually didn't know *why* he'd grown used to it. Essentially, he was no longer surprised by being surprised. Never, though, had his memory condition put him in a situation where he "woke up" getting beaten senseless by a giant rat wearing boxing glove. Never, that is, until today.

An unfortunate result of the human condition is that, often times, our most irrational thoughts come at the least opportune moments. For Ely, his first question was: *Am I a Power Ranger?* His second question was: *How does this thing jab if rats don't have elbows?* Yet jab it did, hard and relentless as a jackhammer. Ely tried to cover his head to weather the mouse's onslaught; he'd received more than enough experience with the wonderful world of brain damage, thank you very much. In between the red flashes of stretched leather and the wall of white fur, he saw another human struggling to its feet, but Ely could only identify the shape as vaguely human, so he couldn't count on it to save him.

He tried to concentrate. *You are the only one who can save you. You have to think. Focus. Where are you?* From what he could tell, he was in a place that looked an awful lot like one of the seldom traveled back hallways of his high school. Maybe he was—

The mouse dropped a "shoulder" and blasted an uppercut into Ely's sternum. It struck him squarely and sent him careening into a cement block wall (painted light gray to avoid emotionally stirring up the bad students). As his shoulder blades bit into the wall, his body felt like a giant hunk of tenderized meat. Most of it anyway; his throat felt like someone had jammed a vacuum cleaner nozzle down his throat and flipped the switch to "turbo."

Okay, his mind blurted out between minor concussions, *you are definitely in your high school.* He peaked under his elbow, peering through his rapidly swelling eyelids. A flicker of hope doused itself. For an instant, he thought that this might be a Senior dressed in a mouse suit hazing him, but that was real slobber glistening on real incisors, and the snow white fur, the furless tail, and the glowing red eyes were every bit as real. Harrison High's Home Ec department couldn't have created something this realistic. Hell, makeup artist and creature-creator Rick Baker couldn't produce something this realistic. Besides, Ely was a Junior, and Seniors didn't haze Juniors.

Just as Ely stepped away from the wall, the rat slipped a punch to his jaw and sent him spinning. His arms flailed out in front of him in a frantic swim motion. It was a familiar reaction: he saw Carl "The Truth" Williams do it... and Jim Bob Kooter, Boxcar Earl, and some of those other hobos who Mike Tyson used to fight when he was climbing the WBC rankings. Their arms usually started twirling around right before Iron Mike would launch an uppercut that almost tore their chins off. Ely didn't want that to be him... and now that he thought about it, it didn't have to be. A pair of jabs glanced off his forearms and gave Ely's scrambled brain enough time to yell, *Run, you idiot!*

Ely ducked under an awkward roundhouse, planted his right foot against the tile, and drove off it. The tiles were recently waxed, but he wore relatively new Rockports, and the rubberized soles caught. *The mouse has stubby little hind legs*, Ely thought as he turned his back fully to his attacker, *any distance over a hundred feet, and you'll torch him.* That was the plan, anyway. Two steps later, he tripped over a prone bald guy lying in the doorway. He tried to catch his balance as he spilled into the cafeteria, his feet desperately stabbing the ground, but the silver, Dutch door barrier didn't have any handles to grab hold of or anything behind them, so he fell sprawling through them. His numb face smacked the tile floor on the other side of the doors, and the taste of blood seeped into his mouth...

*   *   *

It took Ely a couple seconds to catch his breath. He had no clue how much time had passed since he hit the floor, but that was nothing new. What he did know was that his heart was palpitating under his ribcage and his body ached all over, so he knew he was getting his ass kicked. He glanced over his shoulder, and ... *What the fuck? Is that a giant rat?*

Something about it all struck him as de javu-y as he bear-crawled into the cafeteria. Maybe this was a recurring nightmare, even if he never had anything against rats in particular, and they didn't have anything against him. These days, they dissected frogs in science class, not rats. The scenario seemed real, except that it couldn't possibly be happening. Maybe it wasn't. Maybe it was a hallucination, or his brain was still scrambled from the fall that he obviously took. He glanced over his shoulder through the flopping doors again. Nope. Still a giant rat.

Ely fought off a series of full-body hacks and attempted to spit a stream of blood onto the floor, but it clung to his lower lip and formed a single-lane highway down to his chin. The shadow of the rat fell over him now, and he stopped crawling and turned his rapidly swelling face toward the rodent. It paused its advance long enough to lift its paws in a "put up your dukes" gesture. If it were a human, Ely would have kicked it in the knee and run like hell, but since it didn't have knees, he might have to skip to the second half of the plan. A single, random thought dawned on Ely as he scanned for an opening, and despite everything, he clung to it as though it were his own personal Excalibur: *It can't be a rat; it must be a capybara.*

In the time it took him to blink, the rodent bent down and threw a punch that caught him in his tender throat and sent him tilting onto his shoulder. That was enough to break him out of dopy trance, though, and he stopped caring about his opponent's mammalian categorization. Even if it were a giant spiny ant-eater or a crocodile in a rat outfit, it appeared fully prepared to beat him to death. Fortunately, it seemed to be vulnerable to blunt objects to the head, because when the guy with the Jeff Galooli mustache snuck up behind the rat and slammed a full-sized fire extinguisher into the back of its skull, the rodent staggered to its left, toward the dishwasher window, and smacked the tile floor in a stinking, hairy heap.

Ely let out a grateful sigh that took so long that it seemed to suck the air out of his feet. As his lungs regrouped, he let his crisscrossed forearms fall limply to his sides. "Sweet mother of god," he gasped as he eased onto his back and rested the base of his skull against the hard floor. This spent posture only held for a couple of seconds, though, because the blood from his nose and mouth immediately began draining into his throat. His gag reflex kicked in, and despite his body's demand for rest, launched him into a seated position. A couple moments of choking and coughing passed before he felt a hand gently pounding him between the shoulder blades. His scrawny savior stood over him wearing a tan sport jacket and a wispy mustache.

"Are you alright?" the guy asked. Clingy sweat sat poised to drip off his face, almost as if he'd run to Kansas to retrieve the fire extinguisher.

"How do I look?" Ely replied. He probably should have changed the wording to avoid sounding like an ungrateful smartass, but he honestly wondered if he looked as bad as he felt.

The other guy winced out a smile. "Yeah. Point taken."

The awkward, stoop-shouldered expression triggered a memory in Ely's battered brain. "Kelly Edwards?" he said, almost hopeful. "When the fuck did you grow a mustache?"

Kelly closed his eyes for a second, maybe in frustration, but before he could reply, a distant, guttural quack rattled through the cafeteria. "We'd better get moving," Kelly said. "The Home Ec door's unlocked."

"Yeah, sure," Ely replied, struggling to stand on his wobbly legs and wiping away thick strands of blood. He had no idea what was…

"Whoa," Ely said. "What the fuck's that?" His bloody, possibly broken index finger pointed toward a spot on the floor in front of the dishwasher window, where an inert form lay that appeared to be a guy in a disturbingly well-made rat suit.

*   *   *

Chapter Twenty:
10:37 p.m.

Even beneath her heavy work gloves, the tightrope still burned Eva's hands. High places never frightened her, especially, but dangling over a section of packed dirt dotted with elephant droppings wasn't anybody's idea of a good time. She dangled about fifteen feet away from the far pole and over thirty feet above the ground. She'd never thought about it before, but when you get nervy from hanging high enough off the ground that falling will break both your legs, that really didn't qualify you as having a "fear of heights." That was more like, "fear of the very realistic chance of disaster."

A dozen or so feet in front of her, Drek Manifold hovered. He'd already played his hand, and in addition to flight, his power for the day was blowing up his body like a puffer fish (he used it to save the Human Cannonball). To her left, a unicycle balanced on the tightrope. Atop it, looking as though he were on the verge of dropping a deuce in his singlet, Pavel Walessa teetered precariously. Atop him, the other four members of the Flying Walessa's teetered even more precariously via a metal pole braced across Papa Walessa's mighty shoulders.

"I know what you're thinking," Manifold told her, with his flat, Ben Stein intonation, "but don't do it." Below him, clowns, chimps, bearded ladies, and the ring master scrambled about, trying to find something to cushion the impending fall.

Eva scoffed, trying not to look strained, even though her delicate fingers were starting to tire. "You have no idea what I'm thinking. You didn't pick ESP this time, asshole." The crowd of a couple thousand parents and children gasped, but that was probably a general gasp. She

doubted they could hear a word she said. The Walessa's could hear,
though, except for Papa Walessa, who was about to go unconscious from the
strain.

"So tell me," Manifold said. He was talking to her the way you would
talk to a jumper, not a pusher.

"I was thinking how I wasn't going to go back to that prison again,"
she said, which was true. Just the word "prison" brought back a furious
montage that made her jaw clench and her toes curl. The IV drips. The
electroshock any time she brought her hands within six inches of her face.
The strip cells and the feisty, horny guards. She'd do anything to avoid that.

"Rook," Manifold said. "The heist didn't work, but no one has gotten
hurt yet. The judge will be easy on you."

"You don't understand," she reiterated. "I'm not going back. At
all." She removed her left hand from the tightrope long enough to stick her
finger down her throat. The jet of stomach acid tore through the rope.
Manifold went after the Walessas, just like she knew he would.

In the big picture, it was kind of a nothing event. The circus heist
failed. All the Walessas lived because Manifold puffed himself up and acted
as an airbag for the falling family, although little Katya landed on Papa,
breaking his shoulder and ending his performing career. Eva held tight to
her section of rope, swung to freedom and escaped, but the law caught up to
her six weeks later in Salt Lake City when she tried to enter the Tabernacle.
Still, it was a significant event for her, because she learned a lot about
herself, and what was truly important to her.

*   *   *

Eva Destruction stared at Jack Jordan's maimed corpse lying at center
court. Actually, "maimed" didn't quite fit. Not much did, except maybe
"half-digested." She hated using her powers on normal humans. She
threatened to all the time, but the thought of actually doing it made her sick
(no pun intended). It was one thing if your powers consisted of making
people levitate or give you all their money, quite another thing when you
had to watch them disintegrate in front of you. Rather than repeated
experience desensitizing her, she had become a bit squeamish about seeing
another person get killed, much less being responsible for it, much less
seeing someone's flesh dissolving in her stomach acid. This poor bastard
looked like someone had dumped a bucket of toxic waste on the right side of

his body. Unfortunately, his face remained fully intact, leaving those over-rotated eyes to stare vacantly at the rafters. Fortunately for everyone, she could keep her stomach under control during times of acute nausea, or else she might have puked herself all the way to China.

Unlike Donna and her moping ways, in most circumstances, Eva enjoyed the thrill of the super-villain circuit. She liked the money. She liked dating interesting super-villains and bad boy Hollywood celebrities. She even liked the gaudy clothes (might as well wear leather pants while she still could, right?). Taking on the heroes easily became some wild cross between a chess match and a football game, but when real people got hurt, it destroyed the game aspect. When that happened, she always felt like one of those kids who hit a home run through the neighbor's window. One second, everything has clear rules and everyone is wearing primary colors. The next second, everything turns fuzzy and everyone becomes accountable. Times like this reminded her that she had zero chance of a normal future, and that she hadn't spoken to her parents in two years.

The guy on this floor changed from Drek Manifold into Joe Schmoe so fast, she couldn't be sure that the whole transformation wasn't an illusion. Thankfully, her attack only injured him (horribly and critically, but still...). It was Dane who put him down for good with the neural disruptor. After five years in the game, she still hadn't technically killed anyone. That might be the primary reason Donna still agreed to work with her. She'd maimed people, she'd caused them to lose limbs and require organ transplants, but she never crossed the killer's line, and with powers like hers, that was one hell of a thin line. She sure didn't want to cross it now. Granted, in this business, everything was relative; she could start offing people on a daily basis and never reach the body count of someone like Uncle Knapsack or Lord Osis. They'd all be in the same unofficial club, though.

Eva, Dane, and Poindexter stared at the limp body for several long seconds, their thoughts, no doubt, spinning off in vastly different directions. While Eva silently congratulated herself for not killing him, Poindexter undoubtedly tried to calculate some technical aspect of the death, like how fast the transformation took place or whether Manifold's jacket was actually made from denim or conjured out of solid ether. As Dane regarded the body and licked his thin, pale lips, his private thoughts were as subtle as a laser lightshow. "Guarded optimism" would probably describe his mindset best.

He spoke first. "He's dead," Dane whispered, but even his whispering carried to all corners of the gym. "At long last, id iz safe to bring the miracle of Socialism to Western Illinois and Eastern Iowa."

"Congratulations, Dane," Eva said, forcing a smile that might have been sweet had they not been standing over a mutilated corpse. From her spot beside the bleachers, Donna stood with her arms folded and her chin almost resting on her far shoulder, unable to even look at the gruesome scene at center court.

"Tanks," Dane said, then sighed a long gust of air from his mighty lungs. An involuntary smile inched its way across his face. She'd seen him smile before, but it usually contained either cruelty or sarcasm. This one looked categorically different and had only managed to leak out because, for once, he let his guard down. "I vant you all to know dhat each off you played a small, but far from insignificant part in dis historic event."

"Um, does this mean we can go now" a male voice called out behind them. Eva turned toward the bleachers to see a relatively well-built man standing up and wearing a black suit and too much hair gel. Who wears a suit to a public high school reunion in suburban Iowa? Still, it was a valid question, and all eyes turned toward Dane.

He stared down at the mangled, motionless body like the magi gazing upon the Christ child. Finally, his shoulders sagged, his head nodded, and he declared, "Ja. Let's get Uppsala und go home."

A murmur broke out in the bleachers, and Poindexter had to raise his voice to be heard above it. "But Dane," the doctor said, punching numbers into the calculator dangling from a cord around his neck, "my calculations indicate that there may be at least a five percent chance that Manifold isn't permanently gone."

The voices in the bleachers broke off in mid-mutter, and everyone froze in mid-evacuation. "Vhat do you mean?" Dane asked, his large Scandinavian eyes rotating toward Poindexter.

"This one shot laser beams out of his eyes," Poindexter explained. "Before, he was invisible. Plus, I don't ever remember this person, Jackson Jordan, missing from his seat when the wall exploded. How could he beat Donna over the head with a phone if—"

Dane lifted a hand. "Shut up, you!" he bellowed and brought the butt of his fist crashing down on his assistant's skull. "Don't ruin my moment!"

While a dazed Dr. Poindexter used his index finger to force his taped glasses back up the bridge of his nose, Dane took a moment to compose himself before turning to address the standing, leaning crowd. "We need to collect our comrades, and ducks, den we vill release you," he said. "You just need to be patient for a short vhile longer." As the hopeful murmur started to regroup, Dane raised a fist and yelled, "Vote Socialist!"

"That's it, then?" Poindexter said, guardedly. Dane's rages seldom lasted long, but like an earthquake, even after the big one subsided, you still had to worry about the aftershocks.

"That's it," Dane said, running his thick fingers through his short-cropped carpet of hair. "We'll figure out our next move once we've boarded Uppsala and departed."

Poindexter glared at Dane from beneath his bushy unibrow, and when he spoke, the voice that came out was several octaves lower than his regular one. In fact, given the reverberations that trailed in its path, there was no way the two voices could belong to the same body. The voice, combined with the hard, black eyes that were mostly pupil, combined for the most chilling encounter Eva had experienced all day. "Then you've outlived your usefulness, my little pawn," someone said using Poindexter's body. Then, that same someone belted out an eerie laugh. "Hoo Hoo Ha Ha Ha Ha!"

The laugh sounded familiar to Eva. She hoped it was from a movie she'd seen, but she knew better. Eva's brain almost grasped the answer as the white gas began to leak from Dr. Poindexter's pores. Dr. Poindexter would have known whose voice it was; he had an unbelievable memory. Unfortunately, at the moment, he also constituted a large part of the problem.

"It's Lord Osis!" Dane yelled. "All of you: cova your mout!" He dashed toward the exit in his heavy, power-lifter's gate.

Eva didn't have Dr. Poindexter's memory, but for a few seconds, the pertinent information came rolling out like an encyclopedia entry. Lord Osis. From the Vomeronazal Dimension. He was one of the first real villains Drek Manifold defeated, and one of the most dangerous. He had no solid form, but he could inhabit any human or animal body by entering through its orifices. Once inside, he could gradually take control of his host by manipulating the organism's muscular and neural responses. He didn't have to, though; sometimes, he chose to just sit back and watch the show for a while, just like he did this time around with Dr. Poindexter.

The white gas leaked out of Poindexter like smoke from a smoke grenade. They were all in a lot of trouble, and when the severity of the situation registered, Eva gasped, and that was all that Lord Osis needed. When Dane turned back to her and yelled, "Get to da choppa!" she was beyond caring.

*   *   *

Chapter Twenty-One:
10:42 p.m.

"So," the white-haired guidance councilor began as he stared down at the thin, beige file folder in front of him, "what do you plan to do after graduation?" He acted like he'd said it a thousand times before, and of course, he had. It was the sort of thing people in his occupation had to ask graduating seniors. No real purpose to the question; Mr. Connors simply stood alongside a long line of gatekeepers. You could say you planned on going to Harvard or starting your own fertilizer business, just as long as you didn't say anything stupid that they would feel obligated to follow up on.

"I think I'll sleep in," Kelly replied, his body sinking into the chair with an amoeba-like slouch.

Mr. Connors cleared his throat. He and most of the student's he "counseled" spoke to one another once a year for roughly twelve minutes per meeting, and Connors couldn't have picked Kellen T. Edwards out of a police line-up (and god willing, someday he would test that theory), but Connors felt obligated to take a fatherly stand. "No, I mean long-term."

Kelly tried to shrug, but he didn't have it in him. "I don't know. I look at the future, and it just seems like a sucking hole, y'know? I mean, best case scenario, I end up knocking up some chick and working a job I hate for the rest of my life, barely keeping my head above water until it's time to retire and use my savings to pay for my own funeral. Seems like I should just save myself some trouble and drive my car into a telephone pole."

Mr. Connors looked pretty beat, like an EMT working a double-shift. He'd stopped using Just for Men *this semester, and that made him look extra haggard. Professional that he was, though, he decided to tackle this one, even if it meant stretching this meeting to* fifteen *minutes. He grasped both corners of his glasses frames and slowly pulled them off his face. "Kellen, son, I know things might look pretty dark right now: you're about to leave your friends, you're—"*

The word "son" made Kelly panic. During his short life, the best indicator that a speech would instill in him the desire to gouge his eye out with his thumb was if the speaker referred to him as "son." He forced a laugh. "Naw, man. I'm just messin' with you. I plan to start my own matchbook company."

Connors' relief was palpable, but the relief didn't stem from the fact that Kelly would grace the world with his presence: he was just happy to knock out that last file before lunch. "That," Connors said, breaking into a thin-lipped smile, "is a great idea."

Kelly held up his palms to shoulder level and pressed out a smile that matched the old man's. "Everybody needs matches."

*   *   *

Kelly Edward's right hand lashed out and snagged the bent metal rod of the door handle while his left used all its non-dominant might to keep the lower half of Navin Offerdahl's body airborne. He and Ely Lisch were toting Navin into the Home Economics room. The door was only unlocked because, while the Knockout Mouse was busily pummeling the piss out of Ely, Kelly used the fire extinguisher to smash through the rectangular security glass window above the door handle. He had rummaged through the legion of drawers at a World Record clip, searching for a serviceable weapon, but ultimately, the best weapon he could find turned out to be the fire extinguisher. Now, once he and Ely Lisch shuffled inside, Kelly had no idea what they were going to do, but at least a sturdy door and some shadow would buy him some time to make the decisions (emphasis on "him," too; Ely's brain worked for about five minutes at a time, tops, and Navin contributed about as much strategy as a potted fern).

The knob turned under Kelly's hand, and he gave the door a shove with his bony ass. His right hand swung in a little loop in time to catch Navin's falling leg, while his own size-twelve foot kicked out to keep the door from closing. It was a hard decision to drag Navin this far. Calling him "dead weight" was no exaggeration. He would slow them down all to

hell no matter what they did, and no one knew how long the Knockout
Mouse would stay down for the count. That thick, rodent skull could
probably sustain a lot of fire extinguisher abuse. As far as Kelly was
concerned, he only decided to bring Navin along on the offhand chance that
Drek Manifold might be lurking in that crippled little form. That struck him
as a cold-blooded and opportunistic way to treat a fellow human being, but
desperate times... desperate measures... yada yada yada. Of course, since
Ely definitely was Drek Manifold, that kind of complicated matters.

"Let's set him down on one of the tables," Kelly instructed before
they had shuffled all the way inside the room. Thankfully, the Home Ec
room was littered with tables identical to the ones in the cafeteria. They all
stood clustered in the middle of the room, while the cooking implements
(stoves, refrigerators, etc.) lay fused into the walls around the perimeter.
Kelly and Ely waddled in lockstep over to one of the circular tables and set
Navin down. Kelly tried to be gentle, but his willowy frame seldom carried
more weight than a six-pack of beer for this long a period of time, and he
unloaded his classmate like a bag of rock salt. Navin might have sighed, or
blinked, when his back slammed into the tabletop, but the room was dark
and Kelly was going through early stage withdrawal, so it was probably
Kelly's imagination. "Now," he said to Ely, "find a knife in one of the
drawers."

Ely walked toward the set of drawers that, according to a cardboard
sign taped to the nearest refrigerator, comprised part of "Cooking Station
#1." *God, that mouse fucked him up*, Kelly thought as he watched Ely walk
through a sliver of light from the outside driveway. His rapidly swelling
face reminded Kelly of the kid from the movie, *Mask.* Ely's hand reached
out, but before it opened anything, he paused and glanced through the
darkness at Kelly. "Why am I getting a knife?"

"I need to go back and cut the Knockout Mouse's throat," Kelly said
as he stalked over to Cooking Station #8. He frantically pulled open one
drawer at a time, riffling through the dry measuring cups and tea spoons,
then slamming it. The first time he tossed the room, all he could come up
with were steak knives with flimsy blades and rounded tips. They would
have been lucky to carve their way through a Big Mac, which was why he
settled on the fire extinguisher. There didn't look to be anything more lethal
this time, either.

Ely gave a long nod, and then replied in a tone that might have sounded condescending, "What's a 'Knockout Mouse?'"

Kelly slammed the bottom drawer of Cooking Station #8. *This is just so unbelievably…* He put his hands on his hips and took a deep breath. This was not the best time for him. He'd been injecting dilauded into his arms this whole week, and he'd been clean all day. Without his medicine, stress made him jumpy, which meant that dealing with mutant rodents and guys with nonfunctional memory felt like getting crammed into a paint shaker and someone turning it on. Instead of wasting his time and energy yelling, he asked in as calm a voice as he could muster, "Do you have a piece of paper?"

"Um," Ely began, patting himself down. His hand slapped on something crinkly in the back pocket of his jeans. "Uh, yeah. I do," he said and pulled it free. Kelly saw him reading it earlier, when they were first shuttled over the bleachers, and at the time, he deduced that Ely must have written it to himself. Ely unfolded the paper and started to read the typed information on the front.

"Give it to me," Kelly said and snatched the paper out of Ely's hand. The first drawer he'd looked through contained a few pens, and he took one and used his thumb to pop the cap off. Just as he expected, the front of the paper contained some type-written message from Ely to Ely. In the rectangle of dim light from hallway, he saw the line, "God, I wonder how many times I've written these sentences." *How many times, indeed. What the hell did he ever do to deserve a life like this?* Kelly flipped the paper over to the back and started to write.

"If that's a note for me," Ely offered, "it might be better if it's in my handwriting. Y'see, I have this condition—"

"I know," Kelly said, biting his lip. "I know." Streams of sweat rolled off of him now, dripping off his nose onto the paper. Each sweat tributary felt like a line of fire ants marching across his flesh. Plus, his hand was slippery and shaking so badly that he wasn't sure he could write a legible message. *This is insane,* he thought. *That mouse isn't going to stay down forever.* "Fine," he said, finally, pressing the paper and pen into Ely's hands. "Write the words 'Listen to Kelly,' and hold the fucking thing in front of you from now on."

Ely did as instructed, the looked up, expectantly.

"Now," Kelly continued, "find me the sharpest thing you can."

They rummaged for a few more minutes, Kelly's eyes going in and out of focus, but the flimsy steak knives with the serrated edges were the best they could do. Kelly grabbed one, muttering something under his breath about juvenile delinquents ruining things for everyone else, and stomped into the hallway. At this point, he felt too irritated to feel scared. Given his current state and the agony he would be enduring in the next couple hours, death would provide something of a release. So would taking twenty minutes to saw off that mouse's fucking head with a child-proof steak knife. He made it to a bend in the hallway before his caution returned, momentarily. He took a long, slow look down to where the silver double doors marked the start of the cafeteria, but other than a few streaks of human blood on the white tile, there was one other landmark to indicate anything had changed: someone had pushed one of the metal doors open so far that it stayed stuck open. Also, beyond it, almost like an anti-landmark, no white rat lay under the dishwasher window.

Kelly drifted forward, almost involuntarily, and slowly eased the silver door into the closed position. Then, he swallowed and felt the rest of his proverbial backbone leave him. He sensed the presence of the Knockout Mouse behind him, panting its hot rat breath on the back of his neck. He twisted his head around like it was operated by a hand-crank, only to find an empty, air conditioned hallway. *Must just be the inevitable DTs showing up a little early*, he thought as he crept back to the Home Ec room. By the time he closed the metal door with the shattered window behind him, he was still oozing sweat, but it had turned into a cold sweat and sent him into a series of shivers.

"Who the hell are you?" Ely said, peering through the dark.

"Read your note," Kelly directed, his purple lips quivering. As Ely's eyes dropped to the piece of paper in his hand, Kelly reached for a kitchen towel hanging from one of the oven handles and used it to mop up some of the sweat gushing from his brow. *What was the… What were they looking for?* He braced his hands against the table. Sweet Jesus, he was having trouble thinking. From the corner of his eye, he could have sworn that he saw Navin smiling at him with his little, bald cherubic face, but when he glanced over for a full-on view, it was gone. "Aren't we just the most useless trio in the world?" he muttered.

It occurred to him to lock the door. A stomach cramp ripped through his midsection that made him reconsider. Sure, the broken window made it painfully obvious that they were in the only occupied room and painfully easy to get inside, but his goal was to buy as much time as possible until... well, until one of these boys felt like changing into a super-hero.

Kelly walked over to the door in a hunch and locked it. Until he could puke or shit, he would be locomoting about as gingerly as an octogenarian after a car accident. Behind him, Navin lay on the table like a discarded rag doll. It wasn't a comfortable position, with his head listing to the left at an unnatural angle, but Kelly didn't even know if poor Navin could feel pain anymore. He hoped not. Meanwhile, Ely's puffy visage looked about two seconds away from needing to read his note again. It was starting to look like a long wait.

*   *   *

Chapter Twenty-Two:
10:43 p.m.

Chase could actually do a pretty good impersonation of Drek Manifold, with the occasional shuffling and the constant twitching. It cracks up anybody who had seen the protector of the Tri-Cities in the flesh. He modified it from the impersonation of a guy he worked with who died from Huntington's Disease.

*   *   *

Chase Wilder didn't catch the bad guys' reason for running from Dr. Dorkinstein, but they all did it with such gusto that it certainly seemed that they had a valid reason. McVain was running, *really* running... with his chest about four inches in front of the rest of him, and he didn't strike Chase as the retreating type. It implied that the nerd had done something, or *became* something, to be feared. That part seemed like a good thing; "the enemy of my enemy" and all that bullshit. By the same token, the "super-villain code" probably didn't contain a section about having to keep your enemy's hostages alive.

McVain sprinted toward the demolished gym doors, probably toward the helicopter he kept raving about whenever he had the slightest prompting, but as soon as he touched the handle of the doors that led out of the outer concourse, a jolt of electricity sent him flying back toward the baseline. The chick in the black body suit wasn't moving at all. She just stood there with some orgasmic expression on her face, breathing in the white gas. It almost looked like one of those cartoons, where Sylvester the Cat smelled turkey with all the fixin's, and the power of the scent lifted him off the ground and dragged him toward its source.

Dozens of tendrils of mist reached out from Dr. Poindexter, crawling their way toward McVain's twitching, prone form. As the ethereal substance stood poised above the Swedish Superagent, the other chick, the one in the red outfit, launched herself across the gym floor in what certainly appeared to be rocket-powered roller skates. She veered under the basket, snagged McVain by his shirt collar, and dragged his bulk across the recently waxed gym floor, into the back hallway, toward the locker rooms. Just as she began pulling away from the growing, ghostly white amorphous substance that filled the gym, she skidded to a stop at the mouth of the hallway. Turning, she snapped open her makeup compact with the practiced efficiency one normally reserves for a gunslinger in a black and white Western and in one synchronized move, blew some of the flesh-toned makeup particles into the air. Within seconds, the particles had consolidated into a 20 x 20 section of cement wall, temporarily blocking her and McVain from the gaseous attacker.

The mist didn't pout, though. It didn't stomp against the ground or pound on the wall. It immediately made a sharp right and advanced upon its secondary target: the crowd. "Let's get out of here," Chase announced to no one in particular. He had planned to shout the instructions, but in reality, what came out was the same volume as his speaking voice, but with a slightly feminine pitch.

The only other voice came from Reggie Sleeve, who kept muttering to himself, "Stay calm, stay awake. Stay calm, stay awake." Chase would've liked to smack him again. Sleeve had that big shaved head that from the back looked like a giant, coco-colored penis; it was the kind of head made for slapping. There was no time for fun and games, though.

"Run!" someone else yelled, but it was too late. A few people made it around the north side of the bleachers, but then ran into the moat. Others dashed across the gym, toward the northwest entrance, and were consumed by a blast of acidic vomit. A few more desperate souls acted like a pack of Ely Lischs and ran toward the outer concourse's electrified doors. Their fate was predictable. *Idiots*, Chase thought, then realized that he hadn't moved at all. A couple dozen members of the Class of '96, Reggie Sleeve included, had remained in the bleachers, defended only by their slack jaws and bulging eyeballs. The ghostly tentacles expanded and divided, then reached down each of their throats.

Strangely, they had a vanilla taste that wasn't altogether unpleasant.

*   *   *

Chapter Twenty-Three:
10:48 p.m.

"Kelly, pick up," Sally said to the answering machine.

Kelly turned the volume down on Stir Crazy *and reached over for the phone receiver. "Yeah, what's up?"*

"Why didn't you pick up the phone?"

"I'm in the middle of a movie."

"I see," Sally said, curtly, then took a deep breath. "Well, I'm going to make this quick."

"Please do," Kelly said, his eyes fixated on Richard Prior's silently moving mouth. He knew she was calling to break up with him, but he was in no condition to communicate with other humans; he'd taken the shrooms about two hours ago and they were building to a crescendo. That's not fair, though. The drugs weren't making him not care. There were drugs that did that for you, but psilocybin wasn't the right prescription. He just plain didn't care, about anything, and the drugs made him feel less guilty about not caring.

*   *   *

Kelly Edwards pinched the sweaty bridge of his nose. He didn't know whether the sweat came from his nose or his fingertips, he only knew that there was a lot of it. He had taken a seat in a chair in the corner of the Home Ec room, pressing his shoulders against the wooden counter. If he kept his weight pushed back, his constant shaking wouldn't make the drawers rattle. *This is going nowhere*, he thought. Between the shivering and the headaches, and Ely constantly asking the same questions, Kelly couldn't have performed a coin flip much less the mental gymnastics needed to get them out of this building alive. It didn't help that the question Ely kept repeating was "What are we doing?" because Kelly asked himself that question almost as regularly.

One of these two former JV football teammates was Drek Manifold. That was the only explanation he had for how Navin got out of chair and transported himself over two hundred yards down to the industrial tech wing. Circumstantial evidence, to be sure, but in Ely's case, he had even more compelling proof. Kelly was standing in the hallway when something invisible started dropping the dogs on the Knockout Mouse, then suddenly, Ely was standing in the same spot getting his ass kicked. He had no idea why the Manifold in Ely abandoned him in mid-fight, but that was neither here nor there. What Kelly had to do was figure out how to invoke the destroyer lurking within them in time to save the day. Of course, right now, trying not to defecate on himself proved a complex enough task.

"What are we doing?" Ely asked yet again as Kelly sat shivering in the corner with a paper-thin dish towel from Cooking Station # 6 draped over his shoulders. Something wet crawled down his cheeks, but he couldn't tell if it was tears or sweat or blood.

This time, Kelly answered the question with a question. "What do you remember about the day we wrecked Jack's truck?" Ely didn't develop his memory problems right off the bat. There was a gradual increase in forgetfulness, then one day during his junior year, he stopped coming to school and everybody knew why. The doctors scanned his skull about fifteen different ways and didn't find any structural damage, but they did find some whacked out EEG readings. In any case, memory often fades with time and gets confused with other memories, but since Ely was essentially frozen in time, eleven years ago might seem like yesterday.

"What's to know?" Ely said and scratched his now Jay Leno-like chin. Atop that Home Ec table, he seemed awfully serene, annoyingly so for someone who looked like a motorcycle just ran over his face. Of course, Ely remained blissfully ignorant of the fact that a giant, pugilistic rodent was skulking about.... somewhere, hatching a plan to kill them in its walnut-sized mind before the ex-model who could puke apart an armored car found them. Given that, and the fact that Ely wasn't going though withdrawal from pharmaceutical dope, Kelly could forgive his former classmate for his serenity. "It was an overcast day," Ely began, and that observation alone made Kelly perk up and listen. "Jack was driving too slow, as usual. You and me were in the cab. Navin and Reggie were in the back. That song, 'Hold on to the Night,' was on the radio because Jack always played that easy listening shit just to annoy us. There was that flash of orange light—"

Kelly's vision momentarily came online, and his eyelids forced themselves wider. He remembered that. Jack *did* like to piss them off with that adult contemporary shit. He'd even do a twitchy Joe Cocker impression when "Up Where We Belong" came on (actually, sometimes he'd do the exact same impression with other songs, too, even if it didn't feature Joe Cocker, and it worked with almost *anything*...). If anybody ever got annoyed enough to complain about the current piece of sonic shit pumping out of his barely functional speakers, he'd say, "My truck, my radio." So, why was that important? *Oh, yeah...* "Wh-what did you just say?" Kelly asked, slowly, through chattering teeth.

"You don't remember the orange light?" Ely asked, confused.

"No," Kelly said, taking the hand towel off his shoulders long enough to wipe down his face. The orange light was a little hard to forget. "I mean, yeah, but before that. 'Hold on to the Night' was playing on the radio?"

"Um, yeah," Ely said, not sure where this was going. He used a confused tone when speaking so much these days that it was a wonder that his voice box didn't just have one setting anymore.

"Didn't Richard Marx sing that?" Kelly said, already knowing the answer, already trying to fit the information into their problem set.

"Yeah. So?"

"Nothing," Kelly replied. No point in going into it. By the time he explained who Drek Manifold was, he would have to explain what was going on. Then, he'd have to rehash how Richard Marx fit into all this, and by that time, he'd have to re-explain who Drek Manifold was. No, they didn't have time for that. Kelly would have to figure this mess out internally and alone.

So, genius, he thought to himself, *how* is *Richard Marx involved in all of this?* It couldn't possibly be coincidence that a Marx song was playing on the radio when the light hit them, since Manifold was supposed to be the spitting image of late-eighties Marx. If a super-hero had a choice about what musician he would look like, he'd obviously pick Bootsy Collins. But did the light come over the radio waves? Does that question even make

sense? If so, how did they see it? And why did it only affect Ely and
Navin? If it had been only Reggie and Navin that turned into Manifold, that
would have made sense because they were both in the back of the truck, and
it could have landed on them like radioactive fallout. Ely sat in front,
though. This calculus gave Kelly a headache... or maybe it was his brain
cells calling out for more dilauded. Probably the latter.

"What are we doing?" Ely asked through his puffy mouth. He'd
barely moved an inch since the last time he asked the question.

"Trying to stay as quiet as possible," Kelly replied, absently, as he
eased out of his seat in the corner and into a crouch. The sweats hadn't even
stopped and his body had already started to ache. *It's the stress*, he told
himself. *Stress always accelerated the symptoms*. The running didn't help.
Neither did the ass-kicking the Knockout Mouse administered. There were
probably half a dozen other factors, but the fact remained, if he didn't fix up
in the next twelve hours, he'd feel like his blood had turned into liquid fire
and he'd start taking mini-craps every ten minutes. As the moment, he just
had to go Number One, and he'd be damned if he was going to walk down
the hallway to do it.

Kelly pulled open the oven door from Cooking Station #8 and
retrieved the deepest pot in there. The cookware could easily hold half a
gallon of liquid, although he wouldn't have been surprised if his bladder
gave it a run for its money. In an old-man hobble, he carried the pot to the
furthest, darkest corner (a.k.a., Cooking Station #5) so that he could do his
business in relative private.

Maybe Ely and Navin had something like an infection. Kelly watched
a lot of TV (a *lot* of TV) and he had a special place in his heart for medical
dramas. He learned from *House, M.D.* that there are individual differences
for the effect of infections, such that the same disease can produce two
different sets of symptoms. He also learned from *Chicago Hope* that people
have tolerance differences, such that two hundred people can drink
contaminated water every day but only ten get cancer. If his theory held,
then Jack and Reggie might have been infected, too. Reggie blacked out
regular as a fucking wristwatch, and Jack didn't know where he was half the
time. Putting them all under the same umbrella wasn't much of a stretch.

Kelly sighed as he un-kinked his urinary tract. He would sit on the
opposite end of the spectrum from Navin: Navin was really susceptible,

while Kelly was barely susceptible, for whatever reason. Maybe it was all the radio-listening he did as a kid. Navin was a Mormon; maybe his parents didn't let him listen to the radio at all (Kelly really didn't know what their beliefs and rituals were, but he pictured something like John Lithgow's family in the movie *Footloose*). Maybe it had to do with Kelly hating "Hold on to the Night" so much that he was trying to block it out. One way or the other, he certainly functioned the best out of everyone in the quintet. He, Jack, and Reggie were the only one's who graduated high school, and even though Reggie got an online bachelor's degree from the University of Phoenix, he had to work at home because his sleep attacks prevented him from driving. In fact, when you look at it—

"What's that sound?" Ely asked.

Only the initiated would recognize the sound of a mutant duck howling, and it strangled off Kelly's pee in mid-stream. The source of the howl was very close, and that and the extensive echo made him automatically think of the cafeteria. The sound of the swinging doors slamming against the wall resonated from even closer. Kelly zipped up and trotted to the door's broken window in time to see two people running down the hallway, toward the Home Ec room. One limped along awkwardly, probably because she wore high heels. Kelly ripped the door open, and the man and the woman wordlessly piled inside. As Kelly quietly closed it behind them, the woman blew into her makeup compact and caused the door window that Kelly had busted with fire extinguisher to rematerialized, and it was only then that Kelly realized that he had invited Dane McVain and Donna Correction into the Home Ec sanctuary.

*   *   *

Chapter Twenty-Four:
10:52p.m.

"What do you think about Dane?" Eva asked as she finished zipping up her black leather suitcase.

"That's an interesting question," Donna replied, slinging her red leather duffle bag over her shoulder. Compared to Eva, she traveled light, which meant that she only had one piece of luggage that you could fit a full-sized human into. She turned to see that Eva was wearing her bodysuit. Donna still wore sweatpants and an oversized SMU Mustangs T-shirt. They had a two-hour flight ahead of them, and at some point, she would change, but squeezing into those outfits this soon amounted to masochism. She's amazed that she hadn't needed to amputate her hands and feet yet. "How do you mean?" she asked.

"I mean... well, romantically," Eva said, grinning awkwardly, as she looked in the mirror and slid her hands over her leather-clad hips. Eva had a thing for the super-villain-type. It was one thing to date that sort because of convenience: it was their social circle, after all. Donna had the idea that it was something more for Eva, like dating the bad boy and the celebrity at the same time. Let's see... she went out with The Mollusk after he broke up with Shelly. She had more than a few dates with General EO before she found out he was a homosexual and just wanted to be friends. Her most serious relationship was with Nicholas Copernicus of the Super Poles, and they didn't even speak the same language. She even dated the Soft Werewolf, which was safe enough as long as you weren't sending him an email during a full moon. There were more, of course, but those were the ones that immediately sprang to mind.

It didn't seem like a healthy habit to have, but Donna didn't exactly
provide a shining example of romantic success. Deep down, she must have
settled into the role of bitter spinster over a year ago. "Why are we having
this conversation now?"

Eva nodded toward the front of the castle. "I wanted to be as far
away from the helicopter as possible. I don't think it likes me."

"No argument there," Donna said, then took a few seconds to
consider the initial question. "Hmmm. Well, I think he'd be okay if he
didn't have the damned helicopter, but that's kind of like saying a double
amputee would be faster with legs."

"I don't know," Eva said, shrugging as she double-checked the zipper
on her bag. "I think that just means he's committed."

"Whatever floats your boat," Donna said as she eased her way
toward the door. She hated trite expressions, but they probably wouldn't be
trite if they weren't so useful. "By the way, want me to conjure you up a
mover to help you with your bags."

Eva gave her a sisterly smile. "That... would be great."

*   *   *

Even in his forties, Dane kept himself in top physical condition, but it
was top physical condition for a power-lifter, not a distance runner, and after
about ten seconds of sprinting, he looked about another ten seconds from a
heart attack. For her part, Donna Correction spent so much time on the
elliptical machine that she could get her mail sent there, but she usually wore
sweats and a pair of Adidas when she exerted herself, not high-heeled boots
and a leather bodysuit. With the boots, she risked turning an ankle on every
step, but they were less dangerous than the rocket-powered roller skates.
When the ramp to the cafeteria appeared, she came jetting along so fast that
she nearly maimed herself by slamming into a table, so she dissolved the
rocket skates and ran the rest of the way. She'd never used rocket-skates
before; it was a moment of inspiration, but one she probably wouldn't have
again while indoors.

Now, temporarily safe inside one of the classrooms, Donna rubbed her
bruised thighs as she slumped against one of the room's ground-level
cupboard doors, listening for the *clackity-clack* sound as the four-legged
ducks waddled down the tile hallway toward them. The doors at this end of
the school were heavy and metal, and although they deserved points for

ferocity, the Wolfian Ducks lacked the body mass to get into the room. They could, however, alert the others, Donna's former comrades, who had opposable thumbs... and worse. *God*, she thought, *if Lord Osis got a hold of Eva, twenty metal doors won't be enough protection.*

The clicking of maybe a dozen pairs of clawed, webbed feet drew closer. The procession slowed in front of their door, but that might have been Donna's imagination. The sweaty Swede had the pungency of a wet dog, and even though their pursuers were part duck, they were also part wolf, and the scent detectors resided somewhere in that genetic soup. In any case, the clicking feet kept right on moving, and when the sound receded, Donna allowed herself to breathe again.

She glanced across the doorway at Dane, and as if guessing her question, he shrugged. "Maybe dey can't smell as good vit Lord Osis controlling dem."

"Whose Lord Osis?" one of the room's shadowy occupants asked. Donna peered into the darkness at the guy sitting on the table (not to be confused with the guy *sprawled limply* on the table). At first, she couldn't recognize him because he looked like someone had worked him over with a tire iron, but after a few seconds, she saw the blue shirt and red tie and realized that it was the guy with the memory problem. The one who Eva had lost track of but didn't get yelled at for it. "While you're at it, who are any of you?"

Donna took a breath, as if to begin, but instinctively looked over at Dane for approval. She noticed other people do the exact same thing. It was funny: he didn't have a single power. He wasn't that smart. He was prone to rages. He was strong, but only strong for a human. In fact, he wasn't much at all without Uppsala and his cadre of followers. Yet, everyone he worked with deferred to him. Maybe he had charisma. Eva certainly thought so.

Dane nodded, and Donna looked around the room, trying to find the room's third inhabitant, the one who opened the door for them. There he was, a tall, lanky guy seated on one of the chairs, shivering. He acted like he'd been locked in a meat locker for a few hours, but he looked only vaguely familiar. He looked even less familiar than the bald guy lying like a rag doll on the table. The bald guy, at least, she remembered sitting in a wheelchair across the gym from her position. How the hell did he get all the way down here? *Who cares?* she thought. *One thing's for sure: the backside of this high school really does seem to have collected the dregs of the reunion.*

"He's Dane McVain," she began, "and I'm Donna Correction. As for Lord Osis..."

*   *   *

Lord Osis first appeared in our dimension in March of 1996. He is most famous in our world for being Drek Manifold's first and most powerful enemy. Dane McVain would become Manifold's arch-enemy by virtue of their string of epic encounters, but McVain was only a man. In human terms, Lord Osis was nothing less than a force of nature.

He (It?) came from the Vomeronazal Dimension, where molecules vibrated at a much slower rate, causing objects that were solid in that dimension to transform into mists and odors in ours. In his home dimension, Lord Osis had been a politician-turned-murderer who the authorities eventually imprisoned. He continually escaped from their conventional prisons, and since his advanced society did not condone the death penalty, their council of elders placed him in an interdimensional prison from which there was no escape. However, "no escape" meant no escaping back into his home dimension. If a metaphorical brick wall barred him from his home world, a flimsy wooden gate kept him from ours.

Upon materializing in this world as a gaseous cloud, Lord Osis soon found that he possessed the ability to enter into humans or lower animals and manipulate the workings of their brains. Once inhabiting a host, he could extend his influence to other brains via scents created by body processes (e.g., sweat, flatulence, halitosis, etc.). So, he dominated one body, then used it to infect others, kind of like a virus. There did not seem to be a limit to the number of individuals he possessed, although with each additional possession, he lost a little bit of edge to his control, almost like losing power steering fluid, or overloading an electrical outlet.

In his initial escape from his interdimensional prison world, Lord Osis infected every person attending Cityfest '96, a major civic event headlined by the surviving members of the Tri-City DJs. Drek Manifold showed up on the scene and was able to keep the mob from doing any damage by creating a vacuum in the Costco Concert Hall, sucking all the air out, and sealing Lord Osis up on some sort of Mason jar.

Some of the concert-goers attempted to sue Manifold for brain damage due to the temporary hypoxia they endured, but there was no evidence that any of the patrons received any physical damage from the incident. The judge concluded that there were no pre-concert images to compare the brain scans with, and even if there were, there was no proof that Lord Osis did not cause the damage when he possessed them. Some members of the local media hypothesized aloud during on-air broadcasts that you would have to have sustained a *little* brain damage to attend a Tri-City DJ's concert in the first place. In all seriousness, though, had the judge decided differently, the Tri-Cities might have lost their only super-powered savior after one outing.

Osis returned several times over the years, always centering his activities around the Tri-Cities. Most recently, last July, he attempted to take over the Kooterville Town Council to pass an ordinance banning deodorant, thereby allowing him to possess the entire city within hours. In this instance, as with all the other instances, Drek Manifold rose to the challenge and stopped him.

*   *   *

"So," the tall sweaty guy asked when Donna had finished, "what are we going to do now?"

"Do?" Dane responded in disbelief. Thankfully, his breathing had returned to normal; if he had gone into cardiac arrest, Donna was afraid she'd have to jump on his sternum to compress it. "Escape. If I can get to Uppsala, I can get us away from here and leave dis mess up to…" He trailed off, realizing his mistake.

"Who?" Donna hissed. "Manifold? He's dead." She had no love for ol' Drek, but Dane had created this mess, and he'd have to be man enough to clean it up. She had little inclination to work this job in the first place, and she was not about to let him sleaze his way back to Sweden, even if that meant she was stuck in this shit-hole, too. When she spoke next, the volume of her voice had decreased, but not its edge. "It's up to us to stop this thing, and I, for one, am not leaving until we do." She gave Dane a hard glare. "And that helicopter of yours would help out a lot."

Dane scowled as he slumped forward with his hands resting on his knees. His legs crossed under him, Indian-style. "She has a name…"

"Did you say Manifold was dead?" the tall sweaty guy said.

"Who's Manifold?" the guy with the memory problem chimed in.

Donna ignored the second question and turned to the Sweaty Guy. "We found out his secret identity. He was somebody named Jackson Jordan. Dane shot him with a neural destabilizer and he died."

"That's impossible," Sweaty Guy muttered breathlessly. He turned and regarded Dane, sharply. Before he mustered enough boldness to start the name-calling, Dane returned his glower. And Dane was a world class glowerer.

"Don't look at me dat way, little man," Dane growled, "or I'll make you join him."

Donna narrowed her eyes at Sweaty Guy. *Why is that impossible?* she wondered. She almost got a chance to ask the question, but Memory Man cut her off.

"Wait, what's that sound?" the Memory Man asked, and everyone immediately stopped talking in mid-insult. "It sounds like a fan blade."

Donna strained to listen. It did sound a bit like a fan blade, but it wasn't. She knew the sound, because the term "silent helicopter" was a bit of hyperbole. She turned to Dane. "Could they be using the thermal sensors to search for us?"

"Impossible," Dane scoffed. "Da only people who can fly Uppsala are me and... Poindexter."

Donna saw Dane mouth the last word, but the machine gun bullets ripping through the ceiling drowned out the rest of his statement.

*   *   *

Chapter Twenty-Five:
10:55 p.m.

When Reggie woke up, a puddle of spit had collected under his cheek.
"Goddamn it," he muttered, "must have passed out again." He was on the
phone with a client, then he heard a car screeching around the corner, and
now it was... Jesus Christ. Four twenty p.m. The last time he checked the
clock, it was just past noon. He assumed that the cat would be pretty pissed
it didn't get its Fancy Feast, but when he looked over by the window, Karl
was merely sunning himself in the chair.

Being a narcoleptic wasn't easy. For one, a lot of semi-literate
people thought he liked having sex with dead bodies. For two, he didn't
have the treatable kind of narcolepsy. He tried all the treatments, from
pharmaceutical amphetamines to chemical hypocretin, but they never helped
and he got a full scoop of side effects. Still, anytime something new came
out, he kept trying it. That was something he felt pretty proud of: he never
gave up. He managed to graduate high school, then college. He stayed
gainfully employed and made a decent living selling ad space in National
Harvester Magazine.

His relative success, and the difficulty he overcame, didn't bring much
satisfaction, though. He always felt like the world saw him as the retard that
learned to dress himself. The sentence, I was meant to be something more,
popped into his mind at least once a week, but here he was... alone. In his
two bedroom apartment. With his cat.

Reggie rubbed his numb face and dialed the next number.

*   *   *

Reggie Sleeve sat calmly in his bleacher seat. Since the last panicked attempt at a jail break, the crowd of hostages in the gym had thinned by a couple dozen people, leaving almost fifty people in the seats. The Kooterville High Class of '96 was losing people faster than an infantry battalion during the Normandy Invasion. Reggie only felt individually responsible for Sally's well-being, but that was more than enough to weigh heavily on his guilt-prone psyche. The image flashed through his mind of her mangled body being chewed apart by a cluster of Wolfian Ducks, gurgling and snapping like a pack of hyena chowing down on a fresh gazelle. It came and went like a blip on a radar screen, but it felt like a kick in the stomach. He couldn't react to it, though; at this point, he couldn't react to anything.

No one in the bleachers spoke to one another, or even made eye contact, so he wasn't sure what was going on. A few minutes before, Dr. Poindexter had disappeared through the hole in the wall where the gym doors used to be, pushed through the formerly electrified doors, and kept walking toward the football field. Everyone continued staring straight ahead, still as toy soldiers, their eyes fixated on nothing. To be safe, Reggie did the same, although he did his best to avert his eyes from the spot where the remains of Jack Jordan's pulverized body still lay. The red-head in the black cat suit still stood in the middle of the gym floor, just like old times, but this time around, she wasn't wearing a bored expression, chomping on a wad of Hubba Bubba, or checking out her cuticles. She just stared back at the crowd, stiff as a statue, except with the slightest of smiles clinging to her full, glossy lips.

After Donna Correction pulled McVain out of the gym on those rocket-skates, Reggie got stuck in the logjam of people at the edge of the moat, and when the white mist that smelled like sulfur and tasted like vanilla engulfed them, he breathed in the tainted air like everyone else. Without a word, everyone stopped screaming and shoving and wordlessly did an about-face, then started marching back to their seats in a procession that would have made a Marine drill team envious. Reggie followed along, well aware that something was seriously wrong but equally aware that he could do nothing about it. He filtered back to his seat and tried his best to throw his shoulders back and keep his jaw slack so that he could mimic the posture and expression of everyone around him, but after five minutes, his middle back started to spasm and ache. The wooden bleacher seats had been steadily eroding his boney ass all evening, but this "perfect posture" shit marked the final straw.

Reggie chanced an eyeball shift to his left, toward where Sherri Salisbury sat. She wore the same empty expression as all the rest. It made the whole crowd look like a set of identical mannequins with different wigs and different fat-suits. Emboldened by still being alive, Reggie chanced a half-second of elbow-to-elbow contact with Sheri, and the effect was like an alarm clock detonating.

The collective reaction resembled Donald Sutherland's at the end of *Invasion of the Bodysnatchers* (the first remake), with the pointing and the moaning/sucking sound, but in this case, four dozen people were doing it. Actually, "resembled" didn't cut it; the response was identical to Sutherland's. Perhaps it constituted a "natural" reflex among the possessed, but it struck Reggie as being just as likely due to a sick sense of humor on the part of the puppet master. This isn't to say it didn't scare the living crap out of Reggie; it certainly did. For whatever reason, though, the invisible roulette wheel that governed Reggie's brain decided to keep him awake, and he fell into a cringing semi-tuck position.

After several seconds, the crowd ran out of breath and stopped moaning, but they kept pointing at him, their index fingers forming a wall of spikes as they wavered slightly under the breeze created by the air from the ventilation ducts. The only sound came from their shallow breaths and the rhythmic clicking of heels on hardwood. As the latter sound grew closer, the crowd gradually parted, allowing the red head a clear path to the captive narcoleptic.

"Well, well," Eva Destruction said in her regular voice as she crouched down to look him in the eye. Reggie felt grateful: if the super-deep voice Poindexter ended up with emanated form a broad this fine, it would have unnerved him worse than the stereo-moaning. "What's your story?"

Her perfect, surgically constructed D-cups hovered at eye level, and despite his impending doom, Reggie sneaked a peek at her cleavage. It wasn't difficult, and he didn't regret it, either. Hell, if he had to choose between dying and dying while mildly aroused, he'd take the latter ninety-nine times out of a hundred (assuming none of the hypothetical deaths involved saw blades). "Um, what do you mean?" he asked, uncoiling his legs and lifting his chin a couple inches. Her deep green eyes proved far less inviting than her pleasantly fake tits.

"I mean, is your olfactory system shot, or do you have brain damage or what?" Eva Destruction said slowly. She was crouched with her elbows resting on her thighs in a distinctly unfeminine, but not wholly unattractive, pose. "I ask because I've had trouble with people possessing those conditions before."

"I- I'm a narcoleptic," Reggie said, glancing around, but failed to find any friendly faces that might confirm his condition. He thought about explaining that "narcolepsy" in no way involved sex with dead bodies, but hopefully a criminal mastermind knew that much. "But I smell fine..." he continued. "I mean, I can smell... well."

Eva Destruction sighed. Speaking of smelling fine, for a woman who generated super-acidic puke, her breath hinted pleasantly of watermelon. Somehow, Reggie found this tidbit as fascinating as any of the potentially lethal oddities of the moment. "Narcoleptic, huh? That could mean a couple things, but I'm going to play it safe and say that you're him." Her two fingers gravitated toward her ruby lips. It would have been a sensual gesture if her fingertips were going to stop at the lips, but Reggie knew they had a ticket for the end of the line. To him, those fingers might as well have been tugging back the hammer of a revolver.

"Him?!" Reggie protested. He was at least hoping for the chance to argue for his freedom, even if this setup was a thousand times worse than a kangaroo court. "Who him?"

Her fingers dropped a few inches, and her lips, along with everyone else's, shifted into a bemused smile. "Why the one you call Drek Manifold, of course."

"Manifold?" Reggie said, shifting his eyes toward the spot where Jack Jordan's three-limbed corpse still lay. Too many smirking classmates blocked the view, though. "He's out there. McVain killed him."

Eva Destruction retracted her fingers all the way into her fist and eyed him closely for several long seconds. "You really don't know, do you?" she finally said. Without waiting for an answer, she nodded toward center court and added, "That was just one of Manifold's receptacles. That poor sap was just a..." Her ears perked up, and all around him, the collective smirk expanded into a collective grin. Outside the gym, a distant humming resonated. "Good. It's working." She nodded, seemingly at nothing, and about three dozen members of the crowd wordlessly stood up, stomped down the aisle of the wooden bleachers, and marched out of the gym. They wore a broad assortment of pants, skirts, shoes, and socks, but their feet rose and fell in lockstep.

"What—What's going on?" Reggie asked, his head twisting wildly around in search of something that made sense. Above him, the 1985 Boys Basketball Sectional Championship banner rippled in the central air breeze.

Eva and the remaining dozen or so classmates pursed their lips, thinking. "Nothing," she said, finally. "Don't worry about it. Besides, aren't you rather curious why your life was ruined?"

*   *   *

In September of 2000, Manifold trapped Lord Osis in a hot air balloon and with the help of the reality-altering powers of the She-Mare, transferred him back to his interdimensional prison. Upon his return, he soon encountered a fellow native of the Vomeronazal Dimension residing in the vast void. This struck him as strange, because he had never encountered anything at any point during his sentence in the void. That's why they called it a "void," after all. "Identify yourself," Lord Osis said to the green-tinged methane cloud that drifted into his path.

"I am Del Mar, scourge of the Southern Realms," the cloud responded. "Who dares to ask?"

"My name is Lord Osis," he said, puffing up his cloud-chest. "It is I who first populated this otherworldly prison."

The strange cloud made a deep bow. "Lord Osis? I didn't even know that you still lived. One hundred years have passed on our world since your final sentence, and eighty years since Dr. Val Spectrum was dispatched to thwart you."

"Dr. Spectrum?" Lord Osis said with disbelief. "What does that officious little prick have to do with any of this?"

"'Tis written in the history books, m'lord," Del Mar explained. "He was the one who discovered the gap at the other end of this transdimensional prison eighty-one years ago, and it was he who predicted that in another year, you would enslave this other world and use it to conquer the Vomeronazal Dimension."

"Go on," Lord Osis said, feeling the tension building in his long, fluffy spine. It was Spectrum, after all, who foiled Lord Osis' attempt to steal the Xenon Tube and hold the royal family hostage, all those years ago, back when he had thumbs and a face and all the other bodily components. What anti-diabolical scheme could Spectrum have concocted next?

"Well, my Lord, he first considered transferring himself into the transdimensional prison, but it would take twenty years for him to trudge across its length, and you already had a five-year head-start. Instead, he thought to find a faster way to reach this other world. He made several preliminary attempts, using Nightmoots, but none survived the trip. Finally, he found a way to transfer himself into light waves and project himself through the dimensional void. Since the Other World has survived and failed to attack our dimension, it was assumed that Dr. Spectrum was successful in his attempt to defeat you."

"Indeed, he was," Lord Osis, said, grinding his cloud particles together so intensely that it would have felt horribly painful had those particles been solid.

"But you have seen the Other World, have you not, m'lord?" Del Mar asked, eagerly. "Is it as wonderfully solid as described in the books?"

"Yes, yes it's fantastic," Lord Osis said, absently considering all the lovely ways to hurt Dr. Spectrum when he returned to the Other World. "Tell me, Del Mar, what were you imprisoned for?"

"I stole official documents and pretended to a moneyed individual," he said, proudly. "I would steal from their bank accounts and keep the stealings."

"Well, you should be very proud of yourself," Lord Osis said, dryly. Deep down in the pit of his cloud, he knew that he was dealing with an amateur. Apparently, the Council of Elders was so hard up for space that they were willing to send *anyone* to the transdimensional prison.

"We should join forces, m'lord," Del Mar announced, buoyantly. "Together, we can journey to this world of solidity, conquer it, and triumphantly return to the *real* dimension."

"Let me tell you a secret," Lord Osis said, motioning Del Mar to float closer, as though they weren't the only two sentient beings in the entire quasi-reality. Quietly, he whispered, "I... don't... do... partners."

Del Mar's screams carried for miles until Lord Osis finished squeezing the life from him.

*   *   *

"You see?" Eva Destruction said, standing with one shapely hip jutting out slightly in front of her.

Reggie winced. "Not really," he admitted.

Eva Destruction continued, undaunted. "It is my belief that Dr. Spectrum came to this world as a beam of light and inhabited some humans, and due to your frail forms, it has to be—" High-caliber machine gun fire somewhere outside the building made Reggie jump and interrupted her for several seconds, but as soon as the shooting stopped, she instantly recovered and continued. "It has to be more than two. Your frailty is also to blame for his inability to endow you with multiple abilities."

"I—I don't know what to tell you," Reggie said, as evenly as he could muster. "You have the wrong man. I can't even get a driver's license."

The dozen people who he could see all shrugged, but once again, it was Eva Destruction who spoke. "Even so, if I can't control someone in the building, the least I can do is eliminate them."

Reggie gulped, then experienced a sensation that felt a lot like falling backward through a tunnel.

*   *   *

Chapter Twenty-Six:
11:00 p.m.

"Do you know what you're looking at?" Comrade Wilander, Premiere of the Evil Socialists' Collective, said from the edge of the spotlight.

A young, doe-eyed Dane McVain looked up at the jet black, steel dragonfly looming over him. "Yes," he said, his voice echoing through the airplane hanger. "It's a helicopter." He'd just returned from a training mission in Norway, the last step before gaining full agent status in the ESC, and speaking Swedish again felt like a homecoming unto itself.

Comrade Wilander chuckled to himself. "Is socialism just an economic system? Is Sweden just a nation?" Before Dane could answer, the Premiere answered for him. "A helicopter is a portal, a pathway to a higher plane. For as long as man has dreamed, he has dreamed to fly. From the Valkaries of a bygone era, to the dreams of young Leonardo, flying is what gives man a glimpse of something greater than himself. When you step into this helicopter and take it into the air, you are growing closer to the face of god."

Dane didn't believe in god. He wasn't allowed to, but he believed in the ascent of man, because that was what socialism preached. Could it be that this steel killing-machine could be the objectification of all that Socialism stands for? He turned toward the Comrade Wilander to ask, just as the Premiere held out a golden key ring from which a pair of silver keys dangled. "Her name is Uppsala," he said, "and she is more perfect than you or I can ever hope to be." As Dane reverently lifted the keys from his

upturned hand, Comrade Wilander added, "The, uh, round one's for the
door. The square one's for the ignition."

*   *   *

After ten seconds of bullets blasting through the ceiling tiles and
windows like the hailstorm from hell, ten thousand bits of shattered glass lay
on the floor of the multi-kitchen classroom, and the perforated ceiling
looked on the verge of collapsing. All but two of the fiberglass panels had
either exploded or fallen out of their slots, and a thick, hazy dust lingered in
the air. Before the first bullet had ricocheted across the floor, Dane McVain
alertly launched his bulky frame against the side of the refrigerator from
Cooking Station #1, opened the door, and all but climbed inside. Others had
taken refuge under tables or chairs, or in Donna's case, a bullet-proof,
Plexiglas shield she had conjured from some drops of Maxfactor.
Miraculously, none of the bullets so much as grazed anyone in the room, not
even the idiot with the memory problem who must have forgotten why he
was hiding, because now he stood in the middle of the room.

Miraculous, Dane thought, wistfully as the survivors muttered and
stirred in their hiding places. It sounded like the right word to explain how
that fool survived the swarm of bullets. Like all good Socialists, Dane was a
staunch Atheist, and even with all the fantastic meta-human powers he had
seen over the years, he never saw something that he considered a miracle,
until now... possibly. But, divine intervention or no, Uppsala would blast
that idiot apart when she made her next pass.

Dane scanned the room again, or as much of it as he could see in the
crack between the refrigerator door and its housing. The dust had started to
settle beneath the rush of outside air sneaking into the room, and he could
see the idiot more clearly. "Wait a minute," he muttered as he peered out
from his refrigerator fort. That was no normal idiot standing there, staring
through the gaping ceiling holes at Uppsala; that was Manifold.

Before Dane could even begin to pat himself down in search of his
neural destabilizer, Manifold crossed over to Dane's corner of the room and
hefted the entire refrigerator above his head as though it weighed no more
than a softball. He rattled it once, and Dane tumbled to the floor, screaming,
"Vhat da fuck awe you doink?" Only he could hear his own question,
though, because the bullets started flying again. Manifold's only response
was to silently pivot on his heels, reach back, and with one arm, hurl the

Frigidaire unit through the largest hole in the roof, toward the black blob of helicopter hovering outside. A loud crash followed, the sound of metal and plastic breaking, followed by the labored whooping of the helicopter blades as it trailed away from the school. Dane waited, expecting to hear a crash, but only the receding sound of his wounded helicopter reached his ears. With a mighty sigh, Dane let his head hang down. The crisis had passed.

He lay crouched on his hands and knees amid the dusty tiles, blinking back the tears from his eyes. *It must be the dust,* he thought, *causing my eyes to water.* Surely it wasn't the fact that he felt betrayed, not only by his trusty assistant, but by his beloved helicopter. Uppsala had a computer brain that could be overridden, like any computer, but Dane always liked to belief that there was more to their relationship than could be explained with talk of circuits and wiring, something that, when up against it, you couldn't disabled, not with a thousand viruses, and you couldn't hack, not with a thousand… hackers. Alas, the transcendence existed only in his head. Like a good Socialist, though, Dane tamped down his rage and channeled it into action, finally leaping to his feet and ripping the gun from his belt. Before he could lift it into a proper firing position, though, Manifold turned his way and crushed the prototype with the squeeze of the hand. "Didn't your mother tell you not to pray with guns?"

So, Dane thought, *more than a bit nervously, this version came with super strength,* as if grounding a helicopter with a refrigerator had not provided sufficient proof. Manifold took a slow, deliberate step forward, his dark eyes barely visible under his curtain of naturally curly hair. He could pulverize Dane into hamburger meat at this point, and Dane shrank against the now bare, cobweb-chocked wall space where the refrigerator recently stood. *This is how Poindexter must feel,* he thought, mirthlessly, *every day of his life.* Manifold always behaved in a sporting, non-homicidal manner in the past, but Dane really hit him where he lived this time around, literally. Who knew how many of these people were his friends, his lovers, his comrades? Of course, there was also that whole business about Dane frying Jack Jordan's brain. And this version of Manifold needed only to administer what the American's call a "pimp slap" upside Dane's head to put him in traction. As Manifold raised his fist, though, he froze, his ears pricking up under that mane of hair like a dog who just heard a can-opener running.

Manifold rushed to the door of the Home Economics room, punched his hand through it, grabbed the edge of the fist-sized hold, and ripped the door off its hinges. It was a dramatic, if not horribly efficient maneuver, to exit a room, but the instant that the door thudded to the tile floor, Manifold dashed down the side hallway on booted feet, toward the industrial technology rooms, and disappeared around the corner.

"God damn," Donna said through a wince as she struggled to her feet. "Didn't he ever hear of doorknobs?" Dozens of slivers of moonlight trickled in through the holes in the ceiling, illuminating the devastation. Two consecutive, rubble-free inches would have been hard to find. It looked as though someone had dumped a box of hand grenades into the room and slammed the door.

As Dane pulled himself out of his full-body cower and began to assess the situation, his newfound comrades in hiding emerged from their individual shelters. The neural destabilizer gun was useless, its barrel bent upward so that the weapon looked like a capital "Z." He took a head count. Donna, of course. The drug addict. The one with the swelled face and the memory problem. All accounted for. "It's da cripple," Dane muttered in disbelief. His face hardened and turned upward toward the Swiss cheese moonlight filtering into the room. "Da cripple injured my baby."

The room's other three occupants glanced around, trying to deduce what he was talking about, but Dane knew all that he needed to know. The cripple was Manifold. He was the only one missing. Perhaps the imbecile back in the gymnasium was Manifold as well (or used to be…), but the cripple was definitely Manifold right now, and he definitely threw a refrigerator at the mechanical wonder that made Dane a whole man. Dane slammed the broken remnants of the neural destabilizer into the floor tiles and ground his fist into the palm of his open hand. "I'm going to crush dat fucking cripple's spine."

The sound of a swinging steel door slamming into a stone wall interrupted Dane's mounting tirade, and the legion of marching feet coming toward him threatened to suspend it indefinitely. Dane and the other three crept to the doorway and peered down the hall in time to see dozens of unblinking humans rounding the corner, approaching their section of the hallway. *Of course*, Dane thought. *Staying here was probably a bad idea.* Even if throwing the refrigerator drove off Poindexter, it confirmed their location to all the people that Lord Osis had infected. Now, the mob of puppets rampaged toward the Home Ec room, looking to tear them apart.

The interlopers moved more like a wave of protestors than a zombie hoard; their movements were synchronized but not tranquilized. Genuine bloodlust lingered in their formerly docile, suburban eyes. When they spotted the four heads poking out from the doorless doorway, they might as well have been a team of marathoners hearing the report of a starter's pistol.

"Run!" Dane yelled and sprinted in the direction to where Manifold and his mullet had disappeared.

Two comrades followed. The one who remained had just enough time to call out, "Wait a minute? What's going on? Who are those people?" before the tidal wave of humanity swarmed him under.

*   *   *

Chapter Twenty-Seven:
11:03 p.m.

Reggie Sleeve blinked himself back into consciousness in the boiler room and immediately checked the watch on his left wrist. It was a reflexive thing, an oh-crap-how-bad-is-it reaction that he developed as a form of damage control. He did it first thing in the morning, too, even though he didn't wear a watch to bed. 11:03 p.m. No more than a couple minutes could have passed. New record. Normally, his spells lasted at least fifteen minutes.

The only light in the room came from his Indiglo watch light, but that fact alone meant that he was not in the gym anymore. The musty smell provided just as reliable an indicator of where he wasn't. He wasn't in a coffin. He wasn't at the police station. He wasn't in a department store or at a greenhouse. He'd awoken in totally unfamiliar places before, but it wasn't a terribly common occurrence. He kept pressing the button for his watch light as he swept his wrist in an arc to get a better idea of his surroundings. He didn't see much, just a bunch of pipes, but that sight alone dramatically narrowed down the possibilities.

Not only did he know that the endless, meaningless system of pipes and gages twisting about overhead belonged to *a* boiler room, he knew they belonged to the Kootervill High School boiler room. He'd only visited there once before, but that was one more visit than most people who attended the school. Early in his sophomore year, before his life fell completely apart, someone had ripped the pipe of one of the urinals in one of the boy's restrooms out of the wall, and Reggie reported this fact to his Spanish teacher, who naturally assumed that Reggie had broken it (and what's not to love about Gestapo tactics among high school authority figures?).

Long story short, the Spanish teacher sent Reggie to fetch Kenny the janitor from his "office" in this very boiler room. To a fifteen-year-old, this place looked like the ninth level of Hell, and Kenny didn't help: he resembled the sort of person who summered in the Ozarks as a slasher-movie villain who lived off the flesh of stranded motorists and used their bones to fashion Snowbaby replicas to sell on the roadside. Searching among the labyrinth of pipes was a ten-minute ordeal that remained burned into Reggie's memory cells to this day. On the plus side, the memory was clear enough that he still remembered the location of the exit.

It felt like a gallon of blood rushed out of his head when he stood up, but Reggie regained his balance after a couple seconds. With only his little blue light to guide him, he managed to stagger to the metal door without falling over anything and flip the door latch. Directly overhead, a few dozen sets of feet stomped around on the gym floor. Maybe Kenny heard the same sound every time a class ended. It might have been enough to disrupt his hourly masturbation sessions (or increase their ferocity...).

Reggie slowly opened the door, and the cool shock of the hallway air blasted over his face and cold, wet, stubbly scalp. The head-rush wasn't the only side effect of his condition. Whenever he had a sleep attack, his pores would start leaking ice cold sweat. This wasn't altogether unpleasant, but this late in the year, it usually caused a severe case of the chills, especially when stepping out of a boiler room.

During the day, the stairwell up to the land of the high school Eloi was at best, shadowy, as if the school administrators had decided to save the tax payers some money by eliminating a couple light fixtures in that section of the building. Now, with the rest of the school having supposedly closed for the weekend, it looked like a stairway into oblivion. Reggie gripped the handrail, ready to dash up the stairs when he steadied himself... but to where? The gym probably stood empty by now; all those stomping feet were surely headed somewhere. That meant that the Village of the Damned meandered around up there, somewhere, and even if he managed to get past them, the mutated giant ducks undoubtedly were performing search and destroy missions on anything that wasn't either Swedish or a giant rodent.

The last thought re-conjured the image of Sally's half-chewed remains, but he shook it away.

A faintness swept over Reggie, and he bent down far enough to rest his forehead in the crook of his right elbow and against the brick wall. Any strategy that involved walking up those steps struck him as borderline suicidal; he probably should turn around and slither back in the boiler room and barricade himself inside. If he did that, he stood at least a fifty-fifty chance of surviving the night. Was that *really* the best move, though, if not for his life then at least for his sanity? He'd been waiting three long hours to get away from the traveling freak show holding him prisoner, and now that he was free, he refused to sit in his closet and keep playing the good hostage. He could go find a phone. *That* shouldn't be too difficult for him. Granted, with Lord Osis entering the game, the only person he could trust was himself, but the Tri-Cities had a police task force supposedly equipped for this sort of thing. They soaked up more tax dollars than the public school system and Planned Parenthood combined, so it was high time Reggie cashed in on his contribution.

With a plan in hand, Reggie actual made several strides up the stairs before a bigger question hit him. *Didn't Lord Osis say he was going to kill you?* he thought, searching his sluggish memory. *Didn't he say that you might be Drek Manifold? Yeaaaah, that did happen.* Osis promised to kill Reggie, then Reggie woke up in the basement. Unless they dragged him down to the boiler room (which they couldn't have done in the two to three minutes that passed)... *and* left him alive, unbound, and unguarded in a door that required a key to lock from the outside... he *must* have passed through the floor. Yup, there's a bastardized version of Occam's Razor for you: the easiest explanation was that he magically passed through the floor.

He pinched the bridge of his cold nose. "Idiot," he muttered. Self-derogation served as his default response when things went wrong, but this time around, it didn't have much force behind it. In truth, all the pieces of the puzzle seemed to fit so nicely, like when the River Street bridge collapsed when he was standing three blocks away, he passed out, then read in the paper the next day how Manifold had saved a busload of third graders who were traveling over the River Street bridge. Incidents like that filled the nooks and crannies of his life, where he had been geographically close to an act of heroism by Manifold but became incapacitated and never saw it. It almost felt like having a roommate you somehow never met.

"I'm Drek Manifold," he whispered, and even though a sense of unreality accompanied the words, saying them untied a knot in Reggie's guts that had been tightening like a tourniquet for years. Every failure, every time his brain let him down over the years, now fit into a big picture. Better still, the bigger picture showed him to be more than just another well-meaning fuck-up. Quite the opposite; his torment had purpose because he was an honest to gosh hero.

Reggie let go of the banister and pressed his hands into his knees. *Try to focus*, he urged himself. *Try to look for some heavily used switch in your brain to jumpstart your inner Drek.* He tried visualization. He tried meditation. He even tried hyperventilation, but a couple minutes passed and he still stood alone in a darkened stairway. Maybe Manifold didn't show up whenever you blew a whistle. Hell, it wasn't beyond the realm of possibility that Lord Osis was either wrong on this one or just plain fucking with him. In any case, he didn't need to transform into a super-hero to find a fucking telephone.

*   *   *

Chapter Twenty-Eight:
11:05 p.m.

Kelly Edwards felt bad running away from the rabid mob. Mostly, he didn't want to leave Ely's permanently confused ass for the Legion of Super-Puppets to dismember. It pained him enough to watch that monster mouse mash up his face, but this time, he couldn't save ol' Ely if he had ten fire extinguishers. In part, though, Kelly just felt *bad* running: his joints might as well have been made out of hamburger meat and paper mache, and he moved with all the grace of a drunk sprinting through someone's back yard at night trying to escape the cops (not that he had any experience with that...). At least Ely might have a way to defend himself, even if he didn't know how to access that ability. *Better him than me*, Kelly thought, mirthlessly. *I always did bad in crowds.*

McVain labored forward about ten feet ahead of Kelly and made a sharp turn to his right to cut down the back hallway. Nothing but cold air and trees waited on the other side of that concrete wall. Of course, lurking somewhere amid those trees and that cold air was a bunch of mutant ducks. Kelly couldn't think about that, though, because he had to stay focused and keep pumping his arms and breathe: sadly, it took all he had in him to keep up with the bulky Socialist. Hell, he could barely keep pace with a chick stuffed into a leather bodysuit and high heels, so if a living advertisement to quit smoking ever existed, he was it.

The instant Kelly made the sharp right turn, he almost crashed into McVain's wall-like back. Over a dozen members of the Class of '96 stood in front of them, blocking the other end of the hallway. They must have split off from the main group the instant Dane fled the Home Ec room. It struck him as a diabolically brilliant tactic, but Kelly supposed that it was easy to do when a few dozen people all had extensive experience with the layout of the high school, and when all of them shared the same brain.

Chest heaving, McVain silently contemplated his options. For Kelly's money, there couldn't be that many: they could charge forward, try to negotiate or... "Donna," Dane said, reaching behind him but not looking at her, "make me an AK-47." Or conjure a machine gun out of makeup particles.

Donna didn't even bother nodding. With a flick of her wrist, the makeup compact had left its holster, and with a flick of her thumb, the compact flipped open. They were playing with less time than any of them thought, though. Mark Templeton stood at the front of this auxiliary group of zombies, and for good reason: he had a freakishly large jaw, and when his mouth dropped open, out slid the white mist. There was no way to fight mist. You couldn't shoot it or stab it or do anything much but run from it, but an even larger horde marching up behind them pinched off their escape route. It was at that precise moment that Kelly glanced to his left and saw the door to the auto shop sitting slightly ajar.

"In here," he shouted and all but dove through the door. One step inside, though, and for the second time in nearly an hour, Kelly tripped over Navin's ragdoll body. In this instance, instead of falling through some Dutch doors, he careened forward and slammed his boney chest into the side of the instructor's aluminum desk. The sensation it provided was what he always imagined getting shanked felt like. An exquisite pain rocketed through his ribs at the point of impact, and he felt all the oxygen leave his body. Kelly crumpled to the ground in his best Navin impersonation. Fortunately for all of them, McVain alertly squeezed into the room and forced the door closed behind him. Considering it was a high school auto shop and not a hermetically sealed vacuum, though, that managed to stave off their problems for about five whole seconds.

"Oh shit," McVain droned through a grimace as he pressed his considerable bulk against the broken door. Apparently, whoever came through before them (i.e., Navin) must have busted the door latch, and now the Swede was trying to counter the weight of a couple dozen people. Squirming on the floor like a wounded deer, Kelly wondered if McVain competed in an event like this in the World's Strongest Man Competition;

right after the Atlas Stones and the one where they pulled the eighteen-wheeler, they could have you see how many people you could keep from coming through a door. Kelly focused through the raw, searing pain in his chest long enough to scramble to his feet and take a step toward the door. McVain's voice halted him, though. "Vind a Van," the Swede insisted.

At first, Kelly thought the arch-villain wanted him to find a van suitable for an escape, which made sense, what with their being in the auto shop and all, but then he saw McVain wincing in the direction of the four-foot-high, industrial fan pointing at the auto bay. The motor-heads probably used it to dissipate toxic fumes and the smell of their chewing tobacco, but in this case, the principle was the same. Kelly crossed the room, becoming more functional with every step, and grabbed one of the legs. It wasn't heavy, just bulky, and he marched it over to a spot five feet from the door, just as the white mist started to seep into the room from under the closed door. Kelly threw the red handle all the way to the right, and with a steadily building hum, the fan roared to life.

The victory, however, was short-lived. The rush of air shoved the white mist back under the door and out of the room, much the same way members of the Class of '96 leaked their way past the metal door, one set of hands at a time. McVain stared over at Donna Correction, wide-eyed. "You got it?" he said, his voice so muffled by the rush of air and rattling hum of the fan that Kelly had to read the Swede's thin, pale lips to decipher the exchange.

Donna gave a tight-lipped nod, and when Dane gave the door a final shove and used the momentum of the crowd to launch himself backward into the room, everything seemed to happen in slow motion. The instant that Kelly deduced what was happening, he knew that the sight would haunt him for years to come. The most unnerving aspect of it, though, was the utter necessity of it. It almost paralleled his view on the abortion debate: innocents were dying, but what exactly was the alternative? That's why he didn't lift a finger to stop it: he didn't know what option constituted the lesser of two evils, only that he surely would pick the wrong one.

The rush of humanity flung the door against the wall so hard that, if it had been made of wood, it would have shattered. They lurched forward and spun Navin's limp body out of the way as if he were a napping housecat. No fewer than a dozen people spilled into the room in the first couple seconds.

As Dane still slid toward the auto bay, Donna flipped the new AK-47 with a collapsible metal stock into the air, and Dane caught it with one hand, wedged it into place in the crook of his right arm, pivoted on his heels, and opened fire. Kelly never saw a more graceful move from a man that size, and it all took less than a second to execute.

Once, when Kelly drove to Chicago to buy five hundred tablets of Oxytocin, he saw a friend, Tucker Greene, get shot in the chest. The teenage drug dealer who shot him, the one with the White Sox baseball cap with the price tag still attached to it, just pulled out an automatic, squeezed the trigger, and instead of a thunderclap, the report of the gun sounded like a firecracker. It took Tucker about five seconds to even realize that a bullet had just violated his chest cavity. Both he and Kelly winced and held up their palms, defensively, then looked around to see if by some miracle, the bullet had zigzagged past them. They were almost surprised to see the blood seeping through Tucker's shirt.

The entire event remained a remarkable memory only in that it provided far less drama than Kelly had anticipated. So much more so for this burst of machinegun fire. The exploding bullets sounded like a lawn mower going over a twig as they flared from the barrel and chewed the human targets up, little by little, until the people folded up like wet paper dolls. A couple people almost reached Dane before they fell forward into the rapidly expanding pool of collective blood, but even if they had reached him, they wouldn't have had the strength to do anything but lay their slippery hands on him for a few seconds.

Just as Dane finished draining the clip, the flood of glassy-eyed humanity began to recede back through the doorway. "Get da door," Dane instructed anyone listening. Kelly shook off the shock and sprang forward, shoving the metal door closed. A metal table stacked with textbooks sat about a foot to the right of the door, and Kelly reached down, grabbed one of the legs, and threw all the weight of his malnourished body in the opposite direction. It was a pathetic attempt, moving the desk less than a foot to the left, but the feat did manage to cover the doorway by a few inches.

Dane popped a freshly conjured banana clip into the AK-47. "That vas close," Dane reported, his thick eyebrows arching over his steely gray eyes. Then, he noticed Navin's inert form lying spread eagle near the doorstop, and leveled the barrel of the gun at it.

"What the fuck are you doing?" Kelly said, but for a second time, didn't step forward. This time, he knew McVain's actions were utterly wrong, but it didn't matter. Maybe it was due to fatigue, an unwillingness to rock the boat, self-preservation, or the belief that a higher power looked out for Navin, but the bottom line was that Kelly wouldn't be providing anything more than a verbal protest.

"Clearing a path for a classless utopia," McVain said, slamming a bullet into the chamber. "Dis is vhat I came to do, so don't get in my vay."

Kelly didn't. He didn't have to. The six-foot mouse creeping up on Dane's flank dropped him with a single roundhouse punch to the temple. Kelly spent a long moment trying to fool himself into thinking that the rodent had attacked out of humanitarian, all-creatures-great-and-small considerations, but even in those beady red eyes, the glassy stare of the possessed was unmistakable, and the charming little illusion shattered like a cheap commemorative plate.

*   *   *

Chapter Twenty-Nine:
11:08 p.m.

It always amazed Lord Osis that his essence could fit like a key into the mental lock of these humans. He would sneak into the lungs, and then, faster than a lightning bolt, he would take charge of everything from their memories to their bodily functions. With as many as a dozen humans, he didn't break a metaphorical sweat processing all the sensory and muscular responses rolling in from their primitive cerebral corti. Even when the numbers reached into the low hundreds, the confusion he experienced only amounted to a millisecond delay. It was almost like some benevolent higher power *made* him to rule over these pathetic creatures.

In the hallway, they swarmed over the human lying on the glistening, white tile. The left fist of the human female known as Tammy Lynne Harding solidly connected with the human's abdomen, and the foot of Garth Wilson drove the point of his steel-toed boot into the human's groin region. The human's face already looked like a mass of unsculpted clay, but it was necessary to go one step further and beat this one to death. Just like the dark-skinned male in the gymnasium, this creature could not receive Lord Osis' gift, so they must destroy him and do it as fast as possible, since there was a substantial chance that he served as a vessel for Dr. Spectrum and his meddling incarnation, Drek Manifold.

Many of his dozen attackers were women, one even carried a child in her womb, but they acted in concert to reduce Ely Lisch into an even bloodier mass than the one in which the Knockout Mouse had left him. Lord Osis' other group of minions experienced even more of what human's call "luck." Dane McVain, Donna Correction, and the sickly stray human had barricaded themselves into the very room where the Knockout Mouse sat lurking. The wondrous rodent had just discovered the body of one of Dr. Spectrum's vessels but hadn't the time to drop a cement block on its skull before the wildly annoying trio burst in. Lord Osis opted to keep that furry, white wild card hidden for the time being, until the derelicts became fully occupied with the frontal assault they now faced.

Debra Telfair grabbed the back of human Ely Lisch's long, curly hair... wait a moment. The human's hair should have been short and straight, barely enough to grab. And it should have been matted with old, coagulated blood, not bouncy and manageable. The jean jacket and flannel shirt completed the equation: Drek Manifold had returned, and that realization was quickly followed by the one that the series of punches and kicks had started inflicting more damage on Lord Osis' minions than their intended target. *So*, Lord Osis thought, *Manifold has made himself invulnerable. My minions can still slow him down and keep him from saving the others.*

Lord Osis jumped on Manifold's back with one of the heaviest of the portly males, wrapping his hands around the smaller man's neck. When a second alcoholic jumped on, Manifold's legs started to buckle, but just because he was impervious to abuse did not mean that that the Denim Defender planned to stand by and let his enemies pile on top of him. An elbow slammed into the heavier male's ample midsection. It sank in a few inches, and the minion slid off Manifold's back and crumpled to the floor like a discarded Dixie Cup.

Others rushed in, grasping for arms and legs and softer parts, but they were commoners, peasants, and did not possess the vice-like grip that Lord Osis had hoped for. *Four dozen humans*, Lord Osis thought, ruefully, *and not one professional wrestler.* With a duck and a slide, Manifold seemed to ooze from their collective grasp and responded with a series of well-placed elbows to noses. Pain did not bother Lord Osis' minions. He could keep them moving forward until they didn't have any limbs to crawl with, but a well-placed shot to the bridge of the nose, like the one Manifold inflicted upon Mary Riley, scrambled her brain enough to render her useless for several seconds. Manifold picked up on this relative weakness years ago, and he seemed to have an unlimited number of pinpoint shots in him.

Further down the hall, an AK-47 opened fire on a dozen of his stolen bodies, and the shock of shifting his conscious caused the entire legion a second or two of pause. Lord Osis had come to expect a set of rigid, tame behaviors from humans during his half-dozen visits to this plane, largely because he always faced Manifold and the local police. Neither foe wished to kill the members of Lord Osis' army of hostages. Lord Osis was familiar with that mentality; the world that he and Dr. Spectrum hailed from also had a delightfully quaint reluctance toward killing innocents. This McVain character, though, was nothing of a kind. When Lord Osis heard him ask the girl to conjure the gun, Lord Osis fully expected the Swede to hold it in a threatening manner, or at most, fire it into the air for effect. The Tri-City law enforcers frequently utilized that tactic. There wasn't even a half-second pause, though, before McVain started blasting bullets through faces and torsos. Through it all, his grim, square face failed to betray a tremor of emotion.

A quick perusal of Dr. Poindexter's mind informed Lord Osis that McVain's behavior stemmed less from bloodlust than from an obsessively goal-oriented disposition, like all Socialists. In Poindexter's opinion, McVain would have shot his own mother had she been running through the doorway to the Automotive Shop and not even kicked dirt on her body if it meant delaying his escape. *A worthy adversary*, Lord Osis decided. *I shall have to mobilize the Mouse.*

The switch in focus to the Knockout Mouse provided an interesting shift in sensory reality. The world seemed to drain of color and became much flatter, but in that space, almost like an additional dimension pushing out from this one, smells blossomed from every corner of the room. Smells that he had never smelled before, like motor oil and chewing tobacco, tickled his nostrils, almost compensating for his locomotor deficiencies. Still, it was a simpler vessel. He could probably control a million Knockout Mice, if that number existed.

While the Knockout Mouse crept from his hiding place, Manifold threw another elbow. This one broke several of Karen Miller's teeth and freed the Mulleted Meddler for a dash down the hallway.

No matter, Lord Osis thought as he lifted what remained of his broken, bleeding puppets off the tile floor. *Eva Destruction is marching toward the Automotive Shop, and she has a bellyful of unholy gastric juices with his name on it. Even if he somehow evades her, he'll come back. No matter the odds, he always comes back for the innocents.* Meanwhile, Lord Osis had already captured one of Dr. Spectrum's vessels, and with one right hook from the Mouse's forepaw, that killer human came under control.

As Dane McVain hit the floor, all remaining minions converged on the automotive shop.

*   *   *

Chapter Thirty:
11:10 p.m.

Ironically, the Office Skills Department at Kooterville High School didn't reside in an actual office; it consisted of only a kiosk. The department came into being a few years after the school was built, and the administration set up a wooden, ovular structure in the widest part of the hallway that separated the Math Department from the Social Studies Department. The result was a cramped little room that reminded those who frequented it of a submarine, but none of these things mattered to Reggie Sleeve as he cautiously approached its locked door. What did matter was that the kiosk had a working cordless phone inside, and that its walls didn't reach all the way to the ceiling.

He had waited patiently in the darkened stairwell for the sound of Eva Destruction marching the Class of '96 down to the industrial wing like some sort of sexy, possessed Pied Piper, and when the footsteps receded into silence, Reggie made his move. He skulked his way forward a few hundred feet to his current position and didn't encounter a thing except a few dozen sinister shadows. A delinquent, hard plastic chair sat further down the hallway, and he pulled it against the wooden outer wall of the Office Skills structure and climbed atop it. Almost a foot of open space separated the ceiling from the top of the kiosk, but if he sucked in his gut and pushed his back against the ceiling panels, Reggie thought he could fit. Still... he looked up at the gap and licked his lower lip, thinking, *Why did I do so much bench press this morning?* Standing atop the wobbly chair, Reggie raised his hands to eye level. When he squatted down and leapt, though, he barely cleared an inch. Something had grabbed his belt and held him down.

Before Reggie could flail or scream, he realized that that something was
Drek Manifold.

"Not so fast, Chief," Manifold said, sounding more like Mr. Myagi
from the *Karate Kid* movies than Richard Marx. That was an attribute that
never made the news broadcasts for some reason. "You call the porice, and
Lord Osis will take them over, too."

"I thought the police were prepared for stuff like this." The words
came out automatically, and he almost pronounced it "po-reese" as well.
The circumstances stunned Reggie to the point of stupidity. After all, he
stood face-to-face with the man who might have dominated his world, one
way or the other, for over ten years. His pulse throbbed in his neck, and he
worried that he might be so worked up that he would pass out. If his
hypothesis was correct, though, than this was the one time when he could
guarantee staying awake.

Manifold shook his head. "McVain. Yes. The girls. Yes. But not
Osis. I'm the only one who can stop —"

With a vicious quack, one of the Wolfian Ducks flew from the
recesses of the darkened hallway and swooped down on Manifold. Drek
instinctively threw up an arm to protect his head. The Duck's bill chomped
down on Manifold's elbow, but the man's face showed less reaction than if a
mosquito had jammed its proboscis into the back of his neck. Even the duck
looked surprised, glancing up at Manifold with its yellow wolf eyes as he
grabbed the creature by the throat and spun its head around like a twist-off
bottle cap until a dull snap echoed in the hallway. As the creature's inert
body dropped to the floor in a downy lump, Reggie couldn't help but
wonder what one of those things tasted like cooked.

Reggie's eyes drifted from the corpse on the floor to the crotch of his
pants. *Good,* he thought. *Still dry.* He might have lost a few drops when
that quack from hell blasted in his ear, but any leakage wasn't noticeable,
and he still remained conscious. Almost as an afterthought, his lungs started
to draw in air... until he saw the white, smoky tendrils leaking out of the
holes in the Duck's bill.

"Don't worry," Manifold assured him. "It onry has reach of ten feet
and will dissipate in a few minutes. It can't hurt you."

Reggie nodded for a moment, relieved, then the implication sank in.
"So, I am part of you... or, at least—"

"Yes," Manifold said. "You are one of my vessels." Once again, Reggie's disorientation prevented him from thinking big thoughts. No one had ever referred to him as a "vessel" before, but somehow, he focused more on the amusing mismatch between Manifold's body and voice. As a kid, he used to watch a show called *Black Belt Theater*, which featured old Japanese (maybe...) Kung Fu movies with bad English voiceovers. Manifold was almost like a reversal of one of those characters.

"So, are you really that guy?" Reggie asked, leaning his back against the splintery outer wall of the Office Skills kiosk. His body still trembled from all the excess adrenaline. He wasn't used to getting this excited and still staying upright. "The one Lord Osis was talking about?"

Even though Manifold wasn't around for that particular conversation, he nodded. "Yes. I am Val Spectrum."

Reggie eased down onto the hard plastic chair next to the kiosk wall. The white mist poked around at him like a neglected puppy searching for a head-scratch, but it never found the seam it was looking for. "Why do you look like Richard Marx?" Reggie said, looking up at Manifold. Despite everything else, he supposed that was *the* question that bothered him the most over the years. He would have thought it was "why did you ruin my life," but it was the goddamn Richard Marx thing.

"It was the image in your minds when I stepped inside," Manifold explained. "I thought it would comfort you."

Reggie couldn't argue against that sort of logic. Manifold was totally and utterly wrong, of course; it struck everyone as goofy, but at least the idea was sound. It could have been worse: Jack liked to crank up the volume and sing along with the B-52s whenever "Love Shack" came on. The heartland would have never cottoned to a superhero who looked like Fred Schneider. There still remained so many other questions, though, such as "Why did you—"

"We have no time," Manifold told him, matter-of-factly, as he made a cutting motion with the flat of his hand. "I need to kill the rest of the Wolfian Ducks. I need you to go find a pair of beakers. Try looking—"

"Beakers?" Reggie asked. "Like in chemistry class."

"Exactry," Manifold replied. "If we had time, I'd exprain everything, but I just need you to find a beaker or two, with stoppers, then find the others… your crassmates; it shouldn't be too hard. When you get there, don't do anything. Just wait for me."

Reggie nodded, wearily. As always, the sleep attacks wore him down more than they recharged him, and at the moment, he felt like he'd been awake for about a week. "Well, it's been a hell of a reunion so far. Why stop now?" As Manifold turned to go, Reggie added, "One thing: Is Sally still alive?"

Manifold frowned as he ran his fingers through the curly mass of dark, lustrous hair. Reggie mimicked the motion over his shaven scalp, trying to comprehend how that was his hair… sort of. "I don't know," Manifold admitted. "I don't have telepathy at the moment."

Reggie nodded, reluctantly. "I don't have telepathy at the moment" was a good line he would save for the future, used in similar contexts as "it's not my day to watch him" or "I'm not a leash, so I don't know." Manifold meant it seriously, though, so there was still hope. Reggie took a final glance at the cordless phone on the other side of the dirty glass, and that triggered another question. "When you say 'beakers'…" he began to ask Manifold, but just like that, he was gone.

                    *   *   *

Chapter Thirty-One:
11:15 p.m.

When Donna Correction blinked her way through the fog and regained consciousness, it felt like she had been watching a movie and got up to use the bathroom but hit the "fast forward" button instead of the "pause" button. She had no idea what was going on. Well, check that: she knew her hands were bound in chains and the chains were looped over the end of a hydraulic lift in a high school auto shop, but in the big picture, those details weren't horribly useful. Within a few seconds, she also knew that her shoulders hurt like hell, and when she looked down, she saw her feet dangling several inches off the floor. Interesting facts, sure, but knowledge isn't always power. Sometimes, it's just annoying.

Like most auto lifts, the one she dangled from was shaped like an "H." Dane and the thin, sweaty guy dangled in similar positions to her left and behind her, respectively. They both looked awake, if not particularly spry. Her captors had even managed to chain up the bald, unconscious guy and hook him up on the lift's remaining leg. He didn't look like he'd been awake in years, so the shackles struck her as overkill. She had no idea why they did this, nor did she know why she still lived or controlled her own thoughts. Fortunately, since Dr. Poindexter stood several feet in front of the lift, there was a good chance that that information would come posthaste.

"You're probably wondering why you're still alive," Lord Osis said through Dr. Poindexter's over-sized lips. He probably chose to communicate using that particular body because there's comfort in familiarity, even for gaseous parasites. She had no idea when the occupation started, but Lord Osis must've been camped out in Poindexter's craw like it was an Extended Stay America. Eva and the Knockout Mouse stood motionless as statues behind Poindexter, sticking out like boils amid the legion of dumpy, bloody twenty-eight-year-olds. "In my society, it's considered good form to place things into context before you send someone away."

From behind her, Mr. Sweaty spoke. "You mean before you execute us?" he said through chattering teeth. Except for the sport coat, everything about him screamed "borderline hippy," and she hoped that he wasn't going to launch into a lengthy anti-death penalty speech. Despite being a career super-villain, she actually thought the death penalty got a bad rap. At the very least, state-sponsored execution thins the proverbial herd and provides employment for a few high school dropouts; those legs don't strap themselves down. Thankfully, Sweaty either didn't have the statistics or the drive to keep going.

"Well, no, I don't," Lord Osis replied, "for two reasons. First of all, my society doesn't believe in executions. I happen to, but I'm only executing two of you." Donna looked up, expectantly, but he pointed alternately at Mr. Sweaty and at Mr. Comatose. For some reason, she felt relieved. "You both can thank Dr. Spectrum for that," he said to the two doomed men, "you would have lived if I could inhabit you."

Mr. Sweaty did his best to scoff, but that's hard to do when you're experiencing a full-body tremor. It came out more like a sneeze. "Hmm, yeah, sorry I missed out on that."

"Well, now you'll never know, will you?" Lord Osis said, arching Dr. Poindexter's thick, black single eyebrow above the thick, black glasses frame. "You have a few minutes before Dr. Spectrum takes you over instead, and he will, because I'll start executing one of the innocents every sixty seconds until he does. Right now, he's outside killing the Wolfian Ducks, even though all the ducks I possess are inside the building." He shook his head, as thought folly of the act was self-evident. "He'll be here shortly, though, and when he arrives, I shall kill him." He held up a neural destabilizer, much like the one Dane used to have. Poindexter must have stashed a second prototype in Uppsala at some point.

"How do you know that will work on Manifold?" Donna asked. "It didn't when we fried the guy upstairs."

"Dr. Poindexter designed this weapon to demolish the neural connections, and that is where Dr. Specturm lurks, not in the physical body. Up in the gymnasium, though, he had already fled that body, right after your bulimic friend burned him with her wondrous bile," he said, gesturing toward Eva with the gun. The weapon probably weighed a couple pounds, and Poindexter's pasty, frail arm still had problems holding it level. Comfort factor be damned, it was that had to be the worst possible body for doing anything physical. She wondered what the *opposite* of working out was, and if Poindexter did it. "He's invulnerable at the moment, and I don't think that he can immediately transfer the same ability into another body. As soon as he takes control of one of the vessels that I hold, I will dispatch him with a squeeze of the trigger… and this dimension will finally be mine."

"Vhat do you vhant vith us?" Dane demanded. "I hate Manifold wit all my heart." Hearing Dane's deep monotone brought Donna some minor relief; a shot like the one the Knockout Mouse unloaded on him was liable to cause a concussion. The long-term consequences to Dane's health didn't worry her, she planned to break some bones if he didn't pay her the money he owed, but at the moment, he was about the only useful ally she had left.

"Competing plans for world domination don't work well together," Dr. Poindexter replied, smirking. Even if he wasn't technically in charge of his body anymore, Donna wondered if somewhere deep inside, Dr. Poindexter wasn't enjoying Dane's humiliation just the slightest bit. Watching your former boss chained to a hydraulic lift might not make up for getting pounded in the skull five hundred times, but it had to come close. "Besides, I think your… resources might come in handy."

The veiled mention of Uppsala caused Dane to writhe about and rattle his chains like Jacob Marley. All his rage succeeded in doing was spin him about like a wind chime. "I von't allow you," Dane declared, sounding awfully defiant for a guy who was bound and bleeding. "I vill hold my breath until I die. Da only vun who controls my taughts is the Evil Socialist's Collective."

Lord Osis sighed. "Though it isn't my preference, I don't have to enter through your lungs," he explained. All the human puppets present closed their eyes and trembled under the same, simultaneous shiver. When all the pairs of eyes opened, a smirk slid across Dr. Poindexter's lips.

"Manifold has just killed the last of the ducks," Osis announced. "Dr.
Poindexter would be heartbroken, were he with us."

Dane kept his features hard, trying to look menacing, but he couldn't
have been that pissed off. At this point, acting angry amounted to a matter
of personal pride and had nothing to do with losing his invaluable assistant.
At worst, Dane despised Poindexter for constantly soaking up the Helicopter
Repair Fund in favor of his typically unwieldy genetics projects. At best,
their relationship was like that of a businessman and his favorite secretary
that he wasn't sleeping with.

Donna ran her tongue over her cracked lips. Her shoulders ached like
crazy, but it was actually a relief to be off her feet; she must've run a mile in
those stupid boots. *How will possession feel?* she wondered. It seemed like
an important question since it might be the last thing she experienced, almost
like wishing for a painless death. Would it be like being raped when he
entered her? Once Osis was in control, would it be like a coma for her, or
could she tell what he was doing with her body? Would she still see and feel
everything, but stay captive, like a prisoner in a sound-proof booth? *You'll
find out soon enough*, she reminded herself, *but not before Dane does.*

Lord Osis moved Poindexter's body forward and made him grip Dane
by the shoulders, like a friend giving a final, heartfelt goodbye. "Well,"
Lord Osis said in his rich baritone, "time we got started." His lips parted
and revealed two rows of crooked yellow teeth. The rows parted, and from
between them, a tendril of white smoke crept out at a ghostly pace.

Donna watched with morbid fascination as the tendril poked around,
trying to squeeze between Dane's lips, then ducking into his flared nostrils.
A few seconds passed as the tendril pushed deeper and deeper, then a jolt
shook Dane like a rifle shot. After he stopped wiggling, he drew in a long
strand of smoke with a deep, rich, flowing breath. Almost as though he was
snorting up a snootful of opium, his whole body sighed in relief.

Maybe it was her nerves acting up from her standing on the edge of a
fate worse than death, or from running around in a leather outfit for several
hours, but Donna could feel a bead of sweat running down her thigh, seeping
between her skin and the leather. While wearing the T-shirt and shorts she
used for workout clothes, she didn't mind sweating, but when she was
encased in leather, it felt like ants were crawling over you, marching down

your... No. Wait. This bead of sweat was on the outside of her outfit. And it ran *up* her thigh.

It had to be an insect, or an air draft, or something simple and explainable. A desperate mind can play tricks on itself, and the layer of leather made it hard to feel anything specific. Still... she could have sworn that the sensation was climbing differently than an insect would. Insects scurry. This felt jerkier, more deliberate, like a telephone repairman or a tree-topper scaling a pole, searching for purchase each step of the way.

When the sensation had traversed the curve of her hip, she pretended to toss a few matted strands of hair out of her face and hazarded a glance in that direction. It was Manifold (of course it was Manifold), about an inch tall with a miniature denim outfit, digging his tiny hands into the seams of her outfit as he climbed up her left oblique. She didn't know he could shrink, but an ability like that can't come in handy too often. He seemed to travel in the direction of her head. If he had a message for her, he'd better hurry it up, because Dane's eyes had rolled back to their whites and his entire body swayed under the gentle force of the central heating ducts. Over by the door, the Knockout Mouse's pink nose absently twitched, perhaps detecting the familiar scent of mullet.

Without announcing anything to anyone, Eva stepped toward Dane and spit a long, thin stream of saliva on the strand of chains wrapped around his wrists. They immediately began to dissolve, as though made from toilet paper, and within seconds, rattled to the floor. Dane made the short drop to the concrete shop floor and strode away from the lift wearing the same smug expression as all the rest of the puppets. He turned toward Donna, eyeing her like a man who still had a sex drive. By the time Dane's eyes made the trip up to her face, Manifold had managed to dive under the layer of Donna's supple, wavy hair dangling over her shoulder. "Your turn," Lord Osis said with Dane's mouth.

Donna gulped. *Stall. Stall you idiot. Say something. Anything.* "One question," she blurted. That was enough to delay Dane's advance, but then she had to wrack her brain for a question. "Do you get access to everyone's thoughts and memories when you take them over?"

The question must have been horribly transparent, like asking the brand of gun the firing squad was using, because several dozen pairs of eyes immediately shifted to the windows of the garage doors at the back of the room, probably searching for signs of Manifold. It would have been great to have fooled Lord Osis into giving a long, technical explanation, but inducing paranoia turned out to work just as well. He trained the focus on his minions toward the shop's potential entrances, because he had no clue that Manifold had entered the room minutes ago and currently tugged on Donna's earlobe. "That's interesting," Lord Osis said, using the same voice, but this time, it emanated from Dane's almost lipless mouth. "You're obviously stalling, but are you stalling for a reason. I'll find out soon enough though, because whether you actually care or not, memories are accessible via…"

Donna listened intently, but not to Lord Osis' explanation. She was focused on the flea-sized man in the tiny jean jacket lurking in her hair.

"I need you to create a syringe containing high-purity heroine and A-positive brood," Manifold said in a Jiminy Cricket voice. "I need you to create it already stuck in one of Kelly Edward's arm veins. He's the one right behind you. It doesn't matter which arm, so rong as no one can see it." She had no idea what this would accomplish, but none of that mattered, because she needed cosmetics to create objects.

"… say I wanted information about flying a helicopter," Lord Osis continued. "All that I would have to do is access the 'vehicles' node, then traverse down to the various…"

"I know you think you need cosmetics to create objects," Manifold told her, "but I've seen you use perfume. Pheromones in perfume are chemically similar to the pheromones released in sweat." Donna nodded, pretending to be interested to the Osis/McVain dissertation. As soon as she did it, Manifold fell silent. *Oh god*, she thought. *Did I just knock him off my shoulder?* It didn't matter. Manifold didn't need to connect the dots for her at that point: Mr. Sweaty was probably pumping out so many pheromones that she could conjure up enough syringes to stone an army.

"… so you see," Lord Osis concluded, "no matter what you're trying to hide, the instant I access our mind, any information that you know you know, I will be able to obtain."

"I see," Donna said, and without warning, took a deep breath and twisted her body around as far as the chains would allow. The links bit into her wrists, but despite the pain, she grasped the chain with her hands to hold her position for a couple seconds. Mr. Sweaty's bleary eyes widened as they met hers, but the contact only lasted a moment. She shifted her focused to the back of Mr. Sweaty's hand and thought of steel needles and plastic casings. Manifold probably wanted it in a place that wasn't visible, but her powers didn't work that way: she had to see her target. At least this way, it would be somewhat obscured by the mass of chains. She had no idea what the syringe was for. Maybe she was merely going to give him an overdose before they could torture him to death. *Funny*, she thought, *I'm about to kill this guy and I just learned his name ten seconds ago.* Hopefully, Manifold had a plan to save the day and this guy was part of it, but maybe he just wanted to give an old pal a painless send-off. If he was risking her well-being for the latter, he could go fuck himself, because she didn't like being tortured any more than the next person. *Focus*, she reminded herself. *Focus.* The sweat cells were hardening, the skin cells were parting, and –

For the second time in ten minutes, the Knockout Mouse slammed a right cross into the back of her head.

*   *   *

Chapter Thirty-Two:
11:21 p.m.

Donna Correction, the chick in the red leather cat suit, had endured one hell of a rough day. A couple more shots to the head, and she wouldn't be fit to model for a Black & Decker catalogue. Despite watching a giant rodent lay into a model like a curvaceous heavy-bag, Kelly Edwards felt surprisingly peaceful, as though some benevolent force cradled his weary head and whispered that everything would be fine. In fact, if Kelly were an Eagles' song right now, he'd be "Peaceful Easy Feeling." Maybe that's how you should feel when death looms just over the horizon. Maybe our brain reacts that way when facing oblivion. Maybe, but upon looking upward, Kelly thought that part of it might have to do with the prepped syringe dangling from the back of his hand. He had good veins there; those are your show-veins, the one's you can't cover up with black, long-sleeved shirts. For a thinking-man's junkie like Kelly, they were as untapped and beautiful as a stretch of Alaskan wilderness would be to an oil man. The Drug Gods who sent him this gift had yet to depress the plunger, but just having it there comforted him enough, like getting a deathbed visit from an old, good friend.

A flea jumped off Donna Corrections limp head. It might have been a tick (it looked a bit big for a flea), but in either case, she never struck him as the sort who needed to be groomed for parasites (although he'd volunteer for the job in a heartbeat). Maybe her infestation came from regularly socializing with a giant rodent. By the time the creature hit the floor, though, there was no confusion as to whether it was a flea or a tick, because it was Drek Manifold.

The now full-sized Manifold landed in a crouch, and when he rose to his feet, ninety percent of the room yelled, "By the Seven Thrones of Narcil!" as though mimicking a choir. Some of Kelly's former classmates started to rush forward, but then froze as Dr. Poindexter raised the neural destabilizer and leveled it at... Reggie Sleeve? "Where did he go?" everyone yelled, even Kelly.

People shifting bodies. Stuff appearing. Everyone seemingly wearing jean jackets and speaking with the same voice. Everything around Kelly had become such a swirling maelstrom of confusion that he barely noticed the crimson flash to his right, and Navin's chains clattering to the floor. Kelly expected Navin's body to hit the floor in a heap, but the body no longer belonged to Navin, it had transformed into Manifold and landed on its booted feet. A second set of eye beams shot out of Navin/Manifold's face, roasting the replacement neural destabilizer. Manifold turned back to Kelly, but instead of zapping the chains apart, he reached up and pushed the plunger on the syringe, slamming the load of smack into Kelly's veins.

It was like a soft, white bomb exploded behind Kelly's eyes. *Dear god this is good stuff*, his shrinking mind gushed. The pain in his wrists and shoulders melted away, and within seconds, he might as well have been lying in a hammock. Everyone in the room took on a fuzzy glow, and for the first time in his entire life, everything made sense. The secrets of the universe unraveled before him: the meaning of life, the cream getting into Twinkie tubes, dogs and cats living together, Keanu Reeves continuing to land acting jobs... it all made sense. Overdosing felt so much better than he had ever imagined.

*   *   *

Chapter Thirty-Three:
11:22 p.m.

One of the pudgy, male minions lifted the AK-47 that Donna Correction had conjured and leveled it at Drek Manifold, but since he could just body-hop to the next vessel, it might as well have been a toothbrush. Lord Osis considered emptying the clip, just for his amusement, and wasting everyone in the room, but McVain had already shot most of the bullets into Lord Osis' charging minions. The key was the human female, Donna Correction. With her, he could create a new neural destabilizer and cut off Manifold's vessels, one by one. First, though, he sent in the Knockout Mouse.

The giant rodent lurched forward, and Lord Osis receded slightly from its conscious so that the creature could fully utilize its primal fighting instincts and reflexes. Manifold surely did not wish to fry any of the innocents with his eye beams unless it was absolutely necessary, and maybe not even then. Blasting the Mouse was a different story, but he could only do that if the raging rodent gave him a clean shot.

The Knockout Mouse fed jabs to Manifold's face as though it was a speedbag with hair, and the moment of unfettered staring necessary to utilize his eyebeam powers never came. Manifold tried backing away, but the Mouse kept advancing, gloves first, forcing him into a corner, toward a table full of various-sized pistons. Then, the Mouse roared in with series of body shots. Their force lifted Manifold an inch or two off the ground, but then Lord Osis's adversary did an odd thing: he jumped in time with the incoming punch, causing the punch to launch him further into the air. Manifold thudded onto the top of the table and rolled to the other side. The

Knockout Mouse scrambled after him, scurrying around the end of the desk, but when Manifold rose, he had time for one long stare before the red gloves again engulfed his face. The stare lasted long enough to conjure up a pair of eyebeams, but the destructive red light flew past the mouse's "shoulder" and plowed into the autolift.

Lord Osis knew the shot was intentional. If he had to guess, he would have said that Manifold had deduced his plan and was trying to eliminate Donna Correction before Lord Osis took control of her. Unfortunately for Manifold, the blast hit the central shaft of the hydraulic lift and sent the entire structure screeching to the ground. *That was too close*, Lord Osis thought. *Time to end this.*

The Mouse lurched forward, swinging wildly so that Manifold would have no chance at a second shot. Using McVain, Lord Osis crouched over the battered, semi-conscious woman and pressed his fingertips into her delicate jawbones. Lord Osis wasn't sure Dane could rip off her head, but she probably wasn't sure he couldn't. "Make me another neural destabilizer," he commanded.

"With what?" Donna Correction wearily protested.

It was a valid point, but fortunately, McVain carried a bottle of Binaca around with him for emergencies, and that was close enough to a cosmetic product to do the job (after all, the limitations to Donna's abilities were mostly psychological). Lord Osis had Dane release her skull, pat himself down, and pull the tiny bottle free, holding it out in front of him like his own personal Excalibur.

*   *   *

Chapter Thirty-Four:
11:22.25 p.m.

Donna Correction's eyes turned toward the bottle of Binaca, then back to Dane. Some sort of supreme, absurd confidence lingered in his steely grey eyes. It looked completely foreign. She used to think of Dane as confident, but it must have been bluff and bluster, a man trying to compensate for shortcomings that not even a giant helicopter could cover up. The maniacal gleam in his eye now, though, represented total, carnivorous dominance. "If I do this," she began, pausing to lick her lips, "will you promise not to... possess me?"

Lord Osis shrugged Dane's mighty shoulders. "Sure," he lied. He made no effort to sound believable, but you could do that when you had your foot on someone's proverbial throat. Without waiting for a response, he sprayed a couple blasts of the minty freshness into the air. Donna's mind pushed and contorted the particles like potting clay, and within seconds, the neural distabilizer had materialized in midair. Dane's dexterous hand plucked it from the air before gravity could take hold. "Thanks," he said, turning the weapon over in his hand, "but I lied."

"I knew you would," Donna said, then rolled onto her back and kicked the weapon out of his hand. She always chided Eva for insisting that they go to Karate class, saying it was pointless to know self-defense if you had superpowers, but as the weapon skidded under the instructor's heavy, aluminum desk, she had to admit that for once, Eva was right. Of course, during that one moment, Eva might as well have been standing in Shanghai, so Donna wouldn't have to endure an "I told you so."

Lord Osis turned toward Donna, and she expected an eruption, but this wasn't Dane. Dane, for all his other faults, had passion to spare. A cool, calculating sadist stood at the controls now. "Joke's on you," he said. "I was going to go through the front door; you might have actually enjoyed that. There are other ways, though, more painful ways, to reach the brain." Donna didn't even notice the smile planted on her lips until it now fell away. Lord Osis took a deep breath and exhaled a tentacle of white smoke from Dane's mouth.

Donna scrambled a couple feet backward on her feet and elbows until her shoulders slammed into the overturned hydraulic lift. The wispy tendril crept toward Donna's head, then dipped south, pressing its way through her cleavage furrow, to a place deep inside her suit. Meanwhile, behind Dane, a trio of the Class of '96 shoved the gigantic aluminum desk loaded with textbooks away from the wall in order to retrieve the neural destabilizer. *Why oh why didn't I create a squirt gun that looked like the destabilizer?* she wondered as the tendril squirmed its way deeper into her suit. At least she wasn't getting pounded into the ground like Manifold. She glanced to her right as the smoky tendril crept down the small of her back, but it wasn't Manifold whose face the Knockout Mouse launched haymakers into, just some bald, rag doll body dressed in bright red Iowa State sweatpants.

All of Lord Osis' bodies stopped doing whatever they were doing, even the tendril, and collectively turned toward the battered body of Navin Offerdahl. Manifold had vanished. Group shift to the right, where the hydraulic lift lay. So was the junkie. Donna felt a pair of hands and some dangling chain links on her shoulder, and all eyes turned toward her. Manifold crouched wordlessly behind her, and without any warning or hesitation, bent fully over her body, shoving his face down by her rack. He started making a slurping sound, and Donna was about to flail around in some grand mal snit fit until she realized that his lips weren't touching her. They were sucking up the tendril like a ShopVac going to town on a giant strand of spaghetti.

Donna had read the Evil Socialists Collective's file on Lord Osis. Whether the human eye could perceive them or not, tendrils comprised of Lord Osis' essence connected all of the bodies he possessed, each connected with the other like joints in a spider web. As soon as Manifold stood up and focused all his attention on inhaling the smoking essence of the Paragon of

Possession, all the strands tensed and became visible, then slowly retracted into the void between Manifold's pursed lips as if someone turned a crank on Manifold's back. And it wasn't like a human sucking through a straw, either, because humans have to pause every few seconds to catch their breath. This was the kind of suction you see in an airplane movie where someone shoots out the window and everything not bolted down gets ripped outside.

So, Donna thought, *that's the secret power he needed Mr. Sweaty for: suction.* Who would've thought that heroin could turn someone into a superhero?

Donna's face was mostly obscured by a mass of curly, voluminous, hair, but she did catch a glimpse of the possessed Dane. The smoky essence still rolled from his mouth, but it wasn't voluntary anymore. Every muscle in his body locked up, like his brain was dialing up a seizure, and his bulging eyes turned milky white. Needless to say, the delirious confidence had disappeared.

*   *   *

Chapter Thirty-Five:
11:23 p.m.

Minds and senses flew from Lord Osis' grasp at a dizzying rate. Just when he would formulate a plan, the integral parts of that plan would slip from his control. He tried to force the Knockout Mouse to step forward and pound Manifold through the wall, but from its position over by the wall, it was one of the first vessels to get torn from his grasp. He managed to force Eva Destruction to randomly vomit on something right as his grip on her brain loosened, but that wild, desperate attempt brought no respite; the something she targeted with her puke turned out to be a soon-to-be-re-bored camshaft. By the time the hunk of dissolved engine fell through the middle of the wooden table and clattered to the floor, Lord Osis had lost Eva Destruction.

Other than McVain, who stood in the vortex of the suck, the last body that Lord Osis clung to belonged to Chase Wilder's, who, back in his high school football days, could run a 4.8-second forty-yard dash (4.7 if it was down a hill). As everything became hazy and monochromatic, Lord Osis had the body break into a sprint, knocking a few of the dazed former vessels out of the way. Back in the glory days, Chase might have outrun the one-man black hole Manifold had become. He might have dashed down the hallway, out the door, down the road to the nearest super market and rebuilt Lord Osis' army within a matter of minutes, but a decade of eating rich food and breathing the air of Marlboro Country had turned this body from a Z28 Camaro into a rusted-out Dodge, and halfway to the welding room, the lights went out.

*   *   *

Chapter Thirty-Six:
11:27 p.m.

Dane McVain stood the closest to the suction, and even though he had
to wait while everyone else's strands pulled through his chest cavity on their
way to Manifold's puckered puss, he was one of the first to recover.
Watching the... misty essence of Lord Osis getting pulled through people's
orifices and pores made for an unnerving experience, even for someone with
a stomach as strong as Dane's. It almost made him swear off ever joining
forces with Lord Osis in the future. Not quite, but almost.

A residual memory from his minutes of possession still lingered in his
soupy brain. It involved a neural destabililizer skidding to a halt under an
aluminum desk. Dane glanced around, but everyone else remained too
wrapped up in their own recovery to notice the actions of the person next to
them. So, while most of the bruised and battered occupants of the
automotive repair shop numbly blinked or patted themselves down to check
for fractures, he picked himself off the floor and nonchalantly slid in the
direction of the instructor's desk.

Amazingly, the entire thwarting process took just over twenty seconds
and left Manifold with bloated cheeks, groping around like a drunken
teenager looking for a place to unload his Stella Artois. He raced out of the
automotive shop to a janitor's closet across the hall. There he found a one-
liter, glass Erlenmeyer flask with a rubber stopper, and in a great, incoherent
"Blaahhhhh!" he expelled the ghostly villain into his brand new glass prison.

Manifold had done it. Somehow, he had tricked the creature into
exposing itself, and saved the people of the Tri-Cities once again (well, at
least the one's who hadn't been gutted by the AK-47, fried by the neural

destabilizer, eaten by the eels… was he missing anything?). The survivors bobbed around like sea monkeys, mumbling to one another, disoriented by the experience and in awe of seeing their savior up close. As for Dane, he stepped into the hallway and waited for his arch-nemesis to shove the rubber stopper into the mouth of the flask before aiming the barrel of the weapon between the shoulder blades of Manifold's jean jacket. He thought about muttering something poetic, but all the sprung to mind was a line from American action movie star Bruce Willis, and that hardly seemed appropriate. Instead, he just pulled the trigger.

This time, there was no escaping. Manifold couldn't jump bodies if he didn't see the attack coming. Still, Dane remained cautiously optimistic. The violet ray struck Manifold in the lower ribs. When the neural destabilizer zapped normal humans, they dropped to the ground like a marionette with its strings cut, then bounced around, like a marionette with its strings tangled. When the beam hit Manifold, the room filled with a blinding orange light that looked like a setting sun. *This is it,* Dane thought. *I'm home.* When he killed Manifold's vessel out on the gymnasium floor, it felt too anticlimactic: he saw a human dying in a human way, and it left him with a feeling that something was missing. This time, though, the sight of the orange light was as achingly beautiful as the warmth building inside Dane's chest.

No one made a sound during that second the orange light radiated down on them, or during the seconds that followed, when everyone sat blinking away spots after having just blinked away the haze of possession. The first sign of life occurred a moment later, when the eclectic audience let out a collective, hopeful gasp as a single, simple man stood in the hallway, holding a beaker. It was the drug addict. Just the drug addict.

A bubble of emotion welled up inside of Dane that made his throat shrink and his tear ducts swell. For ten long years, he had chased this… thing, knowing that if somehow, he could just rid himself of Drek Manifold, Socialist forces could spill into Illinois and Iowa, wrestling control of both the Mississippi River and Interstate Highway 80, the two most important thoroughfares in North America. He had allied himself with monsters, sacrificed both his dignity and every blade on his beautiful helicopter, all in the hope that he would live to see this day. And now, after a breathless display of otherworldly luminance, Manifold had fled this mortal coil, and a distinctly proletarian sun had risen on a brand new day.

Dane stepped back into the auto shop and slumped against the white, recently washed dry erase board and dropped his chin to his chest. Swollen teardrops crept down his face like they hadn't since he watched *Rocky IV* for the first time, but he no longer cared. The civilians murmured to one another in a restless sort of way, but the Knockout Mouse would prevent them from rising up and becoming too much of an annoyance. Dane had finished thinking for the near future, and he had earned the rest. Now, he could finally stop scheming and return to Stockholm, a hero. Perhaps, the government would reward him with a lifetime supply of bread and his own Volvo station wagon, like in the fairytales.

A delicate, manicured hand dropped onto his mighty shoulder. He didn't have to smell the fingertips to know that it belonged to Eva. It could only be Eva. He knew that she had cared for him... had known it for years... and he had neglected her, fearing that there was not enough room in his heart for a woman, a mission, and a helicopter. Those days were gone, because his heart had swelled up to three times its normal size. He turned to her. Maybe they could climb into Uppsala together, and the three of them could—

The fingernails of the hand dug into his shoulder. As it turns out, the hand didn't belong to Eva. "I want my money." Donna said, hoarsely, the chains around her bloodied wrists jingling. "Now."

*   *   *

Epilogue
12:25 a.m.

For the first time in ten years, Reggie Sleeve sat behind the wheel of a moving car. It felt alien, gripping the wheel at the ten and two positions, but at the same time, it felt secure, like when he learned to ride his bike and Dad jogged right behind him to make sure he didn't wipe out. He couldn't legally drive, of course. That would require a few trips to the doctor and one long visit to the DMV, but for tonight, at least, the cops would be occupied with bigger issues than a former narcoleptic on the road.

Former narcoleptic. He liked the sound of that. Something told him that he would never have another sleep attack again. In some infinitesimally small way, he would miss them, in the same way you miss something you've grown used to, but more than anything, he would miss what they had come to represent. The sleep attacks were his link to something great. In fact, if he'd known that he'd spent most of his adult life as one fifth of a super-hero, it would have made the narcolepsy a lot easier to deal with. He used to think of himself as less than human. Barely an hour ago, he had found out that he was so much more, and now that was all gone.

Reggie drove slowly, about five miles an hour below the thirty mile-per-hour speed limit, scanning the darkened street for cats and nocturnal children. Even after he handed the glass flask containing Lord Osis over to the squad leader òf Task Force Alpha, he still felt as though he were walking on eggshells. He'd read about Post-Traumatic Stress Disorder and wondered if constantly anticipating disaster represented its early stages. It didn't help that his lack of driving experience meant that he still had the teenage jitters;

he strangled the wheel more than gripped it, enough to threaten circulation. It also didn't help that he was driving Sally's car.

Sally had escaped the Wolfian Ducks. The first one incapacitated itself when it bit through her fun-sized can of mace. Appropriately, the sliding door of Kelly Edwards' Econoline Van was broken, and she threw herself inside, metal chair and all, to escape the second wave of mutant fowl. There, she slowly recovered from shock, blood loss, and from macing herself (she had to admit: that shit really works). She had no idea how to hotwire a vehicle, but when Manifold walked around the perimeter of the school and methodically snapped all the creatures' necks like kindling, it freed her to tote the chair down the street to the police station and alert them of the international incident taking place in the Kooterville High gym. In the end, she sustained only minor injuries: a sprained ankle, a few lacerations, a wrist abrasion, and a mangled purse. Nothing that a little rest and a lot of Visine couldn't fix.

"Thanks for driving," Sally said, her teeth chattering despite the heat of the car. "I'm glad Manny's at his grandma's tonight; he'd be going nuts."

Reggie'd never been to her house, but he knew where she lived. Google Earth was helpful that way. He pulled her Kia compact up to the curb in front of the brick, single-story ranch house and shifted into "park." "No problem," he replied. "For some reason, I feel better than I have in years."

"I know what you mean," Sally nodded, even though she couldn't possibly have known what he meant. "I mean, I know a lot of people got killed, but can you believe Navin and Ely are okay? I mean, I know I must have, but I can't every really remember hearing Navin talk before."

Reggie merely nodded in agreement. Someday, he would explain everything to the two of them, now that Ely could remember it. Hopefully, knowing you were a hero would cushion the blow of losing twelve years of your life. He had a feeling, though, that out of all of them, Navin knew what was going on the whole time. It was nothing he could prove, but since Navin couldn't communicate, Manifold might have let him stick around when he took over Navin's body. Just a gut feeling, for sure, but among the four of them, gut feelings counted for quite a bit.

Sally reached for the door handle, then looked back. "How are you going to get home?" Sally asked, expectantly.

Reggie looked down at his lap and shrugged. After carrying his condition like an albatross for so long, he reflexively assumed that hints weren't hints. "Ah, I can get a cab or..." Sally's hand eased over toward the gearshift and closed over his.

"Or you could come inside," she said. Hell, that wasn't even a hint; it was a request. "Manny won't be home until tomorrow afternoon. It's alright."

"All night?" he repeated, and waited for her to nod. He knew he shouldn't. It wasn't appropriate, what with Jack and everyone else dying in such bad, bad ways. If Reggie'd experienced regular sexual encounters more, he might have let the appropriateness of the situation stop him. As it was, you might as well ask a starving man to wait for a napkin before he fucks up a Thanksgiving turkey. Etiquette merely gave him pause before he eased to his right, softening his lips to plant a kiss on the girl he'd been pining for since—

"Open our eyes," Drek Manifold said. He now sat in Sally's seat, presumably using Sally's body.

Reggie's eyes flew open and he recoiled back to his side of the car so fast he almost smashed his skull through the side window. "Wha huh?" Reggie began. Several possibilities flashed through his mind. None of them good. "Aren't you—Aren't you dead? I saw you die."

"You saw me get disconnected from Kerry's body. I knew rong ago that you were stuck with me, but I was arso stuck with you. The neural disruptor freed me enough to do a re-entry."

"And you took over Sally?" Reggie said, almost yelping. This was the final proof he'd been waiting for that God, and by extension, Richard Marx, hated him. "What the fuck is it going to do to her?"

"Probabry nothing," Manifold assured him. "When I met you five, I made the mistake of rooking for a correction of people that could support my rife force. I didn't rook at the other side, how it would adversery affect you. Five was way too few. A few dozen should spread the negative response out thinry enough to keep it from being too disruptive."

Reggie shook his head. "You mean you've... *infected* the whole class?" It wasn't the most complementary term, but it seemed appropriate. "They why didn't you stop McVain from getting away? You just let him fly off and –" The smirk spreading across Manifold's features made him stop. "You got McVain, too?"

"I entered everyone who saw or felt the right," Manifold explained. "I'll take care of him eventuary. And Eva and Poindexter and the Mouse. I think I'll let Donna go, as rong as she stays out of trouble. She was a rear trooper at the end, even after I broke the terephone over her head."

Reggie nodded in agreement, as though he had some input on the whole decision. It did seem like a reasonable plan, and Donna certainly seemed like the least dangerous member of the group. "Oh, nice job by the way with your equipment order," Reggie said. As Manifold's expression turned quizzical, he finished the thought. "You asked me to pick you up a pair of beakers, not flasks. A rubber stopper won't fit in a beaker. We'd have been fucked."

"Oh," Manifold said, frowning. "Sorry about that."

"Don't mention it," Reggie said. They spent several awkward seconds amid the hum of the heater and the idling engine. "So, what happens now? I mean, what am I supposed to do? How am I supposed to—"

"Rive your rife," Manifold said, simply. "You… all of you, have earned it."

Reggie leaned back and his chair and looked out the windshield at the row of streetlights cutting a path through the darkness. When he was a child, his Uncle Joe once told him that a car was a time machine, with everything in front of them being the future and everything behind being the past. For once, the future looked like a place worth visiting. Manifold's advice was simple and clichéd… and poorly pronounced, but for once, it actually applied to Reggie; living his life finally became an option. It wasn't something he could describe to a normal, non-crippled person, but it was as though he'd broken free of shackles that he had always assumed were a part of him, and, now he could pursue a life that –

"Sorry to cut this short," Manifold said, "but Dakota Peters just saw a nitric acid truck overturn, so I need to get going."

"One thing," Reggie said, quickly. When Manifold looked at him, expectantly, he had to pause and think up how to word his request. "Try not to… take over Sally when I'm with her. It's a little disturbing, and… I think I like her."

"It's the reast I can do," Manifold said, his lips parting into a smile. "And... I think she rikes you, too."

And just like that, he was gone...

*   *   *